The PROPHETS
and the
EXECUTIONER
── BOOK 1 ──

THE AWAKENING

FRANK FRANCO

PAGE PUBLISHING, INC.
New York, NY

First originally published by Page Publishing, Inc. 2018

ISBN 978-1-64350-733-0 (Paperback)
ISBN 978-1-64350-734-7 (Digital)

Printed in the United States of America

For

Lina, for her encouragement

Lisa, for being my muse

Johnny, for his artistic help

And my grandchildren, Livia, Deluca, Sloane,
Milania and Romeo for being my inspiration.

*B*EFORE THEIR ARRIVAL *on Earth and before the destruction of their worlds, their lives could only be described as extraordinary. They were many civilizations all living and thriving in a system of planets that were connected by peace, harmony, and common respect, but mostly, they were connected by singular thought. For millions of years, these different cultures, as diverse as they were, prospered from the sharing of knowledge and resources and from mutual understanding. Specific laws were not needed as crime was nonexistent. There were no borders as freedom of travel was encouraged and the allegiance to one another was cultivated.*

It was an exhilarating existence filled with the delights of adventure and camaraderie, a life that was virtually everlasting. An entity could only cease to exist if it itself so chose. Death by accident or age meant a rebirth of a new life with all the excitement of a once-again youthful existence, and with time, the full knowledge of its previous lives would return, therefore maintaining the wisdom learned throughout its past adventures.

This knowledge was the key to the harmony of the different cultures, but unfortunately, that knowledge became the catalyst for their demise. In this time before the collapse of their beliefs and customs, the seeds of greed began to take root; with each rebirth, past possessions became more coveted, desire for immediate standing became more urgent, greed had invaded their minds, and disrespect for one another had destroyed their harmony.

PROLOGUE

T HE MASSIVE EXPLOSION put a sudden end to the quiet, almost peaceful night. Shards of deadly shrapnel being hurled in all direction had the rebel forces scurrying for cover.

Directly above the rebel camp, the enemy vessel paused, surveying the damage they had just inflicted on the dissenters. Then as the small group of warriors prepared to return fire, an ear-piercing shriek signaled the devastation that was about to happen. The bright red ray unleashed by the enemy hit the camp with such a fierce force that it flattened the main stronghold, sending the two brothers crashing through the protective barrier where they took shelter and into the dense brush, barely missing the steep embankment on the north side of their camp. Slowly picking themselves up, they quickly hobbled back toward their friends to lend aid when another deadly ray smashed into the second building, halting them in their tracks. Those few rebels still alive fled in all directions while the two brothers reeling in shock turned and ran toward the safety of the abandoned city.

Ducking behind mounds of ruble and burnt-out buildings, they made their way across the devastated city, distancing themselves from the attack that was pummeling their camp and comrades and toward an area long ago destroyed. The smell of decay powered through the rags they held tightly to their nose and mouth, a futile attempt at keeping the stench of death from seeping through and willing the nausea that had built up in their throats to erupt in a violent manner. The vile horror of death was everywhere as the rot from festering corpses littered the streets. Trying not to stare at what remained of those who once lived here was difficult as the two brothers, still covering their mouths, prayed to clear the death zone before they too succumbed to the same fate as the poor souls they now stepped on or around. Using their robes as a shield against the disgusting odor of war, they forged ahead as quickly as their tired legs would take them. Desperate, they sought a place to hide, a temporary safe haven where they could rest, someplace where the violence of war could briefly be forgotten. There, they would be able to determine their next move. Was this war still worth fighting, or was it time to seek him out and finally accept his invitation to leave this forsaken world and find another?

With the sounds of exploding missiles now in the distance and the air only slightly more bearable, they took cover inside a long-ago burnt-out structure. When they were settled and agreed to abandon the fight, they eagerly locked arms and then, pressing their foreheads together, prepared themselves to summon him. Staring urgently into each other's eyes, they focused on him, but instead, they found despair and fear staring back, fear that had been all they've known for two lifetimes now, fear that was not about living or dying but simply about what once was.

Exhausted, they somehow summoned the strength to continue; still they ached, not from the burns that spotted their exposed skin, not even from the wounds in places where their bodies had been pierced by bits of exploding shrapnel, nor from the Soot mingled with blood and sweat that burned as it ran through their brows and into their eyes, no. They ached from the heartbreak of being alone, the knowledge that they had lost their parents forever, and the loneliness that was to be their future. Ignoring the stinging mixture that blurred their vision, they tried desperately to focus on their grandfather to somehow find him.

The relentless war that was now more than a thousand years of brutality, responsible for the bloodshed of millions as well as the devastation of three worlds, threatened to make all the known species extinct. How did this happen? When did it all begin, and why?

They both held on to each other as the memory of exploding bombs echoed in their psyche. The heartbreaking screams of their friends and loved ones were still bombarding their minds and crushing their hearts. Breaking apart from the mind meld they were beyond terrified, but not of dying, no! They knew that if they died that they would live again; they were terrified for the loss of those friends and family that had run out of lives, those that would never live again.

"Did you feel him?" one brother yelled to the other.

"No," responded his identical twin. "We need to try again. Our grandfather will help us. We need to leave this lunacy and go with him to this new world. Come, we must find a quieter place to summon him."

As daylight broke, Davida and Leonsard began to get their bearings as they recognized the landmarks of the Octavian sector. The eight hills that stood majestically over the rubble that was once the jewel of Pegasus seemed untouched by the wars that had pounded the area for hundreds of years. Excited by the familiarity, the two brothers began running at full speed when, suddenly, Davida came to a complete stop, his eyes glistening with moisture. His mouth fell open in a mournful pose while his bottom lip quivered. "Brother," yelled Leonsard "why are you stopping?" Then he followed Davida's gaze to the lush green rock that covered the tops of the eight hills. The way the green rock glowed against the bright yellow sky reminded them of the peaceful mornings that they would be together with their mother and father, sharing a meal and playing games in the shadows of those same majestic hills. The boys stared sadly at the beauty before them, thinking back to that time, a time when life was good, a time when hate was nonexistent and friendship and sharing were the values they lived each day, a time when peace and harmony was a way of life, a way of life they only heard stories about, a way of life the elders perhaps took for granted and then violently ripped it away from them—a sense of peace that was all too brief as it disappeared during their very first existence. A mere thirteen years after their first birth, the war had begun, and nine lifetimes later, the brutality still raged on.

The two brothers, tears streaming through the dried dirt and blood that was caked on their faces, shook off the feeling of despair, and then wiping the sticky mess from their eyes, they continued their search. It was another hour before they found the abandoned home; it was their father's home all those lifetimes ago, the home that they had lived in during their first birth, the home that they suffered their first death when it was destroyed in the first battle of the sociological tiers more than a thousand years earlier. A ruin, yes, but they still remembered it well, and they knew that deep below the ground level once existed their father's prized cellar; the two boys prayed and hope that it was still intact.

A small opening in the floor led them to the room deep beneath the dwelling where the pungent smell of rot was a sour reminder of how much time had passed and how much their world had suffered.

Back then, when friends and family gathered, the grand cellar was a spectacle to behold; their father would beam as he described his special room. The walls were made of the magnificent blue rock cut from the Octavian hills. Their father would boast about the dark wood that adorned the floors and that they came from another world far away, as did the metal support beams that kept the ceiling solid. Now as the brothers entered the grand cellar a thousand years of war later, the steel beams still held, but all the wood had decayed and the stone walls were no longer the brilliant blue as mold and rust had caked a layer of disgust all over them. The air was vile, but the room was quiet, quiet enough to focus on him.

"Brother, we must try again. Come, let us find our grandfather and go to him."

The two boys once again locked arms and then, slowly pressing their foreheads together, searched each other's eyes for their last remaining relative. After many attempts and many hours, with emptiness threatening to overpower their resolve, they finally found him. It was evident that he was also seeking them as the joy of their connection was overwhelming and immediate.

Staring into each other's eyes, they could see him; he was a giant of a man, with long locks of hair that were as golden as the sun. The high cheekbones and prominent nose reminded them of their own father. His tear-filled eyes, green as the greenest hilltop, were soft and gentle and blinked repeatedly with the excitement and relief of finally finding his grandsons.

In that moment in time, with the power of thought spanning between the neighboring planets, a glazed image of their grandfather holding his massive arms wide open invited the brothers to join him, so leaving their physical bodies behind, they transported themselves into those massive inviting arms.

* * *

Many lifetimes earlier and before the destruction of their worlds, their lives could only be described as extraordinary. They were many civilizations all living and thriving in a system of planets that were connected by peace, harmony, and common respect, but mostly, they were connected by singular thought. For millions of years, these different cultures, as diverse as they were, prospered from the sharing of knowledge and resources and from mutual understanding. Specific laws were not needed as crime was nonexistent. There were no borders as freedom of travel was encouraged and the allegiance to one another was cultivated.

In this time, before the collapse of their beliefs and customs, these beings, as advanced as they had become, could travel by simple thought, so wherever they desired to be, they would simply think of that location and their inner being would transport there. When they arrived, they could choose to materialize a shadow image of their physical form or remain as a sphere of living light.

The metamorphoses that allowed such a manipulation of their true forms were engineered millions of years earlier with the study of conscious connectivity; through that knowledge, they found their brains to be limitless, and after millions of years of evolution, the power of thought became a part of their genetic structure as did a somewhat eternal life.

It was an exhilarating existence filled with the delights of adventure and camaraderie, a life that was virtually everlasting. An entity could only cease to exist if it itself so choose. Death by accident or age meant a rebirth of a new life with all the excitement of a once-again youthful existence, and with time, the full knowledge of its previous lives would return, therefore maintaining the wisdom learned throughout its past adventures. This knowledge was the key to the harmony of the different cultures, but unfortunately, that knowledge became the catalyst for their demise.

Knowledge of past wealth created impatience to once again be wealthy; this impatience became infectious as a few took up the cause and began to preach the unfairness of losing the possessions of their past lives. As this theory spread, gatherings formed, causing skirmishes that created disrespect and mistrust of one another. So laws needed to be introduced to protect society, borders needed to be erected to protect property, and weapons were created to protect the citizens.

Subsequently, the laws created more lawbreakers, the borders created conflict, and the weapons facilitated the wars. The wars that spread from planet to planet sadly destroyed the utopia they had come to cherish, and the paradise they had worked so hard to create had turned to bedlam.

Greed and envy had replaced peace and harmony; singular thought was replaced by the chaos which all but destroyed their tranquil existence. The battles raged for over a thousand years, and in the end, the great cultures that took millions of years to build were destroyed and many of the entities were facing extinction.

Twenty-three was highest number of rebirths ever tracked, and those poor souls who surpassed twenty-three deaths never returned.

Early on in their chaotic state as the wars intensified, sides were drawn. But it wasn't planet versus planet or species against species; the hatred was not that simple, or perhaps it was. The hatred was pure envy. In every society, there were the leaders and the followers, there were the richer and the less rich, and you see poverty was nonexistent in this utopia that they had created. So with what they had learned through the knowledge of conscious connectivity, singular thought had divided them into sociological tiers.

Through the millions of years of transformation, these beings could target their thoughts to specific topics and tasks but could also shield them from those that were not welcome into a particular thought wave. With this knowledge, sides were drawn regardless of species, home planet, or neighborhood. The sides reflected the standard of living each of them possessed.

During the turbulent times, a small group of dissenters who refused to continue the fight sought one another out regardless of sociological standing by sending out their desire for peace in open thought. Soon, others shared their distaste for the wars, and together they created a new society whose goal it was to bring peace.

All their pleas for peace, their ceasefires, their rallies went on for hundreds of years but still their attempts at trying to bring tranquility back into their lives had failed repeatedly, so instead, they decided to leave their world and all its woes behind and embarked on a journey, searching the universe to find a new home, to find that one planet that had all the elements suitable to their existence and suitable to recreate their utopia.

The societies made up of souls from the different cultures, and planets would regain the harmony they once shared by embracing one another's beliefs and values. Together they would search for this new home, and together they would find the tranquility they so desperately desired. Their quest went on for many years; no one knew exactly how many as time was not important and tracking it meant little. Still, the journey was not without its difficulties and did test their resolve, but in doing so, the adversities created a strong allegiance to one another.

Through this difficult time, leaders emerged, and as leaders, they needed to rewrite the rules of life to avoid the same fate that so violently robbed them of their homes and peaceful existence, and so the guidelines were created for the protection of the *Namzu Anunnaki*.

The *Namzu Anunnaki*, the book of wisdom of the twelve planets, was a written accounting of all the knowledge that they had amassed since the beginning of time. In fact, it was the very science of how they were able to transform from solid life-forms to what they had now become. It was the genius of the science and all the processes of singular thought that had thrust them into the supreme beings they had become. So the rules were written and an oath to follow them was taken by all. This would ensure that the *Namzu Anunnaki* would be preserved and guarded until their new home was ready for its wisdom.

The first rule that was voted on and accepted by all was that to remember one's past lives was dangerous, and this ability would only be granted to a very small few. This chosen group would have the responsibility of not only protecting the secrets of the *Namzu Anunnaki* but also guiding the society by executing the wishes of the council through the developmental years of this new home when they found it. They would be known either as a prophet or as an executioner.

The second and only other rule was for the protection of the old souls; these souls were the ones who had already experienced more than twenty rebirths and would face extinction should they pass their twenty-second death. They would be known as the founders and would guide the societies from a safe distance, existing as light forms where all the communication and interaction would be done through thought. Within this existence, they would have the ability to travel to their chosen home and observe and sometimes influence the younger souls. This influence would guide them through their tasks of completing a specific purpose by instilling thoughts and ideas to help them along in their journey and, to a degree, experience the new life through their eyes. Still, their existence would be limited to that of living light until their new home was safe enough for them to be reborn in without the risk of death.

* * *

Many years later and from quite a distance, they saw it; it appeared as a turquoise planet that seemed to invite them. When they arrived on its surface, they found a wondrous place filled with oceans and forests, mountains and valleys that were full of unusual species from the tiniest of life-forms to the uncivilized and barbaric society that seemed to rule this beautiful place. They marveled at the reactions of these barbarians who, upon seeing them, fell to their knees in fear and then adopted the visitors as their gods.

Still, dangers lurked in every corner of the planet, so much so that the founders suggested that the society move on, but many of the younger souls enjoyed the godly honor bestowed upon them and pleaded with the old souls for them to stay; most, though, were just tired of searching, tired of not having a home.

With emotions running high, the founders suggested forming a council that would be representative of all the different societies; they would then vote on whether to stay and make this planet their home or to continue their search. To stay would mean that they would need to cleanse the planet of all its impurities and dangers. Also, rather than to be feared as gods, they would need to assimilate with the current inhabitants and somehow adopt their souls to become part of the path. The stakes were high. Failure to accomplish utopia would be catastrophic to their survival as it would certainly take them most of their twenty-three existences to succeed.

With the risks being almost insurmountable, the council voted in favor of making this planet their home, and thus, the rules for their survival were drawn.

First and foremost, before the godly presence, what they enjoyed was forbidden; they would use it to spread their knowledge in all key points of the planet and entice the inhabitants to help them construct markers visible from the heavens. This was in the hopes that if their brothers and sisters were lost and searching for a new home as did they, then they would be able to find them.

Once this was accomplished, to portray oneself as a god would be outlawed. Those who broke this law would be dealt with severely by the elders.

Secondly, and designed to not repeat the mistakes of their past the original rule was again reinforced and most of the souls would be born without the ability to remember their past lives. An unknowing soul would be born with an agreed purpose, which could be to invent, discover, or correct the course of the society. An unknowing soul could only be awakened by a prophet or an executioner and only with the permission and blessing of the council.

Assimilation was next, and it was decided that coexisting with the planet's inhabitants was paramount to achieving their ultimate goal of peace and harmony. When the time for sharing the *Namzu Anunnaki* was at hand many thousands of years into the future, the assimilated souls, those unknowing of their origins, would all be awakened with the memories and knowledge to teach its wisdom to the planet's inhabitants.

In time and when all agreed that this should be five cycles of life for the awakened souls, the prophets and the executioners would begin the shaping of this planet as their new home. Waiting the five cycles would help them to better understand the true challenges of this young planet.

The executioners would be responsible for executing the laws that had been agreed to on this day. These few souls would be awakened to their past existences when they reached adulthood and would chart and correct the progress made by the others who were unknowing of their purpose. They were the souls who would be entrusted to create a path toward utopia and, after their awakening, would, in fact, sacrifice their existing way of life and would be committed only to the wishes of the council as foretold by the prophets. A single executioner and his prophet whose identities would only be known to the founders would be chosen and, in addition to their regular purpose, would also be charged with protecting the *Namzu Anunnaki*. They would be known as the enlightened ones.

The prophets would be born as awakened souls, the knowledge of their purpose would strengthen with age, their wisdom would be recognized as special, and the unknowing souls, would each have as part of their purpose, the instinct to embrace and protect them.

A prophet would be attached throughout the ages to the same executioner and then, when the time came, would have the task of awakening them. Their purpose would be to counsel the executioners and to keep them on the correct path as, together, they would bear the full weight of this new world on to their shoulders, a weight so heavy that if they should fail, then life as they knew it would cease to exist.

Young Earth creationism (YEC) is the religious belief that the Heavens, Earth, and life on Earth were created by direct acts of God during a short period, sometime between 6,000 and 10,000 years ago. Its adherents are those Christians and Jews who believe that God created the Earth in six 24-hour days, taking the Hebrew text of Genesis as a literal account. Some adherents believe that existing evidence in the natural world today supports a strict interpretation of scriptural creation as historical fact. Those adherents believe that the scientific evidence supporting evolution, geological uniformitarianism, or other theories which are at odds with a literal interpretation of the Genesis creation account, are either flawed or misinterpreted (source: Wikipedia.org).

CHAPTER 1

PLATI, GREECE, AD 949

9,151 Years Later
David and Leo

O N THIS DAY, two brothers would die and the people of Plati
would woefully mourn their death.

The tiny village was nestled in a small cove on the southernmost
tip of the Greek mainland. Its boundaries, from sea level, crawled up
the dark copper-colored hills, embracing the olive groves, and spread
through the lush green pastures atop Mount Zeon. The fishermen,
the farmers, and the shepherds would all protest the execution of the
twins, but it was to no avail as the law was the law and those who
broke it would pay the ultimate penalty.

Most of the villages' populace, just under a thousand souls, lived
a comfortable life that was simple but rewarding. They lived for the
day and celebrated their accomplishments at night. They honored
their neighbors and watched out for one another. They respected the
cycle of life, human or otherwise, killing only for food, and grateful
to receive it. To hang the two young boys from their community was
beyond comprehension. Thus, the citizens of Plati demonstrated and
demanded that mercy be shown to the brothers.

The twins, David and Leo, sons of Helena, were unknowing
souls; this life was their twentieth and would be their final existence

19

on earth. The purpose they shared was that of scientists; they were to find a cure for many of the diseases born on earth. When they committed their crime, they stole a sheep that was ill and near death. Their medicines, they hoped, would cure the sheep and, in turn, be used to help the citizens of Greece and elsewhere. The owner of the animal saw this as simple theft and had the boys arrested and charged.

The families of Plati went back generations. Although they embraced the Greek culture and identity, their roots were seeded by the multitudes from neighboring lands that had conquered their Mediterranean paradise. From the Romans to the Persians, the Langobards to the Avars and even the Slavs, they all took their turn at raping and pillaging this peaceful society. Year after year, century after century, they came, they conquered and then usually left.

Almost fifty years had passed since the last invasion, and they prayed another would never come. The armies of Greece, small in numbers but valiant in courage, would fight until death to protect their citizens. The farmers and fishermen would join them in the futile battle, but they knew the outcome would be the same: many would die, the women and children would be violated, and Greece would be conquered yet again. Each night, they prayed for peace and harmony, and for the last fifty years, their prayers had been answered.

For the most part, the villages were self-governed, crime was minimal, and culture and religion were dominant. Severe penalties were enforced if one broke the law. To do so was to disrespect your neighbor, and to disrespect your neighbor was a violation punishable by death. It had been forty-eight years since anyone had been executed. Today, the two brothers whose family was among the most prominent in the village would be hanged.

The two brothers had experimented for years but usually only with plants and sometimes with each other. They were healers of the future, their mother would proudly proclaim. They had healed rashes and wounds for many of the villagers with their concoctions derived from various plants. They claimed that, in their dreams, the gods showed them how, and they felt compelled to follow their instructions.

The house of Constantine and his wife, Althaia, was among the oldest not only in the region but also in all of Greece. Constantine himself sat as a governor of Greece and would venture to Athens twice a year to sit at the head of its council.

Constantine and Althaia had three sons—Sebastian, Thaddeus, and Michael. Sebastian, blood of Althaia, lost his birth father to a fishing accident days before he was born. It was soon after his first birthday that Constantine, who was then a widower and thirty years Althaia's senior, took Sebastian and his mother in and cared for them as his own. They married immediately and did so with the blessing of Althaia's mother, Helena. She was proud to have a governor as a son-in-law despite his age. Thaddeus was born after Sebastian's second birthday, and as brothers, they were inseparable for thirteen mischievous years. Michael, still a small child at the age of five, would only pester his two older brothers.

Helena had twins who were older than both Sebastian and Thaddeus. David and Leo were the uncles, but because they were older by only a couple of years, the four were more like cousins and together they would run amok throughout the countryside. On many occasions, the four would be seen riding sheep and competing to see who would fall off first. They would dive from the cliffs, challenging each other on who could come closest to the jagged rocks; they would race through the meadows to the delight of all who watched and proclaimed that their swiftness would one day win acclaim for Plati in the games in Athens. Mischievous, yes! Troublemakers, occasionally, but the villagers adored them. And today, to their horror, they would mourn for the two of them.

* * *

Three months earlier, on a cold stormy night, three young boys laden with piles of wood strapped to their backs scurried to get home before the storm trapped them in the woods. On this day, the twins, along with their nephew Thaddeus were charged with gathering the wood to heat their homes during the short Greek winter. Still miles away from their homes, they watched as the dark clouds rolled in and flashes of lightning exploded all around them. The twins, knowing the treachery that they would face should they try to make their way home, instead decided that they would make their way to a shelter that they knew all too well.

The shallow cave was carved into the side of the hill above the turquoise waters of the Mediterranean Sea. The cave was the ideal spot to weather a fierce storm, but more often, in better conditions, they would use the cave to hide from their parents. The entry was angled perfectly so that its opening faced inland instead of out to sea; it was guarded by thick bushes and trees that would protect them from the looming storm.

As they often did when they were in the cave, the threesome sat around a fire and exchanged stories of ancient legends and, of course, the gods. Settling in for a long night, they began to prepare their meal when a loud clap of thunder rocked the tiny cave.

The impact of the thunder was deafening as bolts of lightning tore apart nearby trees. The three boys, startled and frightened, scurried as far back into the cave as they possibly could. Thaddeus was the one to let out the loudest scream, which drowned out the muffled cries of the older twins. Then nervous laughter seemed to calm the three boys as they looked at one another, attempting to be brave.

The torrential rain that had followed the thunder and lightning was now pounding the mountainside, creating streams of mud and debris that crashed past the cave and over the rocky cliff down to the sea below. Still the cave was a perfect shelter against the elements, and now with the fire at a full roar, it was as warm and cozy as their own home and the comfort of the fire seemed to calm their nerves.

"Brother," David called out in a serious tone, his bright eyes reflecting the dancing flames of the roaring fire, "last evening, Mother told me a story of ancient remedies used to heal those ailing of the stomach pains, but her remedy made little sense to me. She said if we scraped the rot from old bread and even the rot from meat, then boil it with milk that it would heal those and many other ailments."

Leo pondered what he had just heard, his hand on his chin, his eyes closed in deep thought. "Odd," he responded, but then just as though some form of clarity hit him between the eyes, he jumped up and started pacing around the fire. "In my dreams!" he declared. "Two moons ago, the gods sent me a vision of a metal cauldron glowing as red as the embers in this fire." Excitedly, he pointed at the red-hot remnants of what was once a branch from an olive tree. "This caldron was shallow and empty and glowing as red as the fires of hell. It had a groove that led to a spout which was angled to pour out onto a plate that sat in cold water. In my vision, the gods poured a mixture of what appeared to be goat's milk and blood. The mixture flowed through the red-hot groove, then what was not lost in steam fell onto the cold plate, creating a thick curd. We shall ask Mother if this vision was that of her ancient remedy."

Young Thaddeus sat silently as he listened to his uncles debate the remedy. Then when it appeared that they were done, he decided to contribute and proclaimed, "I also had a vision from the gods!" His eyes were unblinking as he looked for interest from his two uncles. And then to his surprise, Leo sat down next to him, put an encouraging arm around his shoulder, and begged, "Tell us, nephew, what do the gods tell you?" Excitedly, Thaddeus began telling them of the dream he has had night after night for as long as he could remember, "In my dream, I am much older than I am now." Pointing at himself, he wanted to be sure they understood that the story came from an older version of him. "I was in a large stone house that reached high up into the heavens, its peak as sharp as a needle, just like this." And Thaddeus proceeded to draw a shape of a triangle in the dirt floor of the cave. "Inside this great house, I was not alone. There was a scholar with me who was not much older than you."

Thaddeus, whose heart was racing as he recounted his dream for the first time to someone other than his father, was pointing at his twin uncles. Then he stood up and began pacing as he continued, "In this vision, I am carrying a stone box and am being led deep in to the caverns of this house that was as big as a mountain." His arms arced in a large circle, expressing the enormity of the structure.

Then David jumped in, "Who was leading you, cousin?"

"Why, the gods, of course!" proclaimed Thaddeus. "In every dream, I follow them farther and farther into the cavern but never seemed to reach the bottom." Thaddeus paused, a look of confusion twisted his young face, his nose curled up while his eyes scrunched downward as he wondered why this was so. "Go on," David encouraged, "I think that I have had a similar vision of this great house that you speak of. Was it full of colorful drawings?"

"Yes, yes!" shouted Thaddeus. The young son of Constantine was overflowing with emotion as acceptance from his uncles was indescribable. So he continued, "The drawings are everywhere. There are lions and horses wearing jewelry and strange-looking animals that were both human and creature."

"I've seen them," interrupted David as Leo looked on dumbfounded.

"Why have you never mentioned this to me, David?"

"I will explain later, brother. First I would like to hear more from Thaddeus. Go on, Thaddeus. I beg you to continue."

Now Thaddeus knew for certain that he could finally share his fears, the ones that had been haunting him for the last month since he foolishly angered the gods. Then with a long thoughtful pause, he became more serious. His eyes, now focused at the two older boys, were filled with apprehension while his hands trembled atop his knees. "Well," he began, a sheepish tone taking over his voice, "last moon, on one of the nights when the gods came, I was as curious as I had been for many seasons. These thoughts of desperately wanting to know what it was that I was carrying were hard to set aside, so I foolishly tried to open the stone box, and it angered the gods. They scolded me and said that the time to open the gift was not now and would not be the time for at least a millennium. They said that I must wait until the year MMXII before I would be allowed to open the gift and must protect it even if it cost me my life."

The three boys fell silent; each of them returned to their spots around the fire and sat quietly, their eyes as round as saucers. The gods were not the ones you should anger. *How could this be possible?* the twins simultaneously thought. *Thaddeus would have to become an immortal.* Their questions continued to build and were hard to contain until, finally, Leo broke the silence with an "Um." The glow of the fire danced around the walls and up to the ceiling of the cave. Hot embers popped sometimes, casting sparks toward the opening, seeking the fresh air and the torrential rain that was still pounding the mountainside. Somewhere in the night, the sound of rushing water was uprooting yet another tree, but still the silence in the cave was deafening.

* * *

On the day of the execution, Constantine wept in private. He felt as though his world had come to an end. How would he live with himself after today? He strained to understand the rationale of the founders. He understood that the brilliance of the twins had far surpassed their purpose, and perhaps they should have been born much further in to the future. But how could it be that their brilliance could cause irreparable damage to this world? His face contorted with pain at the thought of hanging the two boys; it was too much for him to bear. Still, the founders had spoken, and in his earthly state, he had no recourse to overrule them, so unfortunately, the outcome would not change. David and Leo would die.

Constantine was born a prophet; thus, he had been awakened to his purpose as well as the calling of others for his entire life. His purpose was to guide Thaddeus in his quest as an executioner and to direct Sebastian in the continued efforts for the formation of an improved governing system. Sebastian and Constantine were both founders, and although they had already experienced their twenty-first existence, for both, this was their first birth on earth. Thaddeus was a relatively young soul living his eighth existence, and although this was his sixth on earth, it would be his first as a knowing soul. Upon his awakening, Constantine would guide him in the understanding and responsibilities of not only an executioner but also as an enlightened one charged with protecting the *Namzu Anunnaki*, the Book of Wisdom.

When the elders, led by Constantine, condemned David and Leo to death, the villagers revolted. "They are special. They have been blessed by the gods," one man shouted with anger.

"You dare not murder them, and if you do, then may all the gods in heaven curse all of you until the end of time," shouted another as the city elders sat quietly.

"Constantine?" Helena called, weeping and pleading for mercy. "These two boys are the brothers of your wife, the uncles of your sons. Surely you must have some compassion. They have helped you with your flock. They cured Thaddeus of the poisoned hives, then saved Sebastian from the treacherous waters of the Mediterranean. My sons have been like sons to you. Why do you not step forward and speak for them as I would do for your sons?" Then she fell to her knees, her arms flailing as they hit the ground beneath; her torso was twisted in agony as she pounded the earth with one breath and then reached for the heavens, gasping and beseeching the gods not to allow this tragedy to unfold.

Helena was also born a prophet; her purpose was to guide David and Leo through their studies in an effort to eliminate the deadly diseases that plagued the earth. In the beginning, Helena and Sebastian were from the same culture and were elected to the council upon arrival on earth. This is her fifth rebirth on earth, all as the birth mother to the twins, and was her eighteenth existence overall. As a council member of the path, her loyalties to the council was very strong, and with Constantine as the head of this council, she could not understand how he could make such a devastating decision. After all, he and Sebastian had been the architect of the path toward utopia, and David and Leo's contributions were paramount to the plan.

Constantine appeared unmoved by Helena's pleas; still, his head hung low as only he understood the pain that was consuming every inch of his being.

"Husband!" The shriek could be heard for legions as she expelled hatred toward him. "Husband, hear me as I speak." Althaia's tone was venomous. For all her beauty, Althaia's anger twisted her face into a frightening mask. "Carry forth this awful deed, and you will lose us for all eternity. If you choose to murder my brothers today, my vengeance will be felt throughout the land. You, as elders, know of what I speak. I order you that in the name of our sacred path, you must release them!" She continued her tirade until her fortitude abandoned her. She then covered her face to hide her shame as she begged and pleaded, moaning and promising anything and everything for their release, and then with one last futile blast of anger, she collapsed next to her mother and wept with her.

Althaia was one of the youngest souls to escape the tragedy that haunted all of them and forced them into this desperate need to rebuild a new world that they hoped would return their way of life. This was her seventh rebirth, always as a knowing soul whose purpose it was to give birth to Sebastian, Thaddeus, and Michael and to support Constantine when the time came to awaken them. In her tirade, she had just vowed to take them both away from the man who was to be their prophet. Collapsed in a heap, her body convulsed with sorrow as the people of Plati continued to barrage the elders with threats and warnings.

Still, the speeches that had paralyzed the entire community went unheeded; the elders ignored the villagers' support for David and Leo. The law had been broken, the elders unyieldingly declared. A complaint had been filed, and justice must be served. Offering no other explanation for their decision and ignoring the pleas and angry shouts hurled at their backs, the elders departed the assembly hall.

Later that morning, the most compelling appeal came from Dianna, Constantine's youngest sister.

"My brothers," she began, "do not allow this. You of all people should understand the consequences. David and Leo are on the eve of success. Their purpose is vital to our survival, and their demise will set us back thousands of years. My brother, they are ready to begin the healing. You have seen the evidence. I beg you, for the sake of the path, stop this lunacy now!" Constantine turned to her with tears brimming in his eyes.

"There is nothing I can do or explain, my dear Dianna. You must trust me and believe that what I allow today will haunt me for eternity, but it is something that I must do, for the survival of humanity is at stake."

Dianna was also a founder but did not sit on the council. This was her nineteenth existence, her tenth on earth. All ten have been as a knowing soul with the purpose of executioner. Dianna had been David and Leo's teacher for all their existences on earth, ten in total. As she left her brother, she vowed never to speak with him again, be it here on earth or in the heavens.

In the forenoon on the very day that would forever change the future, David and Leo were executed. Althaia took her remaining sons and swore that none of them would ever return. Dianna kept to her word and never again spoke to her brother. Helena promised vengeance and proclaimed a new path that would not include Constantine or any of his followers.

"Death to them all," she pledged. "And for all time!" Althaia avowed. And so the division of the path had begun. Constantine would continue to lead his followers, and Sebastian would become the leader of those loyal to Helena. The wars that followed were both unexpected and devastating. Still, the original purpose remained, and despite the conflict, both paths faced extinction should utopia not be realized.

CHAPTER 2

UPSTATE NEW YORK,
DECEMBER 8, 2011

S TEVEN DI CARLO drove his Lincoln Navigator with extra
caution. The falling snow had created a blanket of pure white,
masking the black ice that covered Route 87. The usually safe highway had become a treacherous nightmare in just a few short hours.

The computerized highway sign read, "Albany 12 Miles. *Use
Caution. Icy Sections.*"

Steven glanced over his right shoulder for what must have been
the hundredth time to ensure their children, Tommy and Cathy,
asleep in the back seat, were still safely buckled up; they were. His
wife, Victoria, eyes wide open, was pale and white knuckled. Two
semitrailers had jackknifed a few miles back, and Steven's nervous-
ness added fuel to her own. How good it would be to reach their
Riverdale home just outside of New York City.

"Hey, Vic, you okay? Just another twenty minutes and we'll be
in Albany. If you like, we can get a room there and start up for home
again tomorrow."

"I'm fine, Steve, honest." Then as if regretting what she had just
said, she blurted, "Shit, no, I'm not. I'm scared, honey. As much as
I would love to sleep in my own bed tonight, yes, we should stop in
Albany." Steven smiled at her as she stared straight ahead, her eyes

unblinking, her hands ready to brace the dash, and her feet moving just as though she were trying to help him drive.

Moving slowly down the snow-lit highway, the silence between them was all telling as their attention was focused on the endless ribbon of white unwinding ahead of them, only vaguely aware of the radio playing the Eagles's "Hotel California" in the background. It's not that they were oblivious to the music; it was just an eerie kind of feeling that had them both mesmerized as the truck slowly crunched its way toward Albany.

The untouched powder of whiteness illuminated the evening and the splendor of a snow-covered landscape; still, the treachery of the icy road ahead brought an uncomfortable reality to the mask of beauty that surrounded them.

As Steven eased the Navigator around a sharp curve in the road, he suddenly froze with fear. Out of nowhere, the blinding light had Steven gripping the steering wheel tight. The oncoming semi was sliding out of control and had entered their lane. Steven, with nowhere to go, tried to maneuver the Lincoln over to the right shoulder but was too late as the massive truck slammed in to the Lincoln's back end, forcing Steven to jam his foot hard on the brakes, sending the truck into a full spin, completely out of control.

Victoria, horrified to see that Steven had not buckled up his own seat belt, was screaming at him to do so. Steven could hear Victoria yelling at him but could only think about Tommy and Cathy, and as he turned to check on them, everything seemed to slow down, just as though it was happening in slow motion. He heard himself yell "Hold on!" as the Lincoln's front end hit the railing and sent the black SUV hurtling toward the steep incline at the side of the road.

In complete panic, Steven turned the steering wheel one way while the truck went the other. The more he hit the brakes, the more the vehicle slid. Then in an instant, as the roadside rail quickly approached, he remembered a tip from a friend of his in Montreal, *"Always turn the steering wheel in the direction of the spin, then put the vehicle in neutral and ease the brakes."*

When they broke through the barrier toward the embankment, it was this motion that prevented the truck from rolling over, but to

Steven's horror, it also had the truck sliding straight toward the steep hill ahead. With fear shooting through him like never before, Steven again slammed on the brakes, but it was to no avail. The Navigator crested the incline and powered its way through the low shrubbery.

With Steven's right foot still firmly on the brakes, the truck threatened to slide sideways and into a full tumble down the steep crevasse, so he had no choice but to release the brakes to straighten out the big vehicle, which it did instantly. His relief was short-lived, though, as the Navigator began picking up speed, plowing through small trees and bushes, heading straight for a huge boulder.

He could hear Victoria screaming and Cathy and Tommy crying behind him as the truck slammed hard into the huge boulder, instantly halting the big truck. The airbags shot out, hitting Victoria hard in the face and chest. Steven could smell the airbags as he was sent hurtling past his and through the windshield. His arms took most of the impact, but his head crashed through the glass, sending him over the rock and down a secondary incline. He felt himself sliding face-first along the ice, snow, and mud; strangely there was no pain, and as he wondered why, he lost consciousness.

When Steven awoke, what he saw was beyond comprehension. He was floating above the scene, which seemed surreal. He looked almost dispassionately at himself lying facedown in the snow and at Victoria sliding down the embankment, trying to get to him. Then oddly, he felt a sense joy as he began to ascend high above the trees far away from Victoria and the kids and the accident below.

A warm breeze embraced him and began to carry Steven away. He strained his eyes, trying to get a glimpse of the unfolding events below him, but the breeze carried him farther and farther from the scene which, for some reason, seemed okay to Steven; he was rather enjoying his predicament. When he moved his arms, Steven felt like he was flying. He would glide to the right and then move to the left, then he tucked in his arms and began to nose-dive toward the ground. In a blink of an eye, the ground disappeared and a peculiar light began to materialize. Spreading his arms, he circled toward it.

Hey, I'm getting closer. Shit, I must be dead, unless I'm dreaming. No, I must be dead. There's no other explanation. But why the heck does it feel so good?

"Steven, wake up!" the anxious voice shouted at him. From a great distance, he recognized that it was Victoria's frantic voice calling to him but felt annoyed at her for disturbing his flight.

"Steven, wake up! Please wake up." Her hands were gently shaking him, and then he thought he felt her slapping him just as he tried to steady his descent toward the light. "You're not leaving me, Steven Di Carlo, not here, not now!" Steven could hear her crying, and the light now seemed to be floating farther away. "Steven, please be okay. I'm here, baby. Please wake up." Then he could hear Tommy and Cathy calling to him from a distance.

"Daddy, Daddy . . . Daddy. Mommeee, help him!"

At that moment, the sphere of light flickered and then disappeared. Opening his eyes, he saw a mixture of panic and then relief on Victoria's face. *Where am I? What are those flashes of red? Who is that? Who keeps screaming at me?*

The paramedics had arrived and were yelling instructions. "Get those kids and keep them warm," one man ordered. "I've got some blankets." Steven heard another man say.

Victoria gasped as she noticed the blood streaming from Steven's head and began screaming for someone to help him. Then to her horror, she realized he wasn't breathing. Quickly, she rolled him over, cleared the blood and snow from his nose, mouth, and eyes, and began CPR. When she listened to his chest, she could hear a faint gurgle of air flowing into his lungs. Looking at his face, she saw that his eyes were open.

"Steven, spit for me. Steven, stay awake. Baby, please stay awake."

Why do you want me to spit? he said this half jokingly but really had only thought it. The metallic taste of blood seemed warm and comforting to him.

Steven was once again floating above the scene, trying to understand what the paramedic was saying, but he seemed to be talking in slow motion.

Hey, where are you taking Tommy and Cathy? Why are you taking them away?

"Steven!"

Someone was calling to him, but he refused to be distracted as he was trying to see where the strange men were taking his children.

"Steven," the voice called again.

Annoyed, he turned his head to see who was calling him; there manifested the vision of an angel dressed in a pure white gown with gold and green trim.

As she moved closer to him, she seemed very familiar. Her fiery red hair blowing in the breeze, framing her milky smooth complexion, sent a tingle up his spine. Her voice, as soothing as it was beautiful, seemed to calm him. Then almost shyly, he spoke to her.

"Do I know you? Are you here to help me?"

"My darling," she said, "it is not your time yet. Go back to your family."

Who was this angel who had just called him darling? Where did she come from? Then to his amazement, he saw that she wasn't alone. There were two others with her—another woman and a young boy. Together, they waved at him, the young boy yelling something, but Steven couldn't understand him. Just as the boy came closer, a horrid toxic smell seemed to singe his nose, burning right up through his eyes and into his brain.

* * *

When he awoke, it was still snowing and Victoria was kneeling next him. On the other side of him, what appeared to be a fireman, was holding the lethal little bundle of smelling salt that had put an end to his dream.

Crying and shaking, Victoria Di Carlo's horrified helplessness masked the beauty of her true features. She panicked when the fireman placing a brace around Steven's neck urgently called for help. Then she was consumed with fear when Steven tried to speak but was unable to.

Steven, struggling to breathe, focused on Victoria when, finally, a breath of cold air entered his lungs, he felt grateful for it and tried to smile. Looking at Victoria, he tried to tell her he was sorry about the accident but couldn't form the words. Then panic struck him hard when he tried to motion to her that he was okay, and he realized he was unable to move his arm or legs. He felt desperate as he tried to make out her features and then was terrified to find that the harder he stared at her, the fainter she became. It was as if someone was controlling a dimmer switch to his eyes and turning down the light. Slowly, very slowly, everything went dark.

Somewhere deep in the recesses of Steven's mind, he continued to try to talk to Victoria; he wanted so much to tell her that he was fine.

I'm sorry, baby. I'm okay. Just help me up, you'll see. There's no need to worry, honest. And as Steven Di Carlo's mind spoke those words, he knew that for the first time since they had met, he had just lied to her.

With the reality of his predicament softly infiltrating his consciousness, acceptance began to take over his subconscious, and as it did and with a sort of finality, his mind stopped thinking, and then just like his eyes, his mind went dark and his awakening had begun.

CHAPTER 3

THE AWAKENING

MARIA DI CARLO had not left her son's side in the three days since the accident. Mostly she just sat there very quietly in the bedside chair, watching him twitch and occasionally moan or mumble some unrecognizable word. And then other times, like now, she would sit with her left elbow propped up on the bed, her bowed head resting in her hand while she prayed to God to help him. Absorbed by the gravity of her son's condition, she was oblivious to the nurses coming and going, and she tuned out the constant beeping of the heart monitor. Instead, she focused on her right hand which gently held her rosary while she moved the tip of her thumb from bead to bead, keeping track of her Hail Marys and Our Fathers. Occasionally, she would pause to stare at Steven's chest, making sure that the up-and-down rhythm of his breathing remained the same.

Victoria, leaning up against the back wall of the hospital room, stared right past her mother-in-law and fixated on her husband's eyelids; her own eyes, red and swollen, mimicked his as they twitched nonstop. She watched helplessly as she could see movement beneath his eyelids, movement that seemed to be screaming for help as they shifted side to side and then up and down and then suddenly they would stop dead center just as though he were staring right through them at some horrible happening.

She imagined that his mind was replaying the accident over and over again, just as her mind has done with her. But other than her nightmares, she was lucky; her injuries, mainly superficial, just left her achy and sore while his were devastating—a fractured skull, broken nose and jaw, four fractured ribs, and, worst of all, he was in a coma and had unspecified spinal injuries. What should have been a wonderful holiday for the entire month of December culminating with a family Christmas in Mexico has instead become an unbearable nightmare.

My fault! screamed the terrified voice in her head. *I'm the one who insisted on going home. I'm the one who caused this. It's my fault, and all this happened just because I had more Christmas shopping to do. My sweet, sweet Steven, it was me. I convinced you to cut our trip short. My god, what have I done?* Sinking to the floor, Victoria buried her face in her hands and wept uncontrollably, her body convulsing with each sob; her sorrow, unyielding, was masking the physical pain as she dug her nails through the flesh in her legs and bit down hard on her lip, causing both to bleed.

Roberto Di Carlo sat in the visitors' lounge with both his grandchildren curled up in his lap, asleep. His eyes were dark and sunken, his face, twisted with the pain of helplessness, spoke volumes of the way he felt. His entire body trembled with uncertainty as he stared at Cathy and then Tommy and then Cathy again and then Tommy again, involuntarily hugging them a bit tighter each time. He felt blessed that the children came through the horrific accident without so much as a scratch but worried about the psychological scars that would haunt them forever, especially if Steven . . . He couldn't bear to even think the thought. Lifting his right hand as it shook uncontrollably, he brushed away the hair from Cathy's face and just stared at her peaceful beauty, and then in contrast, he stroked Tommy's head, trying to comfort his worried little face that seemed to be tortured by nightmares as he slept.

Roberto Di Carlo, a quiet man for all of his life, was devoted unconditionally to his family; for the last seventy-two hours, he has been negotiating with God. "Dear God, take me instead of him. He is young. Look and see his beautiful children. They need him,

God. If you take him now, who would care for them? Please, Mother Mary, convince your son to save my son, not for me because I'm not worthy, but for my wife who is named in your honor and devoted to your word. Reward her now and let Steven come back to us. I beg you." And so Roberto Di Carlo continued with his pleas as he gently rocked his grandchildren while they slept.

Steven Di Carlo was oblivious to his condition and completely unaware of the concern that surrounded him in the tiny hospital room; instead, he was panicked and frightened for the safety of his family. They were being held hostage in the bank where Victoria worked. Running as hard as he could, he couldn't seem to get there. One minute the big glass entrance doors were within his grasp, then the next minute he was miles away where the city had vanished, and he was standing alone in the middle of a meadow. At his feet lay a large book that was bound in very old leather, and on the cover of the book was a colorful drawing of a hawk holding a sphere in its talons. When Steven reached for the book, it disappeared and so did the meadow. He was back in Manhattan, and once again, he was charging toward the bank. "What the hell is going on?" he screamed.

Victoria was brought out of her momentary collapse by the sound of a nurse entering the room. Instinctively turning to follow her movements sent sharp pains from her neck to her left temple, then down her spine, convulsing the right side of her lower back. Her painful grunts attracted the attention of the nurse who forced Victoria back in to her own bed, and a new dose of painkillers that would have her sleeping as quickly as Maria Di Carlo could come over to fluff her pillow and adjust her blanket.

CHAPTER 4

THE PROPHETS

ACROSS THE CITY, in a back room tucked in behind the rectory of St. Patrick's Cathedral, three priests sat around a small wooden table. They spoke quietly to one another, worried of being overheard.

The excitement was hard to contain, especially for the old priest who had waited forty-five years for this moment to arrive. Father Michael Ponte was a prophet who was experiencing his twenty-first and last existence; this was his tenth on earth, always as a prophet. Today, the executioner that he has been responsible for in his last three existences begins his awakening. *Much to do,* he thought as his ancient eyes judged young Father Samuel Stewart. *Yes, yes, much to do.* Father Samuel Stewart was a young soul who had only experienced five existences; this was his fourth on earth and his first as a prophet assigned to replace Father Michael.

"When should we awaken him?" Father Stewart looked longingly at his old mentor. "Tell me again about the manuscript, Father. Is it truly a thousand years old?"

"More, my child." He paused as his mind wandered to a life long ago, to a time that marked the end of unity and a path divided. Then with a tone full of recollection, he said, "The first pages were written on his first adventure as an executioner"—then with a bit of a smirk crossing his face—"and the last pages were written when

I was last with him fifty-two years ago. But all in good time, my son. Patience, my dear Samuel, is very important when we awaken someone as vital as—" Father Michael abruptly stopped talking and covered his face with his hands as he rubbed his eyes for what seemed an eternity, then releasing the grip on his eyes, he lowered his hand to cover his mouth, wanting to tell young Samuel everything but couldn't. *At least not yet, not while he was in the room*, the old priest thought to himself as he sat in the shadows of his cloaked hood, invisibly sneering at Father Anthony Jorgenson. *You don't fool me, you traitor. I know who you are. I know why you're here.*

CHAPTER 5

ORIGINS

O N THE FOURTH day of his awakening, Steven Di Carlo was remembering the time before earth, a time of pain and loss. In his first two lives, he was born during a planetary war filled with treachery and betrayal. His first existence saw the loss of family and friends turning him into a warrior with only retribution on his mind. He survived generations, outliving most of his society fivefold. In the end, after hundreds of years of fighting and seeing friends killed and reborn only to be killed again, was anguish he found too unbearable to endure. Recklessness became his adventure as he would transport himself into the middle of his enemies fighting valiantly but wishing that someone would put an end to his misery. Instead, he was captured and taken as a prisoner.

His captor was a giant of a man, his long locks of hair, golden as the sun, hung loosely to his shoulders. His face, enhanced by high cheekbones, sported a prominent nose and a chin that protruded outward. His eyes, blue as the bluest sky, were soft, gentle, and very sad as they stared unblinkingly at him. The silence was eerie, and the sounds of the war could not be heard, no explosions, no screams, and no death.

Steven's mind would replay that time before earth, that time when the giant challenged him to explain what he was fighting for. His name was Constantine, and his mission was to end the wars. So he asked again, "Why do you fight?" And Steven heard himself saying "Why do I fight? I fight to rid the universe of evil ones like you." And the giant looked at him, slowly shaking his head; he seemed hurt by Steven's words. A tear formed in his left eye but was quickly wiped away. "Why do you say that I am the evil one?" Before Steven could respond, Constantine continued, "What if it is you who is the evil one. After all, it was you who attacked us." The angry skies once again erupted with devastating bombs, targeting the ground. The screams of destruction and the familiar smell of burning flesh searing through the senses of his nose was telltale that the missiles had hit their targets. The flashes in the distant skies promised that the devastation would continue, and all the while, Constantine sadly searched those same skies for an explanation. "Perhaps you have reason for your hatred, reasons for your desire to not only kill but your strong desire to be killed. Tell me, young warrior, what is your name?"

Then Steven heard himself respond, "I am Thaddeus, son of Artemus and son of my mother Efthalia, who, because of the likes of you, I will never see again." The giant cupped his mouth and nose as he listened to his accusation; a grimaced look overtook his features. He seemed to lose the ability to breathe, and then and very suddenly, he doubled over in what must have been incredible pain. When, finally, the giant warrior regained his control, he splashed water on his face and sat down crossed-legged, facing Thaddeus.

He looked bewildered as he stared at Thaddeus. Sorrow filled his eyes, and as his lips began to quiver, the giant warrior bowed his head for what seemed an eternity. He spoke in a low voice, a voice that seemed to crack from emotion, "I too will never see my mother or my father again. This war has ripped families apart, destroyed not only lives but also the values we held so dear." Constantine paused in recollection; then, raising his head high, his chin seemed to be poised in either disgust or defiance, his lips were tight to his face, giving off a sad but angry appearance. His arms, crossed at his chest, began to throb as his muscles contracted every few seconds. His eyes were focused on Thaddeus's eyes but looked straight through him, seeing the past lives that he longed so deeply for.

"Tell me, Thaddeus, why do you fight?" he said in a soft fatherly voice. "Do you even know how this war began? Do you know how it will end?" He continued as though he was scolding him. At that moment, Constantine reached over and, with his enormous hands, cupped Thaddeus's face. "I will search your soul, young warrior, to see if you are as worthy as my instincts tell me you are and to see if you are as fed up with this needless violence as we all are and, finally, to see if you are ready to join us in our quest for peace."

At the very moment, when Constantine's callused hands clasped on to Thaddeus's face, silence once again filled the young warrior's mind; he could no longer hear the distant sounds of exploding bombs, and he could no longer see the flashes of terror streaking across the night sky searching for a target to destroy. The sounds of agony and despair coming from the wounded and dying had been silenced and the stench of death had all but evaporated.

Looking into the eyes of his enemy, Thaddeus saw sadness and despair; deep sorrow etched a face already scarred from the battles of this war. Reaching up, he traced the scars with his thumbs, and then as Constantine was doing to him, he latched on to the huge face with his much smaller hands.

Visions of a life before the wars streamed through Thaddeus, lifetimes of peace and tranquility filled his heart. Through Constantine's eyes, he visited all the societies from the many different worlds that celebrated not only life but one another as well; joy was shared with all, and with all, an understanding of harmony between them was unquestioned. Festive gatherings, along with exchanges of knowledge and wealth, seemed to be widespread. Watching through Constantine's eyes, he experienced not only the exchanges but also the feeling of love and respect that they had for one another. He searched the faces of Constantine's friends and recognized friends of his mother and father, and at that moment of amused bewilderment, he saw her.

She was running toward him; her face wore a magnificent smile, her eyes were brighter than he ever remembered them to be, and her voice had an air of excitement he had never had the privilege to hear. It was his mother, and she was a friend of Constantine's, a friend of his mortal enemy, the one he accused his kind of killing her. *How could this be?*

At that precise moment, as the connection with Constantine ended, Steven was thrust once again onto the streets Manhattan millions of years later.

The bank was just a block away. He was running hard; he needed to save them. When he arrived at the bank, Victoria was bound to a chair; she was bleeding and slumped over. Her attacker was staring at him, his evil grin taunting him.

Instant rage had him ramming his body against the door, trying to bust through, but the door barely budged. He slammed his fist against the glass door to no avail. He screamed for help, but no one came. Distraught and helpless, he collapsed to the ground below, his head, buried in his hands, was throbbing with pain, trying to understand what was happening.

Am I dreaming? One minute he was a prisoner of a giant in an unknown world, and the next, the love of his life was being brutalized right in front of him and he was unable to help her in any way. Looking up at the heavens, he screamed up at the architect of his nightmare, pleading for all of it to stop; and then just as he though his demands were being granted, he was instead propelled back in time, and just as abruptly, he was no longer in Manhattan; he was instead sitting on a large rock overlooking a beautiful turquoise sea. On his lap was an old book. The page he was looking at was blank. In his hand he was holding a feather, and as he dipped the tip of the feather into the ink, he began to write.

CHAPTER 6

DOCTOR BRUNSTROM

THE NEUROLOGIST CARING for Steven was considered one of the best in the state of New York. Dr. Thomas Brunstrom had dealt with many comatose patients in the past, but none had the characteristics displayed by Steven Di Carlo. Via the Skype network, Brunstrom consulted with world-renowned neurologist Angelika Jasinski, chief neurosurgeon at Warsaw's Wolski Hospital. From her office in the department of neurology and with the use of cameras, she witnessed the strange behavior of Brunstrom's patient. Three hours of watching and listening to Steven ramble on, not only in unrecognizable dialogue but also in plain English, had captivated her curiosity.

"Thomas, have you called in a linguistic expert to trace the unknown language?" On the large monitor, Angelika Jasinski held the bridge of her nose as she racked her brain, trying to recollect anything remotely close to this kind of behavior. Her dark black hair was tied in a tight bun to the crown of her head; the gray roots, visible an inch above her scalp, gave her the appearance of a woman much older than she really was. Her thin lips were dry and chapped, and her skin, pale from the long Polish winter, had a dull glow that could have come from the ceiling light above her. She looked tall sitting behind her institutional desk as the length of her upper body extended far above the desktop. Like Brunstrom, she was a graduate of John Hopkins University in Baltimore, and over the years, Brunstrom and Jasinski often consulted on each other's cases. Their professional relationship had been one of mutual respect and admiration for the past twenty years.

"Yes, Angie, we had a fellow from Yale come in yesterday. So far, Mr. Di Carlo has spoken in ancient Hebrew, modern Greek and Italian as well as a Gaelic dialect not heard in hundreds of years." Brunstrom walked to the head of Steven's bed, his back to the monitor as he paused to pick up a file, then turned to face Jasinski. He was reading the report prepared by the linguist.

Thomas Brunstrom was born in Sweden and immigrated to the US as a small boy. Growing up in St. Paul, Minnesota, his familiarity with anything other than Swedish or English was nonexistent. Although a tall man, his stature was shortened by a hunched posture and rounded shoulders. What was left of his hair was gray and sparse. He wore horn-rimmed glasses that hung loosely from his larger-than-normal ears and long prominent nose. His beard, also gray, was unkempt. His white smock that was much too large for him hung sloppily from his shoulders. His speech was deliberate and slow as he read aloud the findings of the report. Shaking his head, he said, "I don't get it, Angie. From everything that we've learned about Mr. Di Carlo, the only language that makes sense is the Italian, which, according to his family, he speaks very poorly. He's never been to Greece or Scotland and most definitely never studied Hebrew. But that's all okay too. What's incredibly puzzling is that most of his dialogue in the last two days has been all but unrecognizable. What's even more perplexing, Angie, is that Mr. Waterston, our linguistic expert, claims that it definitely is a language. He says it's complete with the structure for conversation. He's taken recordings back to his lab to try to decipher it. Angie, he claims and says that this is with complete certainty, that whatever Mr. Di Carlo is speaking has no origin on earth but does have some similarities to ancient Aramaic and may, in fact, be the origins of Aramaic, which, as you know, is one of the world's oldest languages."

Both doctors fell silent as Steven once again began speaking in the unknown language. He sounded agitated and angry; he was shouting just as though he was barking out orders. He was struggling in his bed, just as though he were fighting with someone or something. Brunstrom reached over to calm him when, suddenly, Steven grabbed on to his arm and sat up fully with his eyes wide-open, and then in perfect English, he screamed, "Someone please help me."

One floor below, Victoria Di Carlo waited impatiently for the doctors to bring Steven back from the examination room. Sitting in a chair in the corner of the same room, Maria Di Carlo watched her as she paced back and forth and, every so often, stare at the ceiling just as though she could see right through it to the room where Steven was being evaluated. The older Di Carlo wanted so desperately to hold and comfort Victoria but wisely chose simply to be there for her.

Brunstrom, although startled, did not pull away from Steven; instead, he cupped the back of his head and lowered him gently back to his pillow. Peering into Steven's eyes, he saw that he was still in a deep coma. Raising his head to look at Jasinski, he almost screamed, "Angie, did you see that? His heart is racing! Look at the monitor." The heart monitor read 160 beats per minute and climbing; his blood pressure last read 180 over 95.

"Thomas, you need to calm him before his heart goes into distress." Just as the words were being spoken by the Polish doctor, Steven's heartbeat began to slow and his blood pressure began to normalize.

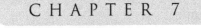

CHAPTER 7

SAMUEL

S T. PATRICK'S CATHEDRAL was cold, dim, and a bit damp on this early December morning. The echo created by Father Samuel Stewart as he paced back and forth in front of the alter was hollow and loud just as you would expect it to be in a big empty church. The saints standing tall on their pedestals were positioned side by side around the front of the cathedral. They seemed ominous in the dim glow of the yellow light coming from the fixtures that were set above every third pew inside the church. The statues were fifteen feet tall, and all of them seemed to be staring at the young priest. St. Patrick stood higher than the rest and was positioned in the left corner just before the sacristy. Dressed in his green tunic and golden headdress, his extended left hand seemed to be pointing directly at Samuel; Samuel paused to look back at his favorite saint.

"Well, Patrick, do you have something to tell me?" he said with a poor attempt at the Irish accent.

The young priest bowed his head as he approached the pew directly in front of the saint. "We have a lot in common, me and you." Samuel paused as he thought back to the days before his faith took hold. Like St. Patrick, Samuel was not interested at all in religion growing up. His thoughts back then were solely of sports, girls, and parties. It wasn't until Samuel was eighteen that the dreams intensified, calling him to the church. And like St. Patrick, he has been charged with leading the flock to a united path while ridding it of all its snakes. "Snakes like Jorgenson," Samuel whispered aloud.

"Yes, we do have a lot in common, my old friend, and I will need your help if we are to succeed." Samuel then knelt and began praying for the guidance he would need. Losing track of time and completely absorbed in his prayers, Samuel did not hear the old priest approach and kneel behind him.

"Samuel, my son, your strength will grow and the challenges you face, you will overcome. The man you have been charged with guiding and protecting is tired of his purpose, and he will need all your resilience and fortitude to be awakened to the true understanding of our path and his renewed purpose." The whispered words were comforting but frightening. Samuel, interrupting his prayers, was all absorbed by how all of this was possible although he believed, without question, what Father Michael had been telling him. Doubt would occasionally surface in his thoughts. Sure, it was the dreams that led him to the church and, ultimately, to this very day. Still, they were simply dreams—dreams that had repeated themselves night after night for most of his twenty-five years. It was eight years ago, at the age of seventeen, that he finally understood the message that led him here to this point, and for the last eight years, he had been absorbing all the teaching of the path according to Constantine. His teacher, Father Michael, has been preparing him and guiding him toward his purpose as a prophet.

Soon, his old mentor would help him complete his awakening; but the anticipation of this day, when it would arrive, and the confirmation that there truly is something beyond death was all-consuming. Being one of the chosen ones that would have the ability to remember all his past lives was more than incredible, but having to wait for it to happen has not only tested his faith and his belief in Father Michael but also played with his belief in his own sanity. Every day, his thoughts were of how it would work: what would he find out about his past existences? How many lives did he live? And the most difficult question of all, did he really want this burden? He looked up again at St. Patrick and wondered if he was one of the chosen ones, then bowed his head and resumed with his prayers.

Samuel Stewart prayed for mankind and harmony on earth; he prayed for peace in his heart and in his mind and then wondered to himself, does he pray to God, or is he in fact praying to Constantine?

When he was about to end his prayer, an encouraging hand embraced his shoulder. It was Father Michael. "My son, your heart is troubled. This is good because without questions, we would never receive the answers, and without doubt, we would never be inspired to be better. Come, my son. It is time to awaken him."

CHAPTER 8

THADDEUS

THE FEATHER TREMBLING in his hand was all he could focus on. Why was he holding it? What happened to the bank? What happened to Manhattan? Where was Victoria? When, at last, he looked up, he saw that he was sitting high up on a cliff overlooking the sea. Small boats were out fishing, and sheep were grazing all around him. Looking down at himself, he was dressed differently. What happened to his jeans, and why was he wearing a tunic? And why were his legs so small, childlike? Looking at his hands, they were the hands of a child. As he wondered, he began to remember, and as he remembered, he began to write.

The twenty-second day of the seventh month
in the year of our Lord, 949
On this day, the darkest day of my life, my father ordered
the execution of my dear uncles, Leo and David.
My mother has since sworn a lifelong vengeance
with promises of hatred against
him. She has taken my brother and I to the house of our grandmother
and has forbidden us to see our father, talk
to him, or even speak his name.
What he allowed happen today will anger me for the rest of my life.

When I asked why, he spoke with sorrow
and wept openly in front of me,
something he had never done before. He swore
an oath that he would explain all of it
to me in good time and asked me to pledge to
him that I would not hate him.
This I could not do.

Young Thaddeus sat alone upon that rock, feeling as though his whole world had come to an abrupt end. He wondered how his life would go on; it had changed so much, so quickly. When would his tears stop flowing? When would the grief and anger leave him? "On this day," he angrily shouted at the heavens, "I have lost two of my dearest companions, and I have lost my father." Collapsing back down on the rock, he wept uncontrollably. Through his tears, his thoughts raced with questions, questions that wouldn't be answered for more than a thousand years. How could they hang mere boys that were two years his senior? How could his father, the chief counsel, have not saved them? They were the blood of his wife, uncles to his children, and were more like sons to him than brothers-in-law. How could he have not saved them?

A sudden blast of cold air along with the smell of acidic filth had young Thaddeus gasping for air and then gagging when he received it. When he opened his eyes, fear struck him violently; confusion had him spinning in circles. Unable to comprehend the vision in front of him, he screamed, but no sound came out. With his heart racing, he grasped his chest as the pain was unbearable. "Has the world come to an end?" he shouted.

CHAPTER 9

A PATH DIVIDED

"What about Father Jorgenson?" asked Samuel Stewart of his mentor.

"I've sent him away on a fruitless quest, young Samuel," the old priest said, chuckling. "He will not be a bother to us for the next two days. Still, we must hurry as the awakening will take some time and we need to hide the executioner's identity from our dear Anthony Jorgenson." Father Michael Ponte, his lips pursed with a sinister smile, cursed his nemesis under his breath. He loathed the charade his once fellow prophet and friend was playing.

When the two priests arrived at the small storage room behind the rectory, a room that they had converted to be their own private office, Samuel decided he needed to know more. Facing the old priest, he said, "I have more questions."

"Yes, my dear boy, of course you do. Please ask all the questions you wish me to answer."

Hearing this, Samuel shook his head in disbelief. For a brief moment, his brow raised up, surprise and uncertainty wrinkling his forehead while his eyes sparkled with curiosity. After all, the normal answer he was used to receiving was "All in good time, my boy, all in good time." Now it appeared Father Michael was willing to talk. Rubbing his hands together in anticipation, he desperately tried to contain the smile that was about to break out, but Samuel was still finding it difficult to hide his excitement. He wanted to hug the old priest but, instead, gently held him by the shoulders. "Anything?" Samuel blurted out.

"Yes, Sammy, anything. After all, the time has come for your awakening, and part of your awakening is asking questions." Father Michael Ponte's ninety-two-year-old eyes sparked like fresh-cut diamonds as he stared into the eyes of his young protégé. "Come, sit down, my son," he said, pointing to a folding plastic chair in front of the small wooden desk that was scarred by the many years of service to the church. "Yes, yes. Where should I begin?" Samuel watched and listened as the old priest slowly made his way to his own chair on the other side of the desk.

"How about we start with Father Jorgenson?" Samuel, once again, suggested.

"As you wish, my young friend, as you wish." A peculiar hesitation distorted Father Michael's attempt at a solemn look as a darker mood took over the old priest's appearance. The sparkle that just, moments ago, made Father Michael look thirty years younger was gone. Instead, his eyes now gave the appearance of shadows, two deep dark rings of black, gray, and pale yellow quickly retreating into its sockets; his eyes, which, just moments ago, shouted with excitement, now spoke of a sadness that was deep and hurtful.

"Where do I start?" whispered the ancient prophet. "It wasn't always like this, you know. There was a time when Anthony and I were like brothers. We would meet each other in almost all our existences. Even in between human existences, we both sat as advisors to Constantine as part of his counsel."

There was a long pause as Father Michael struggled to clear his throat, but more so, the pause was to calm his nerves. He was shaking at the thought of what had happened all those years ago. The right side of his face and neck twitched as it usually did when his discomfort got the better of him. Still, and as his many existences had taught him, he organized his thoughts to remember the fond memories from that terrible time, memories before the path was torn apart, memories of a life at the cutting edge of true civilization, and memories of friendships bound by the common purpose they all shared. When, at long last, he was ready, he took control of his composure and forced an unconvincing smile as he reached out for Samuel's hands.

"My boy, this sad story began a long, long time ago, many hundreds of years before America was even America but thousands of years after our chosen quest had begun. Time enough, you would think for understanding and forgiveness, to understand the mysterious way in that our purposes are fulfilled. Still, with all our knowledge, with all our history, not to mention the many lifetimes we had spent together, we suffered one of the darkest days of our earthly existence."

The moisture from his tears had now caused the dark rings surrounding his sunken eyes to glisten, masking his usual soft appearance and enhancing the skeletal truth of his ninety-two years. "The division of our path happened a thousand years ago almost to the day." The old priest continued with his story but was growing frailer with each spoken word, causing him to gasp as he spoke. "It had pitted brother against brother, husband versus wife, and prophet against prophet. But worst of all, young Samuel, it caused two very special young boys to choose between their mother and their father. The two boys, both leaders and executioners, were the path's most influential souls whose purpose it has always been to preserve unity and to help us reach our ultimate goal. I was the prophet charged with guiding young Thaddeus and Anthony all those years ago, and he was the prophet charged with guiding Sebastian." The ancient one again fell silent; his aura darkened even further and the twitch on his right side intensified.

Wanting to console Father Michael, Samuel gently squeezed his thin frail hands, and before he could tell him that all was okay and to just take his time, Father Michael continued with his story.

"That dear boy was manipulated by him. He had awakened Sebastian with mistrust by not revealing to him his true purpose as an executioner. He led dear Sebastian down a path of contempt for our father, our head of counsel, who led us and loved us for thousands of years. He twisted his mind to believe that the most difficult decision Constantine had ever made was to be evil and full of spite. Yes, yes, it was horrific to watch David and Leo be hanged.

Mere youngsters they were, it made us all question why Constantine allowed it to happen."

Again the old priest paused, but this time, anger flared inside of him. His eyes narrowed in distaste for the memory that had resurfaced after being buried for so long. His hands balled up into tight scrawny fists, ready to strike out, and his teeth bared in a tight pose, causing his chapped lips to stretch his mouth into an angry sneer. "They were my brothers after all," he almost shouted, and then in a barely audible voice, he added, "They were our hope to distinguish the diseases that continue to plague this land we call our home. My god, they were the forefathers of the medical wonders we now benefit from. Still, Constantine must have had his reasons for allowing their execution."

"But what good reasons could there have been? You said that they were just young boys?" Samuel retorted. The old priest ignored Samuels's outburst. After all, it was a question that has haunted him for a thousand years, a question that had never been asked, thus a question without an answer.

"We must focus, my dear boy. Our Thaddeus awaits his awakening."

"Wait!" Samuel said, his face white with disbelief, eyes wide like saucers, his hand pushing back from Father Michael's grip, causing him to almost fall out of his chair. "Are you telling me that Steven Di Carlo is, was, I mean is. I'm not sure what I mean. Are you telling me that we are about to awaken Thaddeus?"

"Yes, my dear boy. Steven Di Carlo is Thaddeus, the son of Constantine. He is the one who will be awakened, and you will be his mentor, his guide, and his prophet."

CHAPTER 10

A Dream inside a Dream

T HADDEUS WAS TERRIFIED as he looked up at the tall structures.

"Where am I?" he shouted as he wondered what had happened to his world.

Had his questions about his father's decision to hang David and Leo sent him straight to hell? Bringing his hands up to cover his face, he noticed they were not his hands. Looking at his reflection in the glass of a nearby building, he eerily remembered where and who he was. Although questions raced through his mind and consumed his thoughts, he answered each one. "Yes, I am seeing the past and also seeing the future. I know this is a dream, but I also know that it's real. I know who I am and who I was, and I know Michael will come for me soon. But right now, in this moment in time, I am Steven Di Carlo and I must let this play out, or I won't know how to save Victoria when fantasy becomes reality and the moment in time collides with the space I'm in." So with all the strength he could muster, Steven Di Carlo began running toward the bank.

* * *

Dr. Thomas Brunstrom had just thanked his colleague and friend, Dr. Angelica Jasinski, for her assessment of Steven Di Carlo.

She would continue to research the world health records to hopefully find some similar cases while he would continue to monitor the very unusual symptoms of his patient's deep coma.

Walking alongside the bed as the orderly slowly wheeled Steven Di Carlo back to his room and awaiting family, the neurosurgeon wondered with a twitch of excitement if the Di Carlo's coma was strange enough to finally get him recognized in the *New England Journal of Medicine*. While they walked, Dr. Brunstrom continued to notice his patient's constant distress. Just minutes ago, he recognized some Greek words being spoken, and now Steven Di Carlo was blurting out the occasional English word. Suddenly, his heart once again began to race. He watched as his patient appeared to be moving his arms and legs just as though he was running. But just as suddenly as he started running, he stopped moving completely; his mouth gaped open, and a hollow scream had the orderly jumping in alarm. His heart monitor was again racing beyond control, and Steven Di Carlo was, once again, in serious distress. Brunstrom acted quickly and had the orderly stop the gurney. He began working on his patient, preparing to medicate him to calm his heart, when, suddenly and just like before his patient's heart began to slow on its own and just as quickly as it had gone out of control, Steven's heart, once again, had returned to a normal rhythm.

Before continuing, Brunstrom entered notes of this latest episode into his journal: "His nightmares, or whatever they are, have been relentless. His heart rate again approached two hundred beats before slowing. Whatever Mr. Di Carlo is experiencing in his comatose state is most certainly taking its toll on his subconscious, but what I'm worried most about is what it will do to his consciousness once he awakens if, in fact, he ever does awaken."

When they arrived at Steven's room, he had visitors waiting. There, sitting with Victoria and Maria Di Carlo were two priests. They were all holding hands in prayer but stood immediately when the bed was rolled into the room. "Hello, I'm Dr. Brunstrom, and I'm afraid that we have a restriction to only two visitors at a time."

"Yes, Doctor," Maria Di Carlo spoke. "We will wait in the lounge while our priests visit with Steven." Then under protest,

Victoria allowed her mother-in-law to usher her out of the room. The two priests waited patiently for Dr. Brunstrom to leave before they approached Steven Di Carlo.

When, at last, they were alone, Father Michael looked at a very nervous Samuel Stewart and said, "My son, it will be fine. You will be fine. First, we will show him the future as these events will be the catalyst for our brother to resume his purpose as our executioner. You, my dear boy, will be his counsel throughout this horrible ordeal. You will help him relive something that has yet to happen. As I have told you, what you are about to experience will also be, in part, your own awakening to the events of the future and how we will need to deal with them. You must help him embrace the pain the two of you will most certainly share, and I'm afraid that, at times, this pain will be unbearable. Samuel, I have seen this future, and I have seen what will happen if he is not awakened and prepared to fight."

"I'm ready," barely audible, Samuel Stewart whispered as he looked down at his feet. Fear mixed with a tinge of excitement had him mostly oblivious to what the old priest had been telling him. After all, he had heard it all before and was already terrified enough as to what kind of future was in store for this man—this man that would become his brother, the same man with whom he would create an unbreakable bond with. Yes, he would be the prophet for Steven Di Carlo, the son of the father of the path.

"He is the son of Constantine!" the young priest said aloud.

"Yes indeed," Father Michael replied. "And also my brother." A smile, hard to contain, beamed from the old priest.

As the two priests approached the executioner's bedside, the ancient one took his right hand while the young priest, now on the other side of the bed, took Steven's left hand; they each then placed their free hand over Steven's heart and began to pray.

CHAPTER 11

DECEMBER 23, 2011

ON THE FIFTEENTH day of his awakening, Steven was about to see the future while being haunted by the past. Running hard toward the bank, he somehow knew that he would once again fail to save her. Still, he had to try, and no matter how many times he needed to do this, he would keep trying. Then as he got to the big glass doors of the bank, there they were. Victoria was bound in a chair surrounded by a group of men; one of the men was pointing a gun at her while another appeared to be yelling at him. Then the man with the gun turned to look at Steven. The evil in his grin was frightening, and the coldness of his eyes was all telling as he began firing the gun.

Steven was frozen in a trance filled with disbelief. How could this be happening? Why was this happening? Although numb and becoming detached from the horrific scene, he was subconsciously counting the shots as the man continued pulling the trigger. Then as violently as one could imagine, Steven escaped his trance and began slamming himself against the doors of the bank. Still, the fortress was impenetrable, and when finally he stopped, perhaps from sheer exhaustion or perhaps from the reality of surrender, he wished for the meadow to reappear. It did not.

Feeling defeated, he somehow forced himself to again look through the glass doors at the carnage that was his wife, but strangely, he could only see his own reflection. So he strained hard to look through his reflection. Still, even with his hands cupping his eyes, he could only see himself looking back at him. Then he felt it happen again. Things were changing; the air suddenly turned warmer, and the darkness of the Manhattan night had turned to a pale yellow glow that, for a brief moment, caused him the need to refocus his eyes. The horror at the bank had, once again, failed to play itself out, but this time, instead of finding himself in a meadow or on a cliff overlooking an ocean or in the middle of a war, Steven surprisingly found himself in familiar surroundings. He was in the bathroom of his cottage at Lake George.

He was looking at himself in the mirror and barely recognized the face staring back at him. In his comatose state, he was trying to process the events that were happening to him. Considering the eyes staring back at him, sadness began to consume him; flashes of the past showed him that death followed him wherever he went.

Slowly receding from those flashes, Steven began to absorb the events of the future. He could no longer remember how he had arrived or where he had just come from as a reality that wasn't began to overtake the dream that was. Crumpled in his hand was an old, worn newspaper; its pages were frayed, creased, and permanently folded at the obituaries. On that page, one name stood apart from the others—Di Carlo. This alone had him questioning the memories of the meadow, the war, the coastline, and even the memory of the bank, and this alone had forever changed Steven's life.

Below Di Carlo, smudged from the dampness of tears that had repeatedly landed on the page, were the names Victoria, Tommy, and Cathy.

The Steven of this future was tired; the bags beneath his eyes were dark and sickly. The nerves controlling his emotions had him twitching like a man drugged out on antidepressants and pain killers. Leaving the bathroom and slowly making his way to the den, he collapsed into his favorite chair.

In this new nightmare, with clear memories of a future that has yet to happen, Stephen Di Carlo was beginning to lose himself to the next stage of his awakening. His body was slouched; his spirit, crushed by the events of his life, cast a shadow around his existence. Forcing his eyelids open, he was unimpressed with the two priests who claimed that they were there to help him. Still, he sat there about to bare his soul to these strangers.

* * *

Samuel Stewart broke the connection as he jumped back from Steven's bed. His face, white with fear, framed his dark eyes that were bulging out of their sockets. His hands were trembling uncontrollably, and his legs felt like rubber about to give way to the floor below. He was unprepared for what he had just witnessed; he was shocked at how real it felt and was terrified at the thought of continuing. Slowly making his way to the nearest chair, he sat and bowed his head, unable to look up. He instead covered his face with his hands and stared blankly in disbelief.

The old priest still standing over Steven's comatose body. His hand, remaining over his heart, was looking down at his longtime friend and brother. Then in a fatherly way, he moved his hand to his forehead just as though he were checking him for a fever but was more out of the affection he had for this man, the friend he had so desperately missed over the past many years. Lightly stroking Steven's face with the back of his hand, he looked up at his young protégé who was near tears in the corner of the hospital room. Without saying a word, a smile creased the old prophet's face as he returned his attention to the executioner. Bowing his head and cupping his hands in prayer, he thanked all the old souls for allowing him to see this transition through.

At last, his purpose was near completion. Young Samuel was indeed ready to take over, and the awakening had most certainly begun.

With his head still bowed, the old priest stared deeply into Steven's face, and at that precise moment, he saw them all; Steven, Giuseppe, Francis, and Thaddeus, all the lives his brother had lived with him at his side. With the memories of those lives flashing through his mind, his emotions began to overtake his feelings of accomplishment. In truth, he thought, the reality of the ages gone by and those yet to come had his sense of achievement feeling insignificant. Still, he lowered himself to Steven's ear and whispered, "We're almost there, dear brother. We're almost there."

The ancient one's thoughts were interrupted as the young priest began speaking in a gruff raw whisper caused by the tightness in his throat. "I saw what happened! I felt his pain! We were there with him in the future. It felt so real." Samuel Stewart was in disbelief of what he had just experienced. He remained terrified at the thought of seeing this through. He looked helplessly at his old mentor, his eyes wet from the tears, his body shaking from the adrenaline. His eyes that, just moments earlier, were bulging had now receded into his skull, his face had turned from white to ashen, and his voice trembled as he spoke. "They were all murdered! His entire family was murdered?"

CHAPTER 12

THE DARKNESS

A MERE BLOCK AWAY, sitting in a small diner that was mostly occupied by hospital workers, the tall, thin man was alone. His winter jacket was buttoned up fully so that the collar covered all his skinny, elongated neck; his pointy chin hung below the oversized zipper that held the collar together like a loose turtleneck. With his head slightly bowed, he peered out at the sparse crowd of mostly nurses and wondered which one he would take that night. A sneer not visible to anyone in the coffee shop stretched his thin lips up the left side of his face, causing his pencil-thin mustache to almost disappear. His eyes, unblinking, sought out his prey, and when he found her, she was sitting alone, nursing a strong cup of coffee, perhaps to energize herself for the second of her double shift or perhaps to drown her sorrows. Connecting his eyes to hers, he began to steal her thoughts; thoughts of loneliness and solitude consumed the middle-aged woman. *Why does no one like me?* she was asking herself. *Sure, I make everyone laugh. Yes, I make myself the brunt of all my jokes, but still, in the end, no one invites me to join them for coffee, not even a drink after work. No one really cares about me.*

A perfect candidate, thought the tall thin man as he sat in the concealed corner of the coffee shop. Concealed, yes, but he still had a complete and clear view of the priest's car while maintaining a strong bond with his new prey.

Earlier that night, hiding in the dark shadows of his own car, he watched the two priests as they entered the hospital. As soon as he was sure he wouldn't be seen, he had followed them in. Then to not be felt, he did his best to keep his thoughts away from the task at hand. Instead, he tried focusing on all the distractions a hospital ward had to offer, but even at that, he was unable to tear his mind away from the vengeance he so rightly deserved, so before he was detected, he fled the hospital and found the darkest corner of this coffee shop to plan his next move.

Even from this distance, he could feel the energy of the happenings in that hospital room. He could sense the euphoria of the old one and the fear of young Samuel. *Oh, how easy it would be to capture his soul right now, but I must wait. First, I will capture the executioner and then let him bring me the old souls, and once I have them, all that ancient wisdom will be mine. Patience, Gabriel, just a bit more patience.* A smile curled his upper lip as he thought of the victory that he was destined to have. Then stroking his thin mustache that sat beneath his long obvious nose, he turned his attention back on to the portly nurse that sat a few tables away from him.

What will I do with her? he pondered. *Should I simply have her end it tonight, or should I send her farther down the road of despair? Ah decisions, decisions.* He chuckled. Then still looking into her eyes, he sent her a vision; in this vision, her coworkers were laughing at her. They were remarking on her weight, and they were betting on whether she had ever been with a man and joking about which man would even want her. As these thoughts bombarded her psyche, her shoulders sagged and her cheeks that, just moments earlier, were rosy from the frigid air turned pale. Even her eyes seemed to sink back into their sockets. That's when she began to cry quietly, alone at her table, wondering what good she was and was life even worth living. He sent her visions of another Christmas alone, visions that while everyone was with family, exchanging gifts, she would be a part of the skeleton crew who volunteered to work every holiday. With her mood darkening, she closed her eyes to escape her thoughts. Instead, she was shown the Brooklyn Bridge and her, standing on the ledge, about to jump. Reveling in the easy conquest, the tall, thin man began his mantra, "Embrace the darkness, dear one, and it will embrace you. Come to me, and I will love you and take care of you. Embrace the darkness, and it will embrace you." Suddenly, his mantra was interrupted as a loud spear of energy pierced through him like a scream in the night. Immediately, he forgot about his prey and focused on the source of the disturbance that had almost knocked him out of his chair. It was the young priest; he had been hit with an incredible dose of despair himself. *What happened?* he wondered with an air of excitement. *Have they begun the executioner's awakening? What did he see that caused an energy wave so big that he would have felt it halfway around the world?*

Evil thoughts began to thrill him, and if someone would have looked at him, they would have seen a wickedness in the dark ink that filled his eyes, and if they were near him, they would have felt a cold chill that emanated from his very soul. "The time is near," he almost shouted to himself. "I can already taste my victory. Soon, Steven Di Carlo, you will be mine, and when I'm done with you, it will be you who is fed to the rats."

* * *

The silence that followed the young prophet's outburst lasted the entire walk back to his car. The quiet release of Samuel's thoughts within himself was medicinal as awareness of his purpose began to infiltrate his soul. The higher calling slowly began to cast aside the fears and doubts that this reality brought with it. He had to admit to himself that no longer was the thought of the path and all its challenges and wonders a fantasy that he had dreamed about all his life. No longer was it a tall story being told to him by an eccentric old priest. The connection he had with the executioner was real. The future events he was shown, as terrifying as they were, will happen. The question he had been unable to let go of since entering Steven Di Carlo's future was, could they change it?

Looking at Father Michael in the pale yellow light cast down through the car's windshield, he saw concern etched on the old priest's face. "What is it, Father?" The ancient face had a sickly glow to it as its bulging eyes stared straight ahead into the darkening night. The old priest was thinking back to the uneasy feeling he had when they left Steve's room, a feeling that had yet to leave him. When he placed all his focus on it, the dread that he felt was immediate and intense.

"We must go back," he said this without looking at Samuel. Then looking up into the heavens, he thanked the elders for the vision. "We were being watched, Samuel. We must go back."

"Being watched by who?" demanded the young priest.

"Did you not feel him? Did you not hurt from the evil that lingered in from the darkness? It starts in your very soul and feels like an empty ache that creeps into the pit of your stomach, a feeling of despair, a loneliness, Samuel, that consumes you completely. When it's finished with the pit in your stomach, it finds its way to your chest and it becomes hard to breathe, just as though your rib cage squeezes all the air out of you. Did you not feel him, my son?" The old man's tone became urgent. "Quickly please, we must go back."

Once back at Steven's room, Father Michael went in alone. He spoke briefly with Maria Di Carlo, and when he was sure that the evil presence was not a threat to Steven, he then returned to his young protégé. "Can you feel him?" he said, almost demanding a yes answer as the old priest ushered Samuel down the corridor. "Search for it deep in your soul, my boy, for this is a lesson that I thought I would never be able to teach you. The feeling will get stronger the closer we get to the source. Tell me, do you feel him?"

"I'm confused, Father. Yes, I do feel something. I feel anxious for Christ's sake." He blurted this out with all the frustration that was building within him. "I need to stop. I need to block everything out because I don't know if what I'm feeling is you making me nervous or if it's the evil that you speak of."

"Yes, yes, of course, my son," Father Michael said this somewhat hesitantly, but deep down, he knew that to teach Samuel properly, he must allow him to sense and feel the evil that slithered toward wickedness. The old priest watched his young friend; his face was contorting with the discomfort he felt, and his eyes were wide-open with a tinge of fear as, most certainly, he was now feeling the dark presence that was seeking out its next victim. Almost doubled over in pain, Samuel pointed toward the nurse's station. "There!" he said, gasping for air. Then with a quick step, Samuel Stewart knew what he had to do and almost ran toward the portly nurse who looked lost and confused, her eyes red and filled with sadness and her shoulders sagged as though the weight of the world had found a home atop them. She was oblivious to the charging priest and appeared to be in a state of incoherence. She stared straight ahead but saw nothing. When Father Samuel finally reached her, he grabbed both her hands, and when he did, it was as though an electrical current unleashed its power straight through him, jolting his arms straight and exiting out his elbows. Still, he did not let go. Instead, he directed her toward a quiet corner of the corridor.

The images were immediate, and the despair was overpowering. Samuel saw a woman on the verge of collapse; visions of loneliness filled her with a fear of not being accepted, never being loved, and dying alone. He could also hear the constant drone that was planted in her psyche: "Embrace the darkness." With thoughts of suicide that were overpowering and consuming all her feelings, she indeed was at the edge of hopelessness, a hopelessness that Samuel intended to defeat.

Digging deeper into her soul, he found a woman who was indeed lonely but far from despair; he found an engaging personality that was hidden by insecurity. He found a soul who, in a previous life, was not only a mother of two beautiful children but also a pioneer in the movement for woman's rights. She was confident and respected despite being overweight. She was a hero to many, especially her family. These were the visions he began to show her, influential visions that slowly eliminated those that were planted by evil. And then as Samuel delved deeper into her mind and her present existence, he showed her a vision of her saving the life of a little girl after she was brought into the hospital for choking. He then reunited her within her own mind with her present-day family, a family that, by no other reason than distance, had grown apart and, in the process, were lost from one another. These visions were powerful, and as they imbedded themselves into her psyche, the evil mantra ceased its wicked chant, attempting to draw her into the darkness.

When Samuel released her, he now saw a woman with bright eyes and a brighter smile. She grabbed his hands and shouted, "I'm going home for Christmas."

Father Michael was the first to feel Gabriel's rage, and in feeling it, he charged toward it with Samuel following close behind. The two priests exited the hospital and were immediately met by a frigid blast of winter. Bracing themselves against the cold, they forged ahead toward the evil presence. In all his years and many existences, the old soul had felt the evil as it cast its despair and wreaked havoc on the weak and the young, and in all those occasions to confront him, he was always a step behind. The devil would disappear like the phantom that he was, but this time, he was closer, and this time, he would summon the power of all the elders and send the evil back into the darkness where it belonged.

Standing in the icy air outside the coffee shop, the tall, thin man, with his coat zipped up to just below his nose, was amused at the two figures charging toward him. Their robes, blowing uncontrollably behind them, reminded him of the priest charging toward him at the last inquisition a couple of hundred years earlier. Chuckling inside his zipped-up collar, he spoke aloud to himself, "Yes, yes, the more things change, the more they stay the same. Foolish priests, we will meet, I promise you, just not today." At that point, Gabriel removed his hat, and as though he were in front of royalty, he bowed deeply, swinging his arm across his body and, with a straight back, lowering his head well below his knees and yelled with as much sarcasm as he could muster, "Gentlemen, I bid you adieu!" With that, he turned and walked toward the shadows of the night.

The younger priest, using his athleticism, ran hard toward Gabriel. When he arrived at the corner seconds after the tall figure turned away, he was gone, vanished. In whichever direction he looked, not a soul was in sight. *Impossible*, he thought. *He could not have disappeared so quickly.* Yet he was gone.

Later that night, Samuel sat alone in his small bedroom; sheer exhaustion from the events of that day had taken its toll on the young priest. His body sagged under the pressure of who he really was and the knowledge of his purpose on earth. His mind raced with the what-ifs and if he was really and truly up for this. He stared through unblinking eyes, hoping that the courage he wasn't sure he had would somehow just show up. When it did not, he cradled his head with his hands and prayed for help. Then with a whisper of wind, St. Patrick entered Samuel's thoughts. *Aye, last night you said that we are the same, and we are, you know.* The strong Irish accent was melodic as it spoke. *Now when we were as one, we were troubled. That's for certain. But you know, we always managed a way out and we not had Michael there to guide us. Remember, follow your heart and you will defeat the snakes. Look toward the present for the knowledge because understanding the here and now will help you deal with what is to come.*

Bewildered but in awe, the young prophet sat at the edge of his bed, wondering if he indeed just had a conversation with St. Patrick. *What did you mean by when we were as one?* A faint echo of laughter rang softly in Samuel's ear as the jovial saint responded, *Me and you, one and the same, dear boy, one and the same. Yes indeed.* And then the laughter roared before suddenly going silent.

In one hand, there was comfort in knowing that there truly was a life after death, that God really did have a plan, whoever God was, and he, Samuel Stewart, was a part of it. On the other hand, dreaming was dreaming, but what he had experienced in the hospital room was more like teleporting into the future where he could touch, feel, smell, and hurt as though he were there.

CHAPTER 13

A SHARED DREAM

L AKE GEORGE IN upper New York State was where the Di Carlos spent most of their summers and occasional winter months. On this day, Steven has returned to his favorite place on earth—returned in mind and soul while his body lay in a deep coma in New York City's downtown hospital.

He was trying to justify why he was allowing this priestly visit. Steven's thoughts rationalized his motives. *I can never forget them, this I know, but somehow, I need to get the evil that happened to them out of my mind. It's destroying me and everyone around me. Shit, I really do need help, but priests? What's my mom thinking?*

Steven, not yet accepting his predicament, kept his head down low. Resting his chin on his chest, he hid his mistrust of the two men that sat before him. Defeated and angry, all he wanted to do was to get up and run away. *That's right, run away, just like the last time I went through this. That asshole, real good shrink he was, all he did was ask what I thought. Well, Mr. Di Carlo, how do you feel about what happened? How do you think I feel, you prick? What a jackass that doctor was, and now I'm doing it again? I swear if these two.....*

Steven's thoughts were interrupted as one of the priests was about to ask him a question. *Well, here we go again! Go ahead, ask me how I feel, and I'll pick you up and throw you in the frickin' lake.*

70

Smiling at the visual he had just created for himself, Steven seemed to sit up a bit straighter and felt a little testy. He was ready to battle.

The priest, the youngest of the two, began to pace as he looked at Steven, his eyes were moist from either nerves or actual tears. *Probably feeling sorry for me*, Steven thought.

"Hello, Steven. My name is Samuel, and this is Father Michael," pointing at his mentor, but not looking at him. "We are not doctors, nor do we know if we will even be able to help you, but we would like to try. Is this all right with you?" Samuel paused as his question received no reaction from Steven Di Carlo. Continuing, he decided to explain why they had come.

"Steven, your mother has told us about your dreams, and with your permission, we would like to discuss them with you. You see, sometimes dreams, bad or good, may be sending us some sort of message. I know the difficulty you would have in believing this, but deep down, I know you do. We, the church, do believe that you are being awakened to a higher purpose. As bizarre as this sounds, we would like the opportunity to explore this possibility." Steven, surprised at what the priest was saying, straightened up even more as he felt somewhat confused. He was not expecting acknowledgement of his dreams; instead, he was expecting to be told the exact opposite. He was expecting him to say, "Dreams are just dreams. They don't mean shit. Wake up and get on with your life." He was sick of everyone telling him that. It's been all he's heard since this began. *And now, someone's actually understanding! This would be a first.* Relief somehow seemed to wash over Steven. *Wow, is someone gonna truly listen and maybe even believe me? Shit, who am I gonna fight with if he's not just paying me lip service?* The change in Steven's demeanor was immediate. He liked this young priest, and there seemed to be a familiarity about him that allowed Steven to lower his guard. Still, he would tread carefully as he responded, "Yes, Father. I do believe a message is being sent to me, and I believe that it is a message of vengeance against those who did this. Are you here to help me get even? Is the church prepared to condone my actions?"

"Well, Steven, perhaps I am, but unfortunately, I can't speak for the church. That will be up to Father Michael." This time, Samuel looked at the old priest as he pointed him out to Steven. "You see, I'm not quite sure yet what my duty to you is. So with your permission, I would like to begin by asking you about some of the events that led you to this time and place." Samuel, still uncomfortable with his task, nervously played with the collar of his tunic. Sliding his index finger back and forth, past his throat, trying to expand the white collar for easier breathing, he struggled to find the words. Then while tugging at and then smoothing the heavy brown fabric of his cloak, a hint of resolve crossed his face, and so he began, "Steven, for certain we need to hear about your dreams, but right now, I want to know you. I want to know Victoria and want to hear all about the children." Pausing, the young priest was rubbing the back of his neck, feeling the pain of Steven's loss and then almost inaudible. "My friend, I know that some of these memories will be very difficult for you, but I also know that most of them will be full of joy and happy times, like this place." With his arms spread out, palms up, Samuel turned around as if in awe of his surroundings. "Steven, tell me about this cottage and the wonderful memories it holds for you."

Watching his face contort as the memories infiltrated his mind had Samuel wondering if he was moving too quickly. Then when a smile creased the right side of Steven's face, the young priest felt somewhat at ease. Taking the big armchair and positioning it to face Steven, he sat quietly, knees almost touching and ready to offer him any comfort he would need.

Samuel decided then and there that friendship would be his first offering; he knew that more than anything, Steven Di Carlo needed a friend who believed in him. Samuel would become that friend.

CHAPTER 14

RELUCTANT ACCEPTANCE

S AMUEL STEWART AWOKE startled and gasping for air; sweat was dripping from his face, his heart beating violently in his chest, while his eyes squinted repeatedly as he tried desperately to focus them. When, at last, he did, he quickly checked his surroundings, and to his relief, he was in his own bed in his own bedroom in the rectory of St. Pat's. *What the hell?* His trembling hands covered his face as his fingers rubbed the sleep from his eyes. "What just happened?" he said aloud to himself. "Shit, I think I just connected with him again, but I'm nowhere near him. How is this possible?" The young priest tried to rationalize the dream that had just happened. "Was it just a dream? My god, what have I gotten myself into?" Knowing in his heart that what had just happened was a lot more than a simple dream, Samuel ran to wake Father Michael.

"Yes, yes, my boy. I was there too. I think Steven likes you, Samuel, but you must get back to him." Looking at his young protégé standing beside his bed, the old priest felt comforted in knowing that this was the young man who would replace him as Steven's prophet. Then still looking up at Samuel, he shooed him away. "Quickly now you must go. Steven needs you!" Then with a sly smile, he whispered, "See you there."

Samuel, returning to his room, was reluctant to lie down and fall asleep; he needed to think this through regardless of his duty to Father Michael and to Steven. "What would you do, Patrick?" he said quietly as he stared at the wood floor beneath his bare feet. "What should I do? What if I'm no good at this? What if my inexperience is what gets his family killed?" The warm-scented air of the church failed to comfort Samuel as he sat there for what seemed to be an eternity but, in truth, was only a brief moment in time. Then as the reality of his predicament once again played havoc with him, he bent forward as though he were in pain. His fingers began tapping on his knees and his thoughts began to relive the events at the hospital earlier that evening. *My god, I was with him in the future. His entire family had been murdered.* Recalling the memories had Samuel involuntarily trembling. His fingernails were digging through his pajamas and into his flesh. His throat began to constrict as the emotion of what he had seen attacked his humanity. Seeing the pain and anguish Steven was enduring made it too difficult to hold back the fear that, somehow, he wouldn't be able to help him. "Patrick, it is you whom I have chosen as my saint. I beg you to show me the way. Please, Patrick, help me do good. Help me help him, and please give me the strength to fall asleep so that I can go back to him." The young priest repeated his prayers over and over, hoping for a sign, hoping for understanding, praying for the guidance he so desperately needed.

Then suddenly, the air in the room changed; the sweet smell of incense was gone, the warmth that failed to comfort him no longer could, and the chill Samuel felt was immediate; his breath was as visible as though he were outside exhaling the winter air. Instinctively, he wrapped his arms around himself to fend off the cold, but to no avail. Instead, the chill intensified, cutting through him like a frozen wind. Wondering what was happening, Samuel checked the lone window in his bedroom and found it to be closed tight, but what amazed him was the frost that was forming on the inside of the glass. Grabbing his blanket, he wrapped it around his shoulders, and then with curiosity filling his thoughts, he sat back down on the bed and prepared himself for what was to come. Just as sure as he was awake, he was sure that he was going to experience something amazing. Fear had not entered his thoughts, and although chilled to the bone, the cold did not bother him. And when he saw the apparition forming just inside his door, he stared wide-eyed with a feeling of enlightenment. But when it came toward him, the reality of what was happening had Samuel scurrying to the far side of the bed, covering all but his eyes with the blanket. "Who are you?" he squeaked out. "Patrick, is it you?" he whispered, barely audible. As Samuel stared at the apparition, familiarity began to comfort him. "Mother?" He called out the only word he could say as Samuel broke down and wept at the sight of her.

Sitting on the bed next to him, Samuel's mother cradled him like when he was a boy, and without a word being said, the young priest fell into a deep sleep and was once again at Lake George.

"Take your time, Steven," Samuel heard himself say. And then realizing he was back sharing Steven's comatose dream and not really understanding how he was able to, he continued asking the questions just as though no time had lapsed. "We are here for you however long it takes."

"Well, do I call you father or just Samuel?" Steven Di Carlo's comfort level was increasing by the second as the priest pulled up a chair and sat facing him eye to eye.

"Call me Sammy," Samuel responded sincerely and friendly.

"All right then. Sammy it is. So you want to know about my memories. What can I tell you about them? God knows I try to remember all the good ones, but it's difficult. You see Father, I mean Sammy, the better the memories, the greater the sense of loss." Steven paused; his tightening throat unmasked his bravado, and his voice, choking up, barely allowed the last few words to get out. So he sat there quietly for a moment, his core trembling slightly as it normally did when he thought about them. The overwhelming sadness had diminished the strong, confident businessman he used to be. The loneliness that was his new reality had battered him hard, and the relentless blame he thrust upon himself allowed no time for strength and courage, only time for self-loathing mixed in with a whole bunch of pity. The realization that he was about to bring it all to the surface not only terrified him but also had him apprehensive. You see, he would be letting a stranger in, something he had not done since his episodes with the hospital's psychiatrist.

Now to confide in someone was to let your guard down, and to let your guard down usually meant someone would get hurt, and that someone was usually him. Still, it was a story that needed to be told, and in the short time since he met Samuel, he felt something different in this young priest, something that wasn't institutional, questions that weren't written on a cheat sheet or in a textbook. Could this priest have the answers he so desperately needed? He decided then and there that he would find out despite the emotional cost.

Through quiet resignation, and choking back his emotion, Steven began, "Yes, Sammy, you're right. We did share a ton of happy times here, so many that it's almost indescribable. As short as that time was, it definitely was full of wonderful memories." Then as if he were reliving a special one, he smiled, then leaning closer to the young priest, he began, "You know, Sammy, I remember our last night here." Steven journeyed back to that night, and he remembered the night sky; it was as beautiful as it was menacing, the flashes of lightning sending enormous shadows throughout the cottage, bringing the ceiling to life with the most gruesome of imaginary monsters that little Cathy could pronounce. *My poor baby*, he thought as he remembered how afraid she was. Pointing at the shadows on the ceiling, he heard her scream. "Daddy, I'm scared. Look over there. It's a witch." Then he could hear Tommy mocking. "Don't worry, Cathy. It's not a witch." And then he jumped at her, yelling, "It's THE BOOGEYMAN!" Choking back some strong emotion, Steven struggled to recount the story to Samuel. All he was able to get out was "That was my little buddy, always the brave one, and he's gone. All of them are gone."

Steven sunk lower into his chair; his body seemed to shrink as the once-formidable man seemed a broken shell of what he used to be. When Samuel reached to comfort him, Steven pulled away and almost apologetically said, "I'm okay. Really I'm fine." So Samuel retreated back to his chair. "Wow, harder than I thought," Steven choked out.

He tried to smile, tried to remember the children that night, but the attempt quickly turned to anguish; his voice, now cracking, became a whisper, and his head hung down low to not show the tears welling up in his eyes. His hands were pulling up on to the seat of the chair to try and stop the trembling that swarmed inside of him, and his toes were curled down into the floor, trying grab on and steady himself. Then after a long pause, he wept openly as he spoke, "God I miss them," then trying to brave up with a forced smile and trying to carry on with his story. "Oh, how my sweet little Cathy looked when her bottom lip began to quiver and her little hands instinctively protecting her ears whenever the thunder roared above us. And you had to see it, Sammy, Tommy becoming the big brother that he was. He saw that she was about to cry. He was a good kid, you know. He went to her and pulled her in close and then held her tightly, promising his little sister that everything would be okay."

With the memories flooding back to him and his throat once again beginning to constrict, Steven excused himself from the den and the watchful eye of the old priest and went to the kitchen to pour some coffee. Incredibly lonely, he stared out at the early-morning mist that blanketed the lake. The low fog that added to the mysterious beauty of the forest sent a shiver through Steven. Instinctively, he held the cup in both hands, hoping that the warmth of coffee would comfort him. It did not.

Mesmerized by the swirling mist hovering above the lake, his thoughts returned to that stormy summer night. He remembered the menacing clouds as they rolled in and how the distant sound of thunder closed in on them ever so quickly. He wished that he could feel them hug him just one more time just as they did that night. He remembered how good it felt to know that they trusted him and that he made them feel safe. "How could I have let this happen? Why wasn't I there to protect them? God, how I miss them."

CHAPTER 15

VICTORIA

VICTORIA DI CARLO sprang up out of her bedside chair as she heard Steven moan. Instinctively, she grabbed on to his hand and found that he was trembling uncontrollably. In the dim light of the hospital room, she could see his eyes moving rapidly beneath their lids and his hospital gown was soaking with his sweat.

Gently cradling his head, she spoke softly to him, trying to calm his anxiety, "Steven, I'm here, honey. I'm right here, baby. Everything is going to be okay." Victoria Di Carlo, not believing a word of what she was telling to the love of her life, struggled to continue with her assurances to him. She wept quietly as the toll of the accident seemed too great for her to bear. The thought of Steven never waking, of losing him, had engulfed her heart and soul beyond despair and continued to wreak havoc with her mind.

To look at her, you would see a once beautiful, vibrant soul completely disheveled and lifeless; you would see a woman who was defeated, broken down by the pain of loss, by the guilt she thrust upon herself. Her once beautiful eyes were now sunken with dark rings beneath them, and her smile that lit up many rooms had turned into severely chapped lips, teeth that had begun to absorb a yellowish tinge, and an angry sneer that would keep most people away.

Victoria Di Carlo held on tightly to Steven's hand; she laid her head as close to him a she could possibly get, her lips pressed close to his ear. "I love you, my darling," she whispered. "Tommy and Cathy miss you so much." She wept at the thought of their children, the horror they had endured, and the fear of loss they now faced. "Tommy and Cathy love you. They want you back, Steven. Please come back to us."

"All of them are gone." The words startled Victoria who sprung up to look at Steven. There were tears escaping from beneath his eyelids. Suddenly, Steven's hand tightened, gripping Victoria's hand like a vice, causing her to cry out in pain when he said, "God, how I miss them."

* * *

After shaking off his self-loathing, Steven made his way back to the den. He had decided that Sammy was the real thing, and so he would tell him his story, all of it, the bad, the good, and the crazy; and if the other old fart had to sit in, then so be it.

Samuel Stewart stood up when Steven entered the room; the ancient one remained seated, his breathing, raspy with age, was loud in the small room. His hood all but covered his face, his hands were also invisibly hidden inside the sleeves of his cloak, and his body was hunched uncomfortably forward, threatening to make him fall.

"Where would you like me to start?" Steven asked.

"Well, why not start at the beginning?" Samuel sat back in the overstuffed chair, still facing Steven, but instinctively giving him some room to breathe. Steven, leaning forward, rested his arms on his legs, his hand locked together, his eyes felt sore and swollen, his throat felt as though someone had taken sandpaper to it; then taking a deep breath, his gruff voice began to tell his story. "We met ten years ago. Victoria had a pretty good job as a loans officer at the New York Mutual Bank. God, how I hate that place." As quickly as he had begun his story, he just stopped. Anger quickly welled up inside him; his face contorted into a fearful mask and his body tightened up into what could have been a ball of fury, and when he continued, you could hear the hate in his voice. "In my dreams, Victoria is in the bank surrounded by a group of men. These men have no faces, yet I can see their expressions, the taunting, the disgust, the horrible cruelty of what they did, and the actions with absolutely no remorse.

"Although my dreams have protected me from seeing the real horror of what happened, the feeling of total helplessness is more than I can bear night after night for so long now. The stupid thing is, I'm not sure what part the bank plays in all this because it didn't happen there. What happened, happened in our home. They were murdered in our home, and I wasn't there to protect them. Like you said, Sammy, I believe there are messages in dreams, and I believe Victoria is sending me one. I think she's telling me that they, being murdered had, something to do with her job at the bank. I need to know why."

Steven paused as anger took hold of him. For months, his hatred had consumed him and his vengeance is what he lived for. Unable to continue, he got up out of the chair and paced in the small windowless space. The two priests, not knowing what to do, kept silent. Fifteen minutes passed before Steven was again composed, and as he took his seat, he sipped the now-cold coffee. Holding the cup in both hands, he continued, "Look, Sammy, you want to know how we met? I'll tell you, but I would rather get to the crazy stuff!"

Steven looked Sammy in the eye, hoping that he would agree. Instead, the young priest responded, "Patience, my friend. Let's take it slow right now and get to know each other first. If you don't mind, please tell me how you met Victoria."

"If that's what you want, well then, I guess that's where I'll start." Steven's expression was indifferent; he really wanted to get this over with. His crazy dreams is what he wanted to understand. Still, he would humor the priest and tell him about Victoria. His frustration subsided as he thought back to that day when he first met Victoria; he smiled at some of the memories of getting to know her and of falling head over heels, madly in love with her. So after a short time he began.

"It's been ten years almost to the day that I first laid eyes on her. You should have seen her, Sammy. She looked exquisite in her dark suit, her skirt just above the knees, her blouse buttoned up to the collar, and her silky black hair tied in a bun. She looked sharp.

And then her eyes, God, her eyes, were so beautifully hypnotic it was hard to tell what color they were. That's when I got caught staring. Sammy, I was trying to figure out the color of her eyes and she caught me ogling her.

"Anyway, I had come into the bank to arrange a business loan to expand my ad agency. Shit, we were so successful that in two short years, we had more than our share of major accounts. Di Carlo, Davis, and Donnelly, we had become one of the top five advertising agencies in the state of New York. Anyway, I went in to meet with our banker and, instead, fell in love."

Steven, dry washing his face, once again fell silent as his memory of that day came back to him in vivid detail. With his eyes closed and a smile threatening to break out, he allowed himself the moment and then shook his head embarrassingly, remembering the lack of tact he had that day at the bank. The conversation he had back then replayed in his mind.

"Hey, Tracie, I'm here to see Brian."

"Sure, Mr. Di Carlo, but by the way, that's not Brian. He's in his office. You sure you wanna see Brian? You know I can delay your appointment if you like, and if you want to know, Mr. Di Carlo, her name is Victoria, Victoria Weeks."

"Thanks, Tracie. I owe you."

Steven's smile puzzled the two priests as they had been watching and wondering what was going through his mind. And then, out of nowhere, Steven continued his story, "You see, Sammy, my friend Brian Cantrell was the only person I had ever dealt with at New York Mutual. In fact, Brian was the one who helped us get the money we needed to get our agency going. He always told me that we made him look like a genius. I used to tell him that he was the one who was the genius, especially when he introduced me to Victoria.

"A couple of days later, Brian was on the phone, telling me that Victoria was asking about me. Well, about a half dozen phone calls and some schedule adjusting, we were out on our first date, which was Pizza at Gino's, followed by a Rangers game at Madison Square, and then after the game, we had drinks at the plaza. Sammy, I'll never forget how incredible she looked that first night in her tight jeans and New York Rangers sweatshirt. I thought that she bought it just for the occasion but found out later that she was a huge Rangers fan. Anyway, the entire evening was magical. You know, that feeling when you meet someone for the first time and as you get to know them, you feel that you've' known them forever. That's just how it was with us.

"I proposed to her on December 24, 1998, following six months of falling in unconditional love with her. The love that I felt for Victoria was something that I had never experienced with anyone else, ever! Sammy, you ever been in love?" But before Samuel could answer, Steven plowed ahead just as if he wanted his story out and he wanted it out quickly. "Hey, you know how everyone says that becoming a parent was something as natural as life itself? You know what, Sammy? They're all bang on. When Tommy was born, it was the most incredible of feelings, and when Cathy arrived, well, it's an emotion too difficult to explain properly.

"I miss them so much that not a second goes by that I don't think of them, and then it brings me full circle because when I think of my little family, I think of those bastards who murdered them. Sammy, I swear in front of God and anyone else who gives a shit that whoever did this is gonna pay!"

CHAPTER 16

OUT ON THE LAKE

A TRAGEDY YET TO happen was playing out like a horrible past filled with relentless nightmares of unspeakable horror. Steven Di Carlo, twitching and moaning along with the occasional verbal outburst, lay in his hospital bed while future events were creating mayhem in the deep recesses of his comatose mind. Sitting at his bedside, Victoria Di Carlo held on to her lover's hand, trying desperately to calm his despair. Wide-eyed and scared, she prayed that he would just wake up and rid himself of all these horrible dreams. Her eyes stained from the continuous worry and nonstop tears twitched with every spasm that struck Steven's core. Her hands, trembling with adrenaline, made it difficult for her to caress his face. She was torn on whether she should call one of the nurses to tend to him or let the episode play out. She decided that she would let it play out.

For Victoria, this was the first time she had been able to understand some of his ramblings, the first time that she could hear his voice in a somewhat recognizable way. "Maybe he's trying to talk to me," she whispered, justifying not calling for help. "Steven, we're not gone. We're here, sweetheart. We're here with you."

"Whoever did this is gonna pay." Steven growled out while his eyes darted from side to side beneath his closed eyelids.

"Who, baby? Who's going to pay? What is it, Steven? Please wake up!" Victoria was near collapse when Steven's agitation seemed to calm. Still trembling uncontrollably, she wondered what horrible nightmare he was having. Then feeling helpless, she buried her head into Steven's pillow and began to weep. When, finally, she gained some control over her desperation, she slowly made her way to the side cabinet for her pen and journal, then sitting down in her bedside chair, she dried the tears that had given some color to her pale cheeks and began to write.

Day 15 (December 23, 2011)
Today, Steven seemed to be very angry.

Inside Steven's nightmare, it was June 2013. Samuel could see his discomfort as a furrow was slowly forming above Steven's brow. Steven, overwhelmed by the recollections of his life, pushed himself as far back as he could into the big armchair. Feeling totally spent, he locked his hands at the back of his head and just stared into oblivion. Samuel, seeing the distress in the eyes of his new friend, decided to allow him some relief by asking to go for a walk.

"Sure, Sammy, let's get out of here," he said in resignation, then getting up out of the chair and with a bit of a lift in his tone, he continued, "Come on, I'll show you around our little slice of heaven. Uh, he doesn't have to come, does he?" Steven, pleased with his shot at the other priest who had contributed nothing, not even a head nod, could see Samuel trying to hide his smile as they left the den for the outdoors and the sanctity of the lake.

Steven led the way down the dock, and Samuel followed close behind. "Do you like to fish, Sammy?"

"I don't know. I've never fished before, and uh, don't know how."

"Its easy, Padre. Come on, hop aboard." Steven untied the security ropes, pushed off the dock, and they were off.

They rode out in silence for quite sometime. Steven, standing up, eyes forward, enjoying the rush of fresh air and the slight spray of the lake against his face, had the boat at full throttle. Samuel, totally delighted with the speed and the roller-coaster-type ride, sat with one hand grasping the seat and the other holding on to the console, bracing for the next hard slam against the water. They were heading for Steven's favorite fishing hole, a small cove on the northeastern side of the lake.

Thirty minutes later, they arrived. "See that creek over there, Sammy? It's my secret spot. The fish gather there, hiding in the weeds. I guess they like the fresh water running in, or maybe it brings them food. I'm not too sure. I just decided to fish here one day and have been filling my basket ever since."

Steven, putting the motor in neutral, started to set up the fishing poles. Samuel got up from the safety of his seat, eyes wide-open as he took in the majesty of Lake George. He stretched out his body, reaching up high toward the bright blue sky and then filled his lungs with the cool mountain air. "Wow, the air here actually tastes sweet. It is absolutely unbelievable. I love it. How'd you find this place? It's amazing."

"Sammy, my friend, you think the air's sweet. Wait until you take a drink from that creek. Never tasted anything better than the water we get from that creek, not like the city. Take a drink from a city tap? Yuck! Heck, take in a deep breath of air in New York City and you have to rush home and brush your teeth. Yeah, it's pretty special all right."

The thought of comparing New York City to Lake George made them both laugh, and then almost immediately, they fell silent as Steven cast out one of the lines and handed the pole to Samuel. As the second line hit the water, they both sat back in the swivel chairs, drinking beer and watching the green and red floats bobbing up and down, waiting to signal a strike.

"How did we get here? Sammy, it was July 1999. Ending up here was sort of a fluke. You see, we were supposed to be on our way to Lake Placid. I guess we were about fifty miles past Albany on Route 87 when we saw a first sign advertising a bed-and-breakfast. We thought, what the heck, we didn't have anything else to do, why not check it out. Lake Placid could wait. After all, we'd been before. So we just checked the map, followed the signs, and ended up here. I tell ya, when we got here, the sight of this place just blew us away. Sort of like what it's doing to you right now.

"So anyway, we found the B&B. It was right on the lake and we just simply fell in love with all of it. The sounds of the loons, the crickets, the wind rustling through the woods, the mesmerizing rhythm of a babbling brook that ran in behind the house, and, of course, the stuff you can do in the summer and the skiing in the winter. And you know what was best of all? It was only three hours from the city. The decision was simple. All we had to do was find a realtor.

"I remember thinking, who would have believed it? Little Stevie Di Carlo, not only a partner in a very successful ad agency with a house in Riverdale, a twelve-suite apartment building in Queens, and now a cottage at Lake George. I joked with Victoria that my friends and relatives in Brooklyn would ask where the frigg is Lake George and what's with the name. Sure enough, when we invited my cousins; have you met Tony and Stef? You've probably met their wives, Anna and Connie. They're at church every freakin' day. Anyway, when we invited them up for a weekend, Tony looked at Stef and said exactly that, 'Where the frigg is Lake George?' And they laughed and I remember Stef looking at me with this huge grin and Brooklyn accent. 'Stevie, couldn't you find a lake with a better name?' Of course, the joking went on until they saw the place. That's when Tony put his arm around me and said, 'Hey, cous, you done good. I'm proud of you. You got a beautiful family, a knockout wife, and now I know you gotta be rich.'

"Well, you've seen the cottage. It didn't take us long to find it, and it was love at first sight. Only five years old and made from real logs. It has a great cellar, Sammy. I filled it with my dad's homemade wine. We'll crack a bottle open later and have it with the fresh trout that we're gonna catch." Elbowing Samuel in the ribs, he pointed at his float. "You've got one, buddy. Reel it in." Samuel's first fish was a ten-inch rainbow trout that gave him a great fight jumping out of the water a half dozen times before he was able to net it.

After the excitement calmed, Steven sat in silent recollection of when he and Victoria first laid eyes on the cottage. He remembered looking at her and exclaiming, "It's actually made out of logs." He thought back at how impressed he was with the high gloss finish of the wood, then how blown away they were as they came around the front of the cottage and first seeing the two massive windows that went right up to the peak of the A-frame centering the front exterior right above the double doors. He smiled and then choked up a little at how excited they were.

"Victoria loved the brick oven," he said out loud but unintentionally. Then looking at Samuel as if he should know what he was talking about, he continued, "My mother, on the other hand, absolutely drooled over it. Sammy, you had to see her. When she found out we had a brick oven, she practically kneaded the dough in the car on the way to the cottage. Wait until you taste her delicious home-baked bread. Oh, and the pizza! Today's pizza day! Sammy, you're in for a treat. Victoria, after learning a few recipes from Mom, proclaimed that every Sunday would be pizza day." Then with a bit of sadness mixed with a painful longing, he quietly said, "Today is Sunday."

"Anyway, shortly after buying the cottage, we got ourselves this boat. Victoria said that since we had a dock, we should have something to park there. So we chose this, an eighteen-foot Boston Whaler, not what you would call a ski boat but it does everything else. We fished right here in this spot, but mostly we toured the lake to our hearts' content, and when the kids remained on shore, we had very special moments. If you've ever made love on a boat, Sammy, you will know of what I speak. The peaceful rocking of the waves combined with the love and passion made for some of the best sex. Hey, you okay with this kind of talk?"

"What'd you think, Steve? I was born a priest? I could tell you some pretty good stories too, but right now, I just want to hear yours."

"Okay, well, one of the most memorable nights of my life was the third of July 2004. It was an absolutely perfect night, warm enough to be naked yet cool enough to need to embrace. We were out here in the middle of the lake just cuddling and playing. I don't know if I should be telling you this, but it's a good story, so here goes, buddy. We got so intense that there was no holding back. The sex was so passionate that when we heard the fireworks go off, well, the moment for us lit up the sky with an explosion of colors and waterfalls of fire. We rolled over with such an amazing . . . I'm not sure how to describe it. Maybe it's as simple an unquestionable love for each other that we hugged and laughed until our faces were wet with joy. Who knew that they were testing the fireworks for the Fourth of July celebrations?

"You know, Sammy, I still feel her with me every day, and every night when I close my eyes, I can still hear her laughter just as she laughed on that third of July back in 2004, only now when I reach out to hold her, she's not there. My face is still wet though. The tears are very real and come from a heart so broken that life no longer has meaning to me, only vengeance."

CHAPTER 17

PIZZA AND WINE

S TEVEN'S MOOD, CONFLICTING with the luster of the bright blue sky, had changed as his thoughts took on a torrent of emotion. Samuel helplessly watched while a wall of silence replaced the positive dialogue that had evolved during their outing. Not wanting to interfere with the demons attacking Steven's soul, Samuel, instead, quietly prayed for his new friend to find the strength and the courage to defeat the demons once and for all.

Reeling up the lines, Steven readied the boat for their trip back to the cottage; he tried to smile in recollection of that night. The incredible coincidence of the fireworks was one thing, but the passion they had for each other was quite another. Unmercifully, his mind kept flashing back to that awful night, the night his family was brutally murdered.

The sun was perched high above the southern sky as the Boston Whaler made its way across the glassy surface of Lake George. Steven had become oblivious to Samuel's presence, and with images of his slaughtered family running uncontrollably through his mind, the heaviness that had somehow lifted in the past few hours had returned with a vengeance. Arriving at the dock, trembling uncontrollably, he secured the boat and, without another word said, went directly to his room.

Slumping onto his bed, he sat quietly, staring at his favorite picture of Victoria. It was of her driving the boat one warm summer evening, her dark beautiful hair blowing wildly behind her, the profile of her face almost a silhouette against an early evening sky. Her eyes were mesmerizing and full of thought, but the camera had not only stilled her hypnotic look but also the words before she spoke them. His sense of loss playing havoc with his emotions had him holding his head between his hands as he silently wept, and as he did, he hit himself with those same hands. It was as if he were trying to knock the reality of it all away from his mind, or perhaps to wake himself from this unbearable nightmare.

Seeking control, he unknowingly bit into his lower lip, and as the blood ran down onto his chin, he was amazed that he felt no pain. Steven wondered whether he would be able to continue revealing his life to Samuel, a life that, not too long ago, he would have thought impossible, a tragedy that he would have thought only happened to someone else's family, not his own.

When, once again, his emotions were in check, he forced himself to the shower and turned the knob to cold. Soaking his head in the icy water allowed him to let go of this latest episode. However, he knew another would come, so he wouldn't lie to himself about that, but this one had to go. He would save his breakdown for far worse memories than this.

Ready to face the duo once again, he entered the kitchen to a respectfully quiet reception. His mother was serving pizza that was fresh from the oven; Samuel was pouring wine for the other priest and his father. Relieved to see his son join them, the elder Di Carlo pulled back the chair next to him for his son to sit in.

"Come, sit beside me. Look, your mother, she made pizza, your favorite."

"Thank you, Pop. Did you save me a big piece?"

"Il pui grande per te, e solo te figlio mio. I always save the biggest for you, my son. Wine?"

"Sure, I was just bragging about your wine to Samuel, so what do you think, Padre? Good enough for Sunday mass?"

"Mr. Di Carlo, your wine is excellent, but I'm afraid the pizza is better." Maria Di Carlo, beaming at the compliment, quickly dished out more. Wiping her hands on her apron, she went and stood by Steven, softly massaging the back of his neck. Steven responded by turning his head so that she hit the right spot.

After dinner, they sat around, talking about the Yankees and the dismal season they were having. Steven, tuning out the conversation, kept staring at the old priest. His head, still cloaked, was slightly bowed as he sipped his wine as if it were a cup of hot tea. His eyes were visible, and it was in those eyes that Steven silently swore familiarity, but from where?

Father Michael, sensing Steven staring at him, did not allow their eyes to make contact. It was too early to reveal their past together. After all, it could seriously affect his awakening, and this he dared not do.

CHAPTER 18

THE NAMZU ANUNNAKI

MARIA DI CARLO awoke completely confused as to where she was or where she had been. "Please have some more pizza, Father," she said aloud, then realized that it had all been a dream. But what a terrible dream. Jumping out of bed, she woke up her husband, Roberto. "Please tell me, Berto, are my grandchildren okay?"

"Of course, they are. Why are you asking?"

"Jesu Mio, I had a terrible nightmare! It was so bad I don't want to talk about it."

Roberto Di Carlo, his face contorting into a twisted mask, wondered why her question seemed so familiar. Trying to recall his dream, he could only remember that he was up at the cottage with the family, nothing more. Then instinctively, he followed Maria down the hall and into the bedroom where Tommy and Cathy were in a deep sleep.

"Come, Maria. You see, the children are fine. We have a long day tomorrow. I know it will be a difficult one, but tomorrow is Christmas Eve and we will be very busy, so we should get some sleep." With that, Roberto Di Carlo went back to his bed and fell asleep before Maria left the children's room.

* * *

Back at Lake George, caught in a dream they all shared, Father Michael knew that the next couple of hours would be incredibly intense as Steven was about to talk about the day of the murders. Pulling Samuel aside, he wanted to prepare his young protégé. "My son, we should talk," the old priest said in his strongly accented gravelly voice.

"Certainly, Father, but can't it wait? Steven is waiting for us in the den."

"Patience, my son. There is much to discuss before we move on to the next chapter of Steven's life. I want you to wake up now." With that, the old priest seemed to vanish while Samuel was in the hallway of the Lake George cottage in between the kitchen and the den. He stood there, not sure what had happened. "Where did Father Michael go, and why would he ask me to wake up when I'm already awake?"

* * *

Samuel Stewart's eyes slowly opened in the darkness of his bedroom; his thoughts were confusing to him. Where was he? Or a better question was, where had he been? Staring straight ahead, straining to remember, he searched for answers but, instead, received only glimpses of what was or maybe wasn't a dream. Sitting up on the edge of his bed, he wiped his mouth, then, scrunching his forehead in an attempt to remember, revealed that, in his dream, he had been eating pizza and that Father Michael was with him. Pacing back and forth in the small room, he talked through the brief snapshots of his dream. "I was on a boat, I was eating pizza and drinking wine." Then as though someone had just punched him in the stomach, he realized where he had been and why. "My god, they're all dead! His entire family, they were all brutally murdered!" Horrified, he paused at the small window in his room and looked out into the darkness of the cold winter night, and when he did, he remembered that it was Christmas Eve. Immediately, sorrow filled his soul, and the pain of loss engulfed his entire being. Falling to his knees, he began to pray.

"My dear Patrick, how could this be allowed to happen? Those two beautiful children and their amazing mother murdered that way. Why! What purpose could it possibly serve?" Still kneeling on the hard floor of his bedroom, he stared up at the emptiness of his small room, the barren walls that had cracks so old that not even the new coat of paint he had applied the previous summer couldn't hide them, the tiny bed that had become his refuge, and the solitary cross hanging above the maple headboard. Even the cross which he prayed to night after night would not draw his focus. Instead, on this night, his eyes rested on the old commode he had brought from his family home, the same commode that he had had when he was a child, the same picture that sat centered on the top, the picture of him with his parents when he was nine years old, about the same age that little Tommy Di Carlo will be when he is murdered. Samuel, paralyzed at the thought of it, did not weep, but still tears stained his cheeks. The sense of loss confused him. Staring down from the picture to the floor, he continued to talk through his memories. "I've never met them, yet I know them. It's just as if I've known them forever." In that moment in time, as the silent questions worked themselves through Samuel's mind, he received an answer. *They have not perished yet, dear one. There's still time to save them, you know. Will you do this for me then? Will you save them?*

The soft Irish accent was melodic as it spoke and seemed to be coming from directly above him. As Samuel stood up to meet the voice, he responded, "Dear Patrick, my chosen saint, please tell me how to save them, and I will. Tell me how to protect them and chase away the snakes, and I will give you my word that I will be your emissary. For the love of God, please show me the way!" The silence that followed was expected. Samuel, feeling somewhat comforted, looked out the window at the falling snow that glistened as it landed. Drying the tears from his face, he began to feel a warmth that was coming from inside his chest and then a release of the dread that he had been feeling exiting out the top of his head. He managed a smile, knowing that something amazing was about to happen. *By the love of all that is holy and by the love of all the elders who share the path, we will save them.* As he thought this, Samuel could feel St. Patrick's hand gently squeezing his right shoulder.

Looking at his reflection in the small window, he could see his favorite saint standing behind him, smiling, but when Samuel turned and looked over his shoulder, he could not see him. When he turned back once again to the reflection in the window, St. Patrick was there and pointed beyond the images far into the cold winter night. Samuel, following his gaze, stared in wonderment as the night sky turned to day and the snowy streets turned to sand. His room, the church, the snow, and New York City vanished before his very eyes as Samuel found himself standing in a desert, his toes digging themselves into the warm sand.

"Are you coming!" He heard a voice call out to him. "Hurry, Uncle! We have much to do." The voice belonged to a young boy of maybe ten or eleven, dark curly ringlets surrounding a soft round face that sported an impatient frown as he looked up at Samuel. The boy stood in front of him, seemingly inpatient. The slightly built boy wore a white tunic that hung just below his knees, his hide sandals had straps that wrapped up around his ankles, his sun-darkened skin was as smooth as a child's should be, and his chestnut-colored eyes were as bright as the sky above.

In his arms, he carried an ornate chest that had the appearance of a highly polished wood; its top was engraved with some type of monogram that appeared to be circles within circles.

What Samuel found curious was that there did not appear to be an opening to the box, and when he reached for it to have a look, the young boy pulled away. "Uncle, you said by decree of the gods, no other man may touch the *Namzu Anunnaki*." The boy had a stare that let Samuel know that his actions were very serious. "Come, Uncle, we must bring the *Namzu Anunnaki* to safety."

The young boy quickly turned and walked away, and when Samuel looked up to see where, he was awestruck by the sight of a magnificent pyramid whose stones looked freshly cut and polished, each massive piece of granite set with precision from its immense base to the sharp peak hundreds of feet up, reaching high toward the heavens. A closer look revealed that bronze-and-silver-colored veins flowed through the stones, connecting each to the other, and as the boy approached, the veins began to glow brightly in the sunlight, and as he continued to walk toward the pyramid, a massive wall slid open.

The entrance to the pyramid seemed to welcome them as they entered; torches lining the corridor inside the pyramid began to light as they walked toward them, and there were hundreds illuminating the narrow passageway that descended deep below ground level. As they entered the pyramid, Samuel felt enlightened just as though he had been there before and knew exactly where they were going.

The entrance itself was a vision to behold; the walls were massive canvasses of art with drawings of elk, elephants, lions, and tigers all sharing a pasture of green with yellow flowers adorning the peaceful scene. There was a mighty river that flowed through the pasture, then split into two, flanking an island with eucalyptus trees, palm trees, and a whole host of lush vegetation. There were multitudes of birds circling the sky above the island and perched in the trees. When you looked closer at the blue waters of the river, you could see water buffalo treading high in the fast water and fish frolicking in the waves.

While Samuel stared at the utopia drawn on the walls, the young boy who had called him uncle had disappeared from his sight. Quickly, Samuel descended the first level. Still, the beautiful art was everywhere as the landscape continued down with him, flickering in the candlelight of the torches. When he reached the second landing, he could hear the faint footsteps of the young boy still descending farther into the caverns of the pyramid. Although not stopping to fully appreciate the art on these walls, he did notice a dramatic change of scenery.

Painted on this level, the walls were alive with people going about their daily business, some were selling their wares while others were buying. There were soldiers striking people down with their swords while other soldiers guarded a palace. Boys with long braided ponytails rode horses at full flight while young girls watched and giggled at them. In the far background stood a majestic city with brightly colored domes on the roofs of the large white buildings. A high wall surrounded the city, the entrance guarded by soldiers holding lances in front of large golden doors.

Still hurrying to catch up to the boy, Samuel quickly moved down the narrowing staircase to where he finally caught up with him on the third level. On this level, the walls were blazoned with bright reds, yellows, and browns; it was a world at war with explosions, death, and mutilation. In the skies depicted above the battlefields were drawn a series of five planets each had fires burning on them. "Uncle, why is this picture familiar to me? Why do I remember this?"

Samuel understood the familiarity the boy felt. "Because it was our home, young Thaddeus. It was our paradise, and it is why we are here." Samuel then turned to face the opposite wall where there was a small doorway. "Come, Thaddeus, it is time."

The young boy followed his prophet toward the painting of a small stone door. When they arrived, there was an emblem meticulously chiseled into the door; it was of circles within circles, within circles. It was identical to the emblem that was forged on to the top of the box that Thaddeus carried. With the young boy watching in awe, Samuel placed his hand on the engraved circles just as though he were summoning some sort mystical power. He then began tracing the circles with his finger when Thaddeus interrupted his concentration. "What do they mean, Uncle, all the circles? What do they mean?" The young boy repeated himself as though it was urgent to receive the answer.

Samuel stopped tracing the circles, and looking down at the boy, he said, "These circles are the secrets of an everlasting life. They are the keys to the *Namzu Anunnaki*. Many years from now, together we will be led back here to retrieve the *Namzu Anunnaki*, and when that time comes, an apocalypse will signal our new life here." The young boy, looking more puzzled than ever, just stared at Samuel as he continued to trace the circles with his finger when, suddenly, there was a loud click. The boy watched as Samuel pushed the small circle that was roughly the same size as his finger into the stone wall and then continued to trace until there was another loud click, and yet another circle sunk into the door. This was repeated several more times until a startling hiss had young Thaddeus jumping back and then watched in awe as the painting depicting a stone door opened.

Samuel went in first, and when he passed through the doorway, he was suddenly back in his bedroom at St. Patrick's. The snow was still falling, and the frigid night air could be felt seeping through the thin pane of glass in the window. Disoriented as he watched the snowfall, he slowly remembered where he was—his dream of Steven at the lake and of young Thaddeus and *Namzu Anunnaki*. Yes, he remembered all of it and knew that Father Michael would be waiting for him in his office.

With him at St. Patrick's and Steven Di Carlo lying in a hospital bed in downtown New York, Samuel finally knew that his purpose had meaning and that failure or fear would not be an option. With a renewed sense of belief, he went to meet with Father Michael.

CHAPTER 19

RESPONSIBILITY

"Well, my son, I imagine that you have a lot of questions." The old priest looked at the young man sitting in front of him, and when he saw him, he saw himself many lifetimes before when he had experienced his first awakening as a prophet.

"Actually, Father, only one question." Samuel's face was focused and determined; his eyes, glistening with clarity, were wide-open and staring straight ahead at his old mentor.

"Just one question?" the old priest replied mockingly, failing to hide the smile that had further creased his already-wrinkly face and put on display his remaining four teeth that had blackened with age in his ancient mouth.

"Yes, Father, one simple question. When do we wake him?"

"Ah," the old priest began, a touch of remorse in his voice. "Yes, a simple question it may be but a very difficult one to answer it is." The two prophets sat there for a long while, each staring at the other, waiting for the first to speak. Samuel's thoughts were buzzing with memories trying to break through, memories that were thousands of years old. Still, he fought them away as he knew where he had come from and knew that he would have time to remember the past. What was important to him, at this moment in time, was to remember the future, so he waited for Father Michael to answer him.

"My son," the elder priest began. "The reason I woke you was to prepare you for the rest of Steven's journey." Father Michael seemed at odds with himself; his hands were moving from the top of his desk to his face, to tugging at his robes and then back to his desk before they started the rotation again. With tears welling in his eyes and a sadness that had whitened his face, he stared blankly at Samuel. Flickering his eyelids, he tried forcing out the tears caused by what he was about to reveal, and then with his voice cracking, he continued, "So much to learn, so much to teach you and so little time!" The old prophet resumed and then suddenly paused. He looked defeated, and although the young priest didn't think his old mentor could look any older than he already did, it seemed that Father Michael had aged even further as they spoke.

An eerie stillness had enveloped the small room. Father Michael sat motionless as he faced Samuel. His eyes, unblinking, looked straight through him to a vision he so often prayed for but never came, a vision he now wished would hold off just a bit longer. He knew that his remaining time on earth was short but also knew that what needed to be accomplished was daunting. His thoughts wandered through millenniums to his first purpose as a prophet, and that was to assist the elders in safely articling the *Namzu Anunnaki*, the Holy Grail as it would later be referred to as rumors of its existence traveled by word over the past two thousand years until this very day.

The Holy Grail it was not! However, it is the *Namzu Anunnaki*, meaning the Book of Wisdom of the twelve planets, which was translated from their original language. As he remembered his first purpose, Father Michael remembered selecting Thaddeus as the soul strong enough to keep its secrets, and a strong soul was indeed needed because to let out the secretes of the *Namzu Anunnaki* too early would be like condemning the earth and all its inhabitants to a path of self-destruction similar to the one they witnessed all those years ago on their own planet.

As the old prophet remembered, he replayed the memories of passing over the responsibility of designing its hiding place to a young prophet named Patricio, who now sat in front of him as Samuel. Patricio was considered the strongest of souls and, together with Thaddeus, had the resilience to protect the secret hiding place of the *Namzu Anunnaki*.

Like a wisp of freezing wind, the chill that passed through Father Michael brought him out of his momentary recollection of his past and of the ultimate purpose they all shared on this new home of theirs. His eyes narrowed, and his face became stern. The shaking that had erupted from his core had stopped, and color had again returned to his face.

"Samuel, the time is near. The science of the *Namzu Anunnaki* may be needed to save the earth from the ever-growing wretchedness that has become this planet. We will need to act soon, but first you need to know Steven's story, all of it, and you need to know this before we awaken him. His story will help you to understand the demons that have been enlisted to stop us, the same demons who sent the evil entity to hospital last night, the same evil that wishes this place to enter the darkness." And so he began. He told Samuel of the twins who were executed by Constantine more than a thousand years ago and of the children of Francis Mackenzie who were killed because their father would not give up the *Namzu Anunnaki* almost three hundred years ago and of a man named Giuseppe whose only son was killed fifty years ago because the evil in the darkness had become angry and impatient. When he stopped, the old priest broke down, sobbing. The last words he blurted out were "I was there to witness all these atrocities and you, my son, have been spared until now." With that said, the old man got up and went back to his quarters, leaving Samuel to do the same.

CHAPTER 20

THE DAY THEY WERE MURDERED

N O SOONER HAD Samuel fallen asleep than his subconscious returned him back to Lake George and Steven Di Carlo's story.

"It was last September," Samuel heard Steven saying before he understood that he had returned to the lake and the life of Steven Di Carlo. Reacquainting himself to the vision was not difficult this time. He sat there and listened as they both edged closer toward the full awakening that the elders thought they needed.

"It was our usual boys' trip to the lake," he heard Steven saying and then fully tuned in to listen. "Rob Donnelly, Jimmy Davis, Tony, and Stef joined me at the cottage for a couple of days of fishing, a little poker, a lot of Scotch, and the occasional cigar. I guess I haven't mentioned Rob or Jimmy yet, have I? Jimmy sort of reminds me of you, Sammy, but in a strange kind of way. You'll see what I mean when you meet him. Anyway, I've worked with Rob and Jim for years, selling advertising for the *New York Post*, and we were the best. Shit, we brought in so much money for them that the rest of the gang nicknamed us the Closers." Samuel could see Steven's eyes light up when he talked about his business and his partners; his smile was warm, the kind of smile that held fond memories. Samuel couldn't help but smile himself as his newfound friend felt a tiny bit of joy in a world that held nothing but misery for him.

"The relationships that we had developed with our clients had given us the opportunity to go out on our own, so in 1998, Di Carlo, Davis, and Donnelly opened their doors. I should probably say door. We started out with a two-room office in Brooklyn, one filing cabinet, two desks, and my mother as a receptionist.

"With a lot of hard work landing some key accounts, we quickly built our business, and within one short year, we had expanded to a five-office complex just outside Manhattan. My mother was promptly retired, and we hired a staff of three media buyers, four account executives, two receptionists, and, of course, us. Shit, we even had benefits for our employees." Steven paused, his eyes became distant and his smile thinned out as he bit his lower lip.

"The day I first saw Victoria . . . " He paused again, and then lowering his head, he seemed to be shaking away a memory he didn't wish to visit. The white of his knuckles were prominent as his hands gripped the seat of his chair and his legs seemed to rise involuntarily as he continued, "Anyway", his voice cracking, "it was the day we were negotiating a loan to expand our business further, and expand we did." The smile was back, but the warmth had stayed hidden as he looked Samuel in the eye. "Sammy, our offices now occupied one complete floor of the Sears tower in downtown Manhattan, our staff had tripled, and our profits reflected our growth. The best part was that the three of us were not only partners. We were also best friends, and weekends at the cottage were a common occurrence. We fished all day and played cards all night, and sometimes, just for a change, we drove the fifteen miles to Meadow Gardens for a round of golf. After one of our weekends away, we'd usually get back home and still hang out together. We would collect our families and go out for Sunday dinner or a movie or sometimes both." The pain suddenly came through as his voice wavered and cracked. Anger could be heard as his dialogue became more of a snarl than an accounting of a story. With a throat that sounded raw and a delivery that was short on breath, he forged ahead, "Well, this weekend would be different." He came to a full stop and just stared at Samuel for what seemed an eternity as Steven collect the strength to continue.

"I guess I remember the drive home more than anything else. Sure, there was the usual horseshit about who caught more fish, whose was the biggest, who had the lucky hand in cards, and the old 'wait until next time' challenge." And then with his voice completely shaking and as the anger welled inside of him, he continued angrily but with a tone of complete remorse, "Who would have known that there would never be a next time? Unbelievable how, in a blink of an eye, your whole world can change. Anyway, the next time we would come to Lake George, sadly, it wouldn't be for poker and fishing." Steven stood up and went to the window to stare out at the lake as he spoke those last few word filled with a sort of finality.

"As I said," he continued, staring out at the lake, more to hide the tears that were threatening to flow than to look at the calm waters of the lake, "the trip home was different this time. It had me feeling a little more homesick than usual. There was this desperation to get there, which was odd. At the time, it had me feeling anxious and nervous, and I couldn't figure out why, unfortunately, I found out why. The creepy shit. I've been here before feeling I had aside. I'll never forget the anticipation I felt as we closed in on Riverdale."

The smile, although cautious, was back as he turned away from the window and returned to take his seat opposite Samuel. The sparkle in his eyes was again warm as he shyly explained, "You know the one, Sammy, when just the thought of holding your favorite girl would make you breathe a little quicker or would send tremors throughout your entire body, giving you the uncontrollable shakes. Your stomach would feel like butterfly heaven, and your imagination would take you away from your poker buddies and bring you into daydream paradise. Well, Sammy, coming home to Vic was always like that. It would just intensify the longer I was away. Absence makes the heart grow fonder. I don't know who said it first, but I did know it was true. Returning from wherever was always a thrill, from the kids waiting in the window and then running down the walkway to meet me to Victoria standing in the doorway and leaning up against the threshold. She always had this special pose. She would cross her arms just under her breasts, her right leg crossing her left, her predictable expression that said, 'It's about time.' Then she would release this enormous smile and run down the walkway to welcome me home. God, I miss her."

Steven turned to face an empty wall and seemed to stare through it. The warmth was again gone, and the hate was back. Samuel watched silently for quite sometime, knowing that any kind of consoling would be in appropriate. Samuel knew that Steven needed to rid himself of the demons, and the only way to do that was to feel the pain and then inch forward. As he watched Steven, he felt some of that pain. He knew the ending of this macabre story but didn't know the details, so he sat silently, giving his friend all the time he needed.

When he turned back to, once again, look at Samuel, Steven's eyes were distant, probably searching for a visual of those better times; and when, all at once, he found them, a longing that was so intense crossed his face while the loneliness crushed his heart. Falling silent, Steven found it hard to breathe, so he just sat there looking beyond the walls and then through Samuel and the old priest. Thinking of happier moments helped him choke back some of the emotion, and as his ability to breathe returned, he once again focused in on Samuel.

"Sammy, you ever play video games? Tommy was the best. He would challenge me to all his favorite games, and like most dads, I had absolutely no chance. Heck, with kids his age, you just put a play station in front of them and they were instant experts. Cathy, now she would enjoy beating me up too. Her favorite game was *Mario Bros*. She would first clobber me and then she would giggle like only little girls can. What I would do to hear her giggle just one more time."

Steven, again, paused as he thought of the children and the joy that surrounded their presence. Just thinking of where the story was taking him had him paralyzed with fear. Getting out of his chair, he walked over to the corner of the room where he had set up a speed bag. Without looking at the priests, he began, left, left, right, left, left, right, slowly picking up speed until his fists hitting the bag was as rhythmic as a drummer performing a solo.

Steven had a system of handling his despair; the speed bag would allow him to shut everything else out, and when his mind was completely cleared, he would think of the good times, the times before everything went insane. His memories of coming home after a business trip brought a smile of remembrance to his face. So Steven, once again, took his seat and continued with his story.

"Sorry, Sammy, the bag helps me battle the bad."

"No worries, my friend. Take all the time you need."

"I'm done for now. Where was I?"

"I think Cathy was clobbering you at *Mario Bros.*"

"Right, she always did. Did I tell you that Victoria was twenty-seven when we met? I was thirty-five, and as you already know, she'd been married before, a three-year disaster as she called it. I had been in a few different relationships with one lasting almost six years. Still, nothing could come close to the way we felt about each other. The only way to describe our relationship would be to say that we were true soul mates. When we held each other in whichever fashion, we simply fit, like two pieces of a puzzle. There were no uncomfortable positions. We were so in tune with each other that we knew each other's needs and exactly how to satisfy them."

Steven paused again. It was apparent that he was summing up the courage to get to the part of the story that terrified him. His eyes had become dark and frightened. His hand nervously shifted back and forth, opening and closing. His jaw appeared to be locked as his mouth was scrunched up like a wrinkled ball just as though he were trying to speak but his lips refused to mouth the words.

"Well", the word cracked as he forced it out, "as we closed in on Riverdale, with the tremors of anticipation shooting through my entire body, all I could think of was holding her in my arms and keeping her safe. But I would never hold her in my arms again, and I wasn't there to keep her safe. I remember the highway sign read Manhattan Twenty-Two Miles, and thinking back now, they were the final twenty-two miles of my life, as I knew it. We lived in Riverdale in the northwest Bronx. Our home was a turn-of-the-century estate overlooking the Hudson River." Then he tried to lighten his mood. "Hey, Sammy, our house even had a name. Can you believe it? Heatly Manor. We bought it in June of 2006. Although it was in desperate need of repairs, it was love at first sight. The grounds, one full acre was spectacular with its delightful gardens and an incredible swimming pool."

Then with disbelief in his tone and anger in his eyes, he stared cynically at Samuel as he stated more so than asking, "How could everything that was so right, so beautiful, and so perfect be gone just like that! Imagine, Sammy. Your life can change forever at a snap of a finger, only leaving you with the memories of that past life, memories that might bring a smile to your face and a feeling that, sometime, a very long time ago, life was good, it had meaning, you had faith and some belief that this world that we had created was good and that all those bad things always happened to someone else, never you." Briefly pausing, Steven cupped his face with both hands, rubbing his eyes with his fingertips, then just before moving to his temples, he continued, "And then you're hit with the reality of it all, those smiles that briefly visit and those feelings of normality that try to break through, gone, just like that. All the good memories are swallowed up by the pain, the anger, the hate, and, worst of all, the loneliness of the reality, that is.

"I remember calling home when we were about ten minutes away and there was no answer. The feeling of dread was immediate, and there was this sense of something horrible. I can't explain it to that point I had never had anything horrible happen in my life, but somehow, I knew it had happened and I knew it was bad. When we arrived at our home, it was like a scene out of prime-time TV. Police cars were blocking all the streets, lights were flashing, and there were at least three ambulances parked in front of the house. I remember jumping out of the truck and then being grabbed by someone, and that's when my world began spinning. It felt like a ton of bricks crashing down on top of me. Flashes of red and orange with white spots seemed to burn right through my eyes as bolts of white lightning exploded in my mind. It was as if a thousand voices were screaming at me. I felt as though I was being grabbed and pulled at. I felt two hands holding my face and yet another two grabbing my shoulders. I felt like I was being strapped down and couldn't move, a total feeling of paralysis came over me, and as it gripped me fully, things began to slow down.

"Sammy, this is really crazy, but I swear on everything holy that what I'm about to tell you is the truth as I remember it. You see, I sensed this feeling of floating and confusion, and at the same time, I felt this intense heat. The heat seemed to be coming right from inside me. It's hard to explain, but it was so hot that it was unbearable. Then just as I was about to scream, it became very cold." Looking at Samuel and still ignoring the old priest as though he were looking for encouragement to continue, Steven began to tremble. A bead of sweat formed on his brow, and his hands desperately searched for something to rub. Then in a tone that sounded both desperate and forced, he slowly pleaded his sanity. "My memory of what happened is as clear as a bell to me, and even if you think I'm nuts, I really don't give a shit because you know what, you wouldn't be alone." Steven again paused. Closing his eyes, he allowed the visuals of that awful night to enter his mind, and as the lights began flashing behind his eyelids, he was ready to, once again, bare his soul.

* * *

The old priest, his hands twitching, his throat desperate to take a breath, helplessly watched as Steven struggled with the anguish that was his life. Restraining himself from reaching out to him was the one of the most difficult things he could remember doing. But he had no choice, so he remained completely cloaked, head still bowed, his body trembling not only with age but also with grief. Then with difficulty, he swallowed the lump that had formed in his throat, allowing the raspy breathing to, once again, calm his anxiety. Raising his eyes slightly, he continued to listen to Steven's story.

"When the cold hit, I was floating above the Navigator. Shit, I was looking down on my friends and, yes, myself. But that's when I heard her. Victoria was screaming and crying, calling my name. I searched everywhere, but I couldn't see her. Then I could hear the children. God, they sounded so helpless and in so much pain that my mind was exploding with agony. I remember calling to them and listening to the panic that was in my own voice. It sounded like a whimper, like someone so weak and pathetic that they were afraid to look, afraid to find out, afraid to know what had happened.

"Next, I was floating over our house. I remember thinking I must be dreaming and then I remember praying, 'Oh, please let this be a dream. Don't let it be real.' Shit, how could it be real? For God's sake, I was floating in the fricking air. Then I thought that maybe I had died in the car, maybe I just had a heart attack and died. Unfortunately, I was still alive. Disbelief had me desperately trying to wake myself up, but I was unable to. So I continued to hover above the house, and they were still screaming. I willed myself toward the screams and found that I began floating down to the house, and the screams kept getting louder. My head felt like it was about to burst. Again, my thoughts were that I must have died. What other explanation could there have been?

"Then suddenly, I found myself inside Tommy's bedroom. God help me, his little body looked crumpled and broken as he lay on the floor. There was a pool of blood surrounding his head. He was naked from the waist down and was bruised everywhere. A rush of anger took over my thoughts, and then disbelief consumed my hopes. All I could think of was 'Wake up please! Wake up! This has to be a dream.' That's when I heard his voice. He was calling to me, 'Daddy, I'm right here.' I remember asking, 'Where, Tommy? Where are you?' Even to myself, I sounded desperate. Then he said, 'Daddy, help me. I'm scared. They're taking me away. Please help me.' And then there was silence. I called to him over and over, but the silence continued, and my despair was crushing me.

"Then just as I was about to scream, I was suddenly in the library and the hot burning feeling was back. As I looked down on a room full of blood, I could smell the death. Victoria was lying face-down. Her beautiful hair was matted with blood, and the back of her skull seemed to be missing. I tried to turn and run, but I couldn't. I remember first yelling at God to stop it and then begging him. When I realized no one was listening. I bent down to try to hold her, and as I was lifting her head, I was mercilessly transported from the library to the living room. I remember yelling at the ceiling, 'Please stop this! Please let me be! Just leave us alone.' But like the nightmare it was, it just kept on. Cathy was there in the living room. Her little hands were bound with a belt and tied to a coat hook on the wall. She was just hanging there. Her neck looked broken and her little body was covered in blood."

Samuel listened in disbelief; his body was shaking with anguish, and his thoughts were filled with anger and hate against those who did this. The old priest sat paralyzed with grief. His cloaked head was shaking as he was unable to contain the weeping that was now coming from his core. As he was about to scream, he remembered why he was there and remembered that there was still time to stop this from ever happening, a detail that had escaped young Samuel as he continued to listen to Steven's accounting of the horrific events.

"As the realization of what I had found hit me," the two priests could hear Steven saying, "I felt a tremendous pain in my chest. It felt as if I were about to explode, and I did. I exploded with anger. Then when that didn't help, I simply crumpled. I was defeated and broken, so I succumbed, and when I did, I began to lose the ability to breathe, and for that, I was thankful. I remember begging as I looked up at the ceiling, 'Let me die please, just let me die.' And I was ready for it. I was wishing for death. I didn't want to breathe. I didn't want to wake up. You see, I finally realized it wasn't a dream.

"Then as my thoughts left the horrid scene that I had found, I felt someone grabbing my shoulders. Someone else was holding my face, and I felt a pounding in my chest. When I awoke, I was lying on the front walk of our house. Rob, Jim, and Tony were staring down at me, their eyes wide with panic and their hands trembling with fear. They kept repeating how sorry they were. Sirens wailed in the background. Red flashing lights lit up the neighborhood, and my neighbors were standing around, completely distraught and full of fear.

"As I tried to get up, it felt as though I was being held down, but nobody was holding me down. With all my senses and every part of my being, I tried to will myself to move, but it was as if the blanket that was covering me weighed a thousand pounds, and I was pinned to the walkway. Robby, seeing the fear in my eyes, lifted my head and cradled it in his arms like a parent would a child. He was talking to me, but I couldn't make out what he was saying.

"I could see and feel the panic all around me, but it was like a dream state, a surreal type of feeling that you get when you think you're awake, but in fact you're still asleep. Only I knew too well that I was awake, and very soon I would have to face up to what had happened.

"Stefano was now kneeling beside me and was wiping my forehead and face with a cold cloth. I remember how good it felt, but when I looked at him to thank him, that feeling was short-lived. His eyes were red and wet with tears, his hands trembled with anger and fear. He appeared to be, as I felt, totally incoherent. I remember wondering how devastating something would have to be to turn a hardened tough guy who'd been through everything Navy SEAL to a state of helplessness and what appeared to be despair. I heard myself trying to console him, but what amazed and frightened me was that I actually heard myself.

"I had come out of whatever I was in. I sat up so quickly that I startled those around me. Tony and Jim appeared out of nowhere and joined Robby and Stef at my side. They all had that same lost look as I had seen in Stefano's eyes. I remember pleading with them, 'Please tell me this is a dream. It can't be real.' I begged them to tell me what they couldn't. I remember Tony's words as they startled me more than you could imagine. He said, 'Steve, we're gonna get these guys. Whoever did this is gonna pay, I promise you.'

"I remember asking, 'What do you mean, Tony?' Oh, God, it wasn't a dream, was it? And they're dead, aren't they? I looked at Stef and ordered him tell me that it wasn't true, and then I turned to Robby and Jimmy. 'Tell me that it didn't happen please.' As I begged them for some sort of hope, all I got was the promise of vengeance. Then Stef confirmed what happened. I remember the hateful look in his eyes as he spoke to me, 'Steve, I don't know what to say, except we're with you in your pain. You know we will be by your side always, and the fucks who did this, well, fuck if the cops don't get them first. All I can say is they'll wish they never set foot here.'

"That's when I jumped to my feet and ran toward the door and into the living room. Everyone tried to stop me, and I should have let them. When I got to the living room, my darling little Cathy, my little princess, was still hanging on the coat hook. It hadn't been a dream at all. She was dead. They were all dead. The anger I felt was overwhelming and so immediate, and Stefano's words rang clear in my mind. The fucks that did this will wish they were never born. Whatever it cost, I will get them, and they will die."

CHAPTER 21

THE VISITATION

T HE SILENCE IN the room was deafening. Samuel held his right hand over his mouth, not knowing what to say or do. He simply stared. Father Michael appeared unmoved, but a closer look would have shown a trembling lower lip and watery eyes, not to mention the gooseflesh that covered his arms, back, and neck. The old priest was quietly praying, and although no one heard him, if you listened, you would have found the constant sound of whispering irritating.

A door slamming in another part of the house seemed to bring everyone back to consciousness. Samuel got up and walked over to the speed bag and just punched it as hard as he could. The sound startled the old priest momentarily, but then he again continued his praying. Samuel, holding the bag with his left hand, looked as though he was about to punch it again. Instead, he used it for balance as he spoke. "Steven, why don't we call it a day? We can continue tomorrow."

"I'm okay, Sammy. I appreciate your concern. The reality is that I don't want to go through this again tomorrow. So let me continue." And so he did.

"When I summoned the courage to do so, I walked over to Cathy and took her down from her death hook. One of the investigators was about to stop me, but Stef grabbed his arm and, with a gesture, told him to let me be. I brought her to the sofa and sat down, holding her limp little body in my arms. She looked so hurt. There was no peace in her stillness. The pain and fear was telling by the look on her face. I felt numb. I began rocking her just as I did on the many nights before she went to sleep. I remember crying when I spoke to her. Somehow, I knew she was listening. I'm not sure how. I just knew. I felt her presence around me. It was so strong that I felt the warmth of her aura instead of the coldness of her flesh. I told her that she was my little sweetheart and that she would always be a part of me. I told her how much I loved her and that I would never forget her. I promised her that one day, we would all be together again. Every day, I wonder how I'm able to go on without them. What they did to them is beyond comprehension. My sweet little baby, they not only tortured her, the degenerate assholes violated her. Why would they do this, Sammy? Why?"

Unable to respond, Samuel just sat there feeling more lost than at any time in his entire life. His face had a pained look. His eyes, red with hatred, seemed to be blinking continuously. His left hand, gripping the punching bag, had lost all its color, and his right hand formed a tight fist as if he was ready to punch someone. Samuel was distraught; he had never encountered such heartbreak. How would he be able to help Steven if he himself was unable to cope with this unbelievable tragedy? Feeling the hatred build within him, Samuel swore a silent oath to help Steven avenge his family, and as he did, he realized that Steven was still recounting his story.

"I promised her vengeance. I told her that whoever it was that stole her from me would pay and that I would not rest until I got them. And then, Samuel, I was mad at God again and asked him why. Why did he let this happen? I buried my head into her blood-soaked body and cried. I don't know for how long, I just remember someone taking her from my arms."

"Was there anyone with you through all this?"

"Yeah, Sammy, there was this lady. She was sitting with me, holding my hand and stroking it in sympathy. As much as I wanted to be alone, I was grateful she was there. She seemed familiar to me. I knew her but didn't know from where. She even accompanied me in the ambulance and sat with me at the hospital too. I know I was sedated, but I also know she was there and she was an incredible comfort to me. But I guess that this is why you guys are here. You know that she wasn't actually there, right?"

Steven seemed to, once again, be lost in thought. Samuel, wanting to reach out to him, was refrained from doing so with a look from the old priest. The only comfort that Samuel felt was that the most difficult memories for Steven were out of the way, and although the question of his sanity remained, Steven would soon know the truth about the journey he was about to begin.

"Steven, your mother told us a bit about the events that surrounded you in the hospital. Do you think that you could tell us a little about that day?"

"Sure, Sammy, but I got to tell you that, by this point of my story, all the doctors and shrinks that I've seen in the past thought I was going nuts. They didn't say this in so many words, but I knew they were thinking it. Do you think I'm insane? What about your boss over there? Does he think I'm nuts? Tell me, my new young friend, where are we going with this?"

"Honestly, Steven, I'm not sure. But I can promise you that you're not alone, and none of us thinks you're nuts. So if you're up to it, please continue."

Steven, trying to find a reason not to trust them, was unable to. They seemed to be sincere. More importantly, they seemed to really care. For the first time since the murders, someone was willing to listen to what he had to say and not trying to tell him that it was his imagination fueled by his loss that was making him delusional. "Wow, you actually want hear more. Okay then. You know what, let me grab us a beer and then I'll continue." When Steven came back, he wasn't surprised that only Samuel accepted the beer. He smiled at the old priest and held his can up as he toasted their faith and then continued.

"Well, when I awoke, they were there, all three of them. That's right, Victoria with her infectious smile, Tommy with his bright blue eyes, and Cathy with her arms extended like she always did when she wanted to be picked up. They were there in the hospital, and

I remember the excitement I felt seeing them and then me telling them it was all a dream. 'You're alive. You're not dead. Oh, thank you, God.' And then as quickly as I said that, the all-too-brief reprieve was snapped away from me."

"'Steven, listen to me' she said. 'We don't have a lot of time.' That confused me again as I wondered what she meant. So I asked her, 'What are you saying, Vic?' She said, 'Shush, my darling. Please listen.' So I did. 'We're no longer in pain. You need to understand that what happened was meant to happen and that we're okay now! We're home where we belong. Please know that, with all our hearts, the three of us will miss you dearly, but we will be together again one day. Steve, I need to pass along a message to you.' That's where I was a bit floored. They were really dead, and she needed to give me a message. Talk about being fucked up. I tell you, it was bizarre. So still in disbelief, I anxiously blurted out, 'A message from who?' And this is what she told me. She said that everyone on earth has a purpose and that they had served theirs, but I still needed to complete mine.

"You see, she said that everyone on earth has a spirit guide from this so-called place. They apparently help us fulfill our quests. She said that I have three guides and that they were the ones who allowed them to show themselves to me. You know what else she said? She said they asked her to tell me that I have a destiny on earth and that what happened to them was a part of that destiny. Victoria also told me that I came from where they were. That's right, Sammy, the same place where they went after they died. Supposedly, I chose to return to earth to fulfill this destiny. Sammy, to this day, I still have trouble understanding what she was trying to tell me. I remember just staring at her in disbelief that they were even dead. So I asked her what she was talking about, what destiny, and what purpose. I said to her, 'Can't we just go home?'

"She told me that they would always be with me but that I must listen because our future in this other place depended on it. She said that I needed to let my anger guide me and that my heart and mind would take over when the time was right. I would know this with the help of my spirit friends. They would guide me, but I needed to understand the messages.

"Again, I asked her, 'What messages? How would I know? How would I understand?' She told me that I would need help and that I would be shown the way to this help. I just needed to listen and look for the signs. She also said that I had to be on guard because my mind was going to tell me to give up. She said that I had to fight this darkness with all my heart and my anger and that I must never give up because if I did, then we would never be together again. I remember her sort of scolding me. She said, 'Steven, do you understand me? You must be strong. Steve, I need you to be strong, and we need you to live.' That's what she said, and I can hear her words as clear as a bell even today."

"What did you tell her, Steven?"

"I told her that I didn't want to live and that I wanted to be with her. I told her that if I died, then I would be with them. After I told her that, she looked very sad. She told me that if I died by my own hand, I would go to another place far from where they were. She asked me if I understood and then said that they had to go. So she told me to be strong and that they loved me. I was begging them to stay and not to go when I heard the nurse trying to wake me. 'Mr. Di Carlo, wake up, Mr. Di Carlo. Oh, there you are, are you all right?' I asked her where they went. She said, 'Who, Mr. Di Carlo? Hang on, Mr. Di Carlo. I'll get the doctor.' I remember yelling at her and saying, 'They were just here. Surely you must have seen them.'

"'You just hang on. I'll be right back.' She looked at me like I was some sort of nutcase. Then I just remember feeling like shit and wondering what the hell happened, so I kept calling to her. 'Vic, please come back. I know you were here. Please I need to understand. I need to know. Please come back and help me.' Then I was a bit annoyed with her. I whispered because I didn't want anybody to hear me. I said to her, 'You didn't let me say goodbye. I didn't even get to tell you how much I love you and the kids. Come back. I need you. I love you.'

"Back then, that day in the hospital revealed so much to me, but it took me weeks to figure it all out. Before the nurse left the room, I could sense her discomfort. After all, what do you say to someone whose wife and kids had just been murdered, and he just claimed to have seen them? I remember the look in her eyes. She was having trouble holding back the tears, and when she spoke, it was with that same lump-in-the-throat feeling that we all get when sad emotions run rampant.

"I imagined, and I was right that, that was the way it was going to be. It wouldn't matter who I ran into or the multitude of visitors that I was to receive over the next few weeks. It would be that same uncomfortable feeling. Then the funerals. I wondered how I would survive the funerals, but I did, and what I learned on that day helped. We should go back and talk a little more about that day."

* * *

"When the doctor came in, she looked at me for a while, poked, prodded, took the stethoscope out, and listened to my heart; in general, I think she was stalling, just trying to compose herself. Her first attempt at verbalizing began and ended with uhmmmm. Dr. Taylor, who preferred to be called Kimberly, was a longtime family friend and had been my doctor for the past thirteen years. Although Victoria and the kids had their own doctor, they still became good friends. Victoria and Kimberly had gone out for lunch, tennis, and just hung out on many occasions, and I knew this was very hard on her, but I also knew that if I said a word, I would crumble. She attempted to speak again. This time, it ended with both of us sobbing and holding each other."

Steven fell silent, his eyes staring at the floor, his hands clasped together with his fingers nervously fidgeting. He thought back as the encounter with Kimberly played out in his mind.

"Steve, I'm so sorry."

"I know, Kimberly. Thank you."

"Can I get you anything? How about some water for the both of us?"

"That would be good."

"Steve, do you understand everything that has happened?"

"You mean do I know that they are dead? Yes, Kimberly. Do I understand? Fuck no! Kimberly, how could this have happened? Have you heard anything from the police?"

"They're outside right now, waiting to talk to you. I told them you needed some time."

"Kimberly, they were here."

"The police?"

"No, Kimberly, Victoria and the kids!"

"Steve, I know this is hard."

"Kimberly, listen to me. I'm not nuts. I know how this must sound, but please hear me out."

"I'm sorry, Steve. Please tell me. I'm listening."

Vaguely aware of his surroundings, Steven continued to think back, remembering every detail as if it had happened yesterday. His eyes, now up from the floor, captured Samuel's gaze. Looking at the young priest filled him with a sort of peace. His feeling of familiarity continued to grow. He knew Samuel, but from where? These questions would continue to puzzle Steven, but this feeling was the same as the one he has whenever he's with Stefano. He understood that they've known each other all their lives. After all, they were cousins, but he always had an odd feeling that they were more than cousins and now he has that same feeling about Samuel but didn't know from where. His mind continued to wander as Steven drew farther and farther away from the den and his two visitors. Samuel, recognizing this, decided to let Steven be for the time being and motioned for Father Michael to be patient.

A short time later, Samuel decided to bring Steven back to the here and now and, with a timely question, had Steven continuing with his story.

"Steven, what did you tell Dr. Taylor?" Steven shot up as though he hadn't missed a beat.

"Well, I told her everything that I could remember."

"How did she respond?"

"She told me that she didn't think that Victoria would ask me to follow my anger but that the advice on living sounded very much like Victoria and that I should listen to that advice. She said that she believed in guardian angels, but even though it was going to be difficult, it was very important that I was able to separate the dreams from reality. That's when I asked her about the lady that was comforting me. I asked her if she knew where I could find her. I told her that I wanted to thank her. You know what she told me? She said that she was at the hospital waiting for me, and she didn't remember seeing anybody with me. She asked me if I was sure. I told her that I was and that the lady sat in the hospital room, holding my hand. She asked me if I could describe how she looked. I said of course I can. She was quite small, maybe five feet one, black wavy hair, late thirties, maybe early forties, not fat but a little heavy, a very beautiful face, probably Mediterranean.

"Then she told me that she would see what she could find out. She seemed lost and started to cry. When she gained some control, she told me that my parents were outside, waiting to see me. They had been out there most of the night. She had to give my mother a sedative and that she was a little concerned for her. She hadn't stopped crying. Then she said, 'It's very difficult, Steven, and I'm worried that I can't be what I've been trained to be. I'm supposed to be under control and someone to lean on, but instead, I feel like a wreck. Steve, I loved them too.' Again, we just held each other and wept. I remember wondering if it was possible to run out of tears, and how would I face my mother? My mother adored my family. When they were together, they were inseparable. Mom took pride around the relatives, always bragging about her daughter-in-law and her grandchildren. And now they were gone.

"Sammy, I remember when she walked into the room, it looked as if she had aged far beyond her sixty-five years. This was a shock to me because whenever I looked at my mom, I was always amazed at how young she looked. That day was different. On that day, I was amazed at how old she looked. She came over to me, and as she usually did when she was upset, she spoke in Italian."

Steven Di Carlo, using the back of his hand, wiped a tear from his right eye and found it difficult to recall the anguish that over took his mother during those times; he could still hear her words that day.

"Figlio mio, che ti posso dire. Che maladetti potevano fare questa bruta cosa. Gesu manda una maledizione a questi assassini, e farele soffrire Dio mio."

Continuing, Steven seemed exhausted; his shoulders had sunk, his eyes seemed to have deepened, and his voice grew weak. "She told me she cursed them and prayed to God to let them suffer for eternity. Then she put her head on my shoulder and cried. My father was leaning against the wall. His hands were trembling as he covered his face, hiding his tears. He would be my strength, my rock, and my conscience over the next few weeks. My mother would be my support, my friend, and my shoulder to cry on. Thank God for them because without them, I don't think I would have made it."

* * *

"When I told my parents about my dream, they believed every word and went on to explain their interpretation of the different planes of existence as they called them. They both told me not to take this message lightly and to write down everything that I remembered and to try to remember it all.

"When I finished, I had gone to the washroom, I suppose, to try and wash away the sadness. Of course it didn't. What did happen, though, was incredible. As I called silently to Victoria, trying to will her back, a heart materialized right before my eyes on the bathroom mirror. This was nuts. It was absolutely crazy because this was the way Vic signed off on any of her messages to me. I called to my parents, and when they saw the heart, we embraced and cried some more. When we looked again, the heart was gone.

"When Kimberly returned, she found us in the bathroom and asked if we were okay, and then she joined us in our embrace. When we were all composed, she had told me that she asked around about the woman from last night. She said that no one could recall her. She definitely was not aboard the ambulance nor was she with the police.

"That's when I told Mom and Dad about the encounter, and when I described the lady to them, my mother did the sign of the cross and began to weep again. She told us that I had described her favorite aunt who had died when she was only forty-one. Mom was seventeen at the time. Since then, Mom had always prayed to Aunt Rosa to watch over us, and she had always felt her close by. She said that when we got home, she would show me her picture."

Aunt Rosa

Then directing Samuel to a framed photograph above the desk, Steven said, "That's her."

Steven sat back as though the conversation was over. Then standing, he appeared to return to a state of agitation as he began pacing, almost trying to decide if he should go to the speed bag or out to the kitchen.

Samuel, feeling the moment was right to stop and give Steven a break just a few minutes ago, was now worried that he would lose this opportunity, so he stood and walked directly into Steven's path and decided that he would try to guide the conversation back to the paranormal. Stopping Steven in his tracks, Samuel's tone became comforting but demanding.

"Steven, earlier on, there was a lot of talk of retribution, and I know that revenge is on everyone's mind, including mine. That is one thing that we will, for sure, deal with it, but what I need to know right now is about the experiences that have brought you here, you coming to this place at this time to undertake this horrible vengeance, this terrible journey that seems to have consumed your every thought. There has to be something else, Steven. I need to know now what this is truly all about because for me to support your vengeance after hearing what happened is not an issue, but for him," Samuel looked over at the hunchbacked cloaked figure that had still to mumble a single word. "For him, it has to be more than simple revenge."

Steven, slumping back down into the overstuffed chair, appeared reluctant to go on.

"Okay, Sammy, it's just that there are some things that are a little more difficult to talk about. First off, I'm concerned that you will finally conclude that I'm a nut bar or, for sure, delusional or worse. I might really be a nut case. Maybe I have actually lost it, and this is just me having a mental breakdown of some kinds. Are you sure you want to sit through this because I'm not sure I do?"

"Yes, Steven, I do. Firstly, I don't believe that you are having a mental breakdown, and absolutely certain that you're not a nut bar. What I do believe is that there are other influences at work here and believe that these influences have guided us to you. So my old boss over there," Samuel pointing at Father Michael, "told me that if it's our blessing that you seek, then we need to know that the cause is just and that your council is, in fact, coming from a holy place."

Steven just stared at the young priest. He knew that Samuel had a mandate and knew that eventually things would escalate, but right now, he looked amused and then twisted a smile at his young friend. Then waving his finger as though he were scolding him, he responded, "Sure, but you know what, Sammy? It's not me calling it a holy place. You can class it any way you want. Then you can wake your boss up and tell him that it's not me that wants his blessing. I'm just doing this for my mom, capisce? You see, I don't give a flying fuck what the church thinks. With or without your blessing, I will have my vengeance." Then as though he had gotten something off his chest, he calmed and was almost apologetic as he continued, "Sammy, you just need to understand that this is very difficult for me. Remembering makes me very angry and very emotional, but then again, my anger is all that has kept me going."

"Sure, Steve, I understand, but as you yourself told me, you were asked to follow your anger, so then perhaps this is simply a part of your journey. Hey, why don't you start with this mysterious woman that your mother claims to be her deceased aunt?"

"Why not? It's as good a place as any," Steven almost snapped back, his head was throbbing, frustration threatening to have him end this, which was the last thing he wanted to do. Confused by the churches' involvement had him questioning why he was even talking to priests; after all, he still blamed God. *Where was he?* Steven thought to himself. *And why did he let this happen!* He sat silently as he tried to regain his composure, then felt embarrassed at his own thoughts as he knew the answers to his questions, then focusing on Samuel, he sought some comfort from Samuel's eyes. He knew the young priest was there with the right intentions and knew that this journey with him would be a very long one. "Well." Steven, massaging his temples, paused again as he collected his thoughts, then ready to continue, he leaned forward, resting his elbows onto his knees, and stared into Samuel's eyes. "Well, right after I was released from the hospital, I couldn't go home. In fact, that same day, I called my lawyer and asked him to arrange for a realtor and put the house up for sale. Tony and Stefano were an incredible help to me. Not only did they help with my belongings from the house and the hiring of a cleanup crew, they were also a huge help with the funeral arrangements. I wasn't of much use to anybody or myself for that matter for quite a while.

"That day, my mother came and sat beside and me. In her hands, she had some very old pictures. At first, I just wanted to be alone and silently wished that she would just take those pictures and leave. But as you know, mothers tend to have this comforting quality about them. They know what to say, when to say it, and when to just simply say nothing.

"We sat there together in a comforting type of silence for quite a long time. She held me close for most of it, stroking my head the way that she did when I was a boy. When she finally spoke, I knew that she had chosen her words very carefully. She began by telling me that she wished she could take the pain away from me but said she couldn't. She told me that it would take a long time, probably the rest of my life, to understand. She said that times like these usually cause us to question our faith. Boy was she right! And then she said that I was probably very angry at God for allowing it to happen. Right again! So she told me that she would try to explain our faith and the way that she understood it to be and perhaps this would help restore and, possibly, even strengthen my belief. She began by saying that the things that happen on this earth happen for a reason, and most times, those reasons don't make any sense.

"So as if bombarding me with a bunch of question, she began asking things like, 'Why are our loved ones taken from us, especially our children? Why do we suffer all these diseases like cancer, AIDS, and the thousands of other viruses plaguing our lives on this earth? Why are there wars and terrorists and murderers and pedophiles and all the other hideous crimes committed against the innocent? Why does God allow humanity to suffer such as it has since the beginning of time?'

"So I asked her why. She said that the answer could be as simple as 'He's testing our faith.' And in a way, she believed that this was precisely what he was doing. She believes that earth is destined to be the benefactor of his master plan. She told me that she thought that throughout the ages, she believes that God's goal has been to rid the earth of all its impurities, and to do this, many innocent lives must be sacrificed and their souls returned to heaven to await their next journey to earth, which, of course, would include a new assignment. That assignment, she said, could be to contract a deadly disease or to cure one. It could be to rid us of an evil soul that has escaped from hell, or it could be to discover part of what is needed to keep this earth healthy for the time when it truly does become paradise.

"You see, Samuel, her belief is that of all the planets in our universe, God has chosen earth to become a part of heaven, and to become a part of heaven, it must be cleansed. When this happens, she figures maybe a thousand years in the future, we would all be able to return here and live forever. Nice thought! Oh," Steven hesitated. His cheeks blushed, and his eyes focused on the ceiling. He stared at a crack that was starting to spread near the light fixture. Then as he brought his gaze back down and into Samuel's eyes, he went on, "Um, she also told me that she thinks that I'm a part of his master plan, and Victoria coming to visit me with that message and with her dead aunt at my side could only mean that I'm needed."

"Needed?" Samuel contributed to encourage Steven to go on.

"Yeah, that's what she said! I said, 'Needed for what, Ma? What could I possibly do for God?' As much as I wanted to believe her theory, really, I just want to be left alone, hating whoever I wanted to hate even if it was the Almighty. Then just like smacking me between the eyes, she said, 'Here, look at my beautiful Zia. Is she the one from the other night? Was she the one that was with you?'

"As I took the photograph and looked at it, my expression told all. There was no doubt in my mind that my mother's aunt was the one comforting me on that awful night. No doubt at all. My mother simply looked at me and told me that her aunt would continue to take care of me just as she always has. She said that she had prayed to her every night for almost fifty years and that she had answered her prayers by being with me at my time of need."

"So let me get this right, Steve. You're telling me that the woman in the picture was the same woman that you saw? Amazing! Please tell me more. Tell me what happened next." Samuel, anxious to hear more, tried desperately to hide his enthusiasm from Steven, but failed.

"Okay, bud, but let's grab a coffee first and then I'll tell you some more."

Steven felt as though an enormous weight had been lifted from him. Talking to Samuel was indeed therapeutic, so much so that he was eager to continue. And so they grabbed their coffee and then headed straight back to the den.

"Where was I?"

"You just told me about your reaction after seeing the old picture."

"Right," Steven said as he sat there like the thinker, cupping his chin with his right hand and his forefinger resting atop his upper lip, his right leg, which was crossing his left, was supporting his elbow. His eyes were intense as he gathered his thought, and then lowering his hands to his shin, he held on, rocking ever so slightly. "Well, Sammy, the rest of that day was spent receiving all the well-wishers, friends, and family that came to pay their respects. As difficult as it was, I was genuinely touched by their condolences and their respect for my grief. Very little words were exchanged, but still I knew what they wished to say."

Steven again paused as he thought back to that day at his parents' home; he remembered the faces of those who came to visit and then let a tear escape from his eye as he remembered the sadness in his father's face as he came to console him. Wiping the tear from his cheek, he continued, "It's funny but one of my strongest memories from that day was the aroma of espresso. It filled the air. My dad brought me a cup. He'd always say espresso is not espresso unless you spike it with Sambuca. We sat there, me and my dad, sipping from our tiny cups, talking about nothing in particular, but his message came through loud and clear. He said, 'Son, I don't know much of what your mother speaks, but I do know that Victoria was there with us at the hospital.'

"He said it amazed him, and up until that point, he used to humor my mother about her beliefs but didn't really believe in angels or saints or, for that matter, God. He went on to say that this experience has left him confused but had also left him with sense of peace. He believed that Victoria and the kids were indeed in a better place, and for the first time in his life, he believed that a better place did exist. He told me that I must remember Vic's words. And then trembling so much that he spilled some of the coffee, he reminded me of what she said, 'She told you that you must live because it's the only way for you to be with them again. Understand?' He told me that he needed me to let him know that I understood that. Then he told me that he couldn't bear to lose me too and that he loved me. Then we just sat there silently, both of us in our own kind of despair, both of us in a shared understanding of his message."

Steven sat back in the chair and uncrossed his legs. At that moment, he just wanted to go to his father and hold him. He wanted to rest his head on his mother's lap and have her stroke his hair just as she did on that day. Fighting off the strong desire, he again leaned forward, massaging his temple and then rubbing the back of his neck before continuing, "Still, my mother's aunt Rosa haunted my thoughts. Sammy, as much as I tried, I couldn't get her out of my mind. I simply couldn't. Picking up the picture, I looked at it again and again, and the more I looked at it, the more I was convinced that this was the woman that comforted me that night. I continued to doubt myself. After all, how could it be? She was long ago dead. It wasn't possible. Yet there she was in this very old black and white picture. Here, have a look."

Steven got up from the chair and walked over to his desk, then taking the picture down from the wall above his desk, he handed it to Samuel. It was of a woman probably in her thirties. She was wearing a traditional type of dress ornamented and worn down below the knees; it was dark with white trim and embroidered with flowers. She had posed with her left hand on her hip and stood square to the camera. Samuel thought of the Mona Lisa when he looked at her, not quite a smile yet sort of. He imagined that getting a picture taken in those days must have been a rare occasion. Then Steven handed him another picture that his mother had left for him. It was no doubt of her, young and pretty; she must have been in her teens. She posed with a very solemn look, a look of troubled sadness; her piercing eyes were glistened with tears as she held a picture to her chest. Then Steven began to tell Samuel of the second picture.

Sammy, as I looked closer at the framed picture, there was a boy, perhaps as young as twelve or thirteen. Although it was difficult to make out his features, I knew his face. I knew that I had seen it before. Man, I remember feeling very strange. It was almost like a severe déjà vu. Shit, even the background was familiar. See the stone house with the single door? Well, looking at it back then gave me this strange feeling, and as I continued to look, the strangeness became even stronger, and

Young Maria Di Carlo

suddenly, out of nowhere, I knew this house. I knew what it was like inside, even the colors of the walls. I could see the small kitchen and the bedroom, which had three beds. I even knew the house number without looking. It was 9612, but when I did look, though, I could only see the number 9.

"It was totally mind-numbing, my friend. Shit, the feeling was so strong that I knew I had to be right. So I closed my eyes to absorb all that I had felt in those last few minutes, and, Samuel, this is where it gets a little crazy because, suddenly, I was aware of a bustling tiny little street. There were people pushing carts, selling their wares, others bartering at stands set up near the road, children running and playing. Older men were gathered around a card game, arguing about the outcome, and you know what, I knew all of them. I knew their names, I knew their faces, and I knew where they lived. And suddenly, I knew where the numbers were.

"My mind went to the door and on the door to the right of the number 9, I could see and touch the other numbers 612. These extra three numbers appeared to be carved into the door with a knife. When I opened my eyes, I was trembling with panic, soaked with sweat, and looking into my father's face. He was holding my shoulders as if he was trying to wake me. I could hear the panic in his voice as he asked me if I was okay. I told him that I was fine and that I would explain later and then ran up to my room.

"Once in the privacy of my room, I grabbed my briefcase to find my portable magnifier, you know, the kind I use in my business to check the quality of ad reproduction. Anyway, I had to dump everything out to find it. When I found it, I knew I would be able to see if, in fact, there were numbers carved on the door. I remember thinking what would I do If they were there and then wondering if the numbers were, in fact, there, what would it all mean. Had I simply fallen asleep and dreamt all of it? That's when this wave of nausea hit me like a ton of bricks. I ran to the bathroom, wretched out whatever little I had in my stomach, and then just sat there, and as I sat there, I began questioning my sanity.

"You've got to understand, Sammy, at this point, I had everybody's attention, but it was concern I think more than anything else.

They must have thought I was having some sort of breakdown, and why not? That's what I thought. What the fuck, I was allowed. Shit, I just lost my wife and kids. Of course, I was going nuts. Sorry about the swearing, but shit, even thinking back to that first experience gets me all emotional and very intense."

"Go on, swear all you want, shit . . . I understand." Samuel tried to smile as he swore but instead felt the visible heat swell up in cheeks. Covering his face, he motioned for Steven to continue.

Steven, wanting to laugh at his young friend, thought better of it and, instead, continued with his story.

"Okay, where was I? Right, there was a light rap on the door as both Stef and Tony forced their way into the bathroom. They sat down beside me and said nothing for quite sometime. Then Stef broke the silence and began with his usual Bronx tough-guy slang. You should have heard him." Then Steven imitating Stefano's exactly lightened the mood. "Whatever you want, Steve, whatever you need. You know I can get it." Then with his best impression of Tony, he continued, "That's right, Steve. We're with you, and together we're gonna get these guys. Tell him, Stef. Tell him about your dreams." And then out of nowhere, Stefano almost snapped, and with a very stern look, he yelled at Tony, 'Man, I told you now's not the time. Just cool it, Tone. We'll get to that later when were all thinking straight.'"

"Then we were all silent again as the three of us became absorbed in our own time passing thoughts. For me, looking at Tony and Stef as we sat on the bathroom floor seemed all too familiar. What came to mind for me was when we were nine years old and hiding out in that very bathroom. I guess I must have smiled because Tony looked at me and said, 'What?' I told them that I was thinking about the time when we stole Mr. Rossi's cherries and he chased us for blocks. I told them I remembered old Mr. Rossi pounding on the front door. Christ, was he pissed. I remembered my mom telling him where he could stick those cherries. When I recounted this to them, Tony started laughing first and then we all laughed together. Stef continued and said what we were all thinking, 'Those were good times, weren't they?'

"When we settled down, I told them about the picture of Mom's aunt and my vision and then told them that I thought I was going nuts. To my surprise, they both verbally attacked me and said that I should take that stuff very seriously. Tony said that I should go see Father Andrews, the old priest at Sacred Heart and tell him about this because he knew about these things. I never did.

"Instead, I chose to believe that I was somehow imagining all of it or perhaps conveniently sidetracking my mind. I knew I was sane all right. What I didn't know was how I was going to keep it. Anyway, back to the magnifier. About an hour after entering the bathroom, the three of us emerged to the relief of not only those needing to use the facilities but to my parents.

"Going back into the living room, I quickly acknowledged the well-wishers and, just as quickly, grabbed the now-famous photographs and escaped to my father's study with both Tony and Stefano close behind me. Locking the door, I again described what had happened and explained about the numbers. I told them that I couldn't look because I didn't know what I'd do if I was right, so I handed the magnifier to Stefano, who was curious as hell, and he grabbed it willingly. He sat down at the desk as I fired up the ancient 386 clone and the scanner. I figured that we were going to need to enhance the picture within the picture to figure out why the kid was so familiar. When I looked over at Stefano and Tony, they were crouched down over the magnifier, taking turns at the analysis. I remember, they both had this profound look as they gawked at each other, then Stef looked at me and asked me what I thought it meant.

"Numbers 9612. In my heart, I knew that the numbers had been carved there for a specific reason, and that reason, Sammy, escapes me, but the significance of the numbers hit me squarely between the eyes. Numbers 9612 is September 6, 2012, the day they died. Well, feeling overwhelmed, I asked Tony and Stef to leave me for a bit, claiming I was tired and confused. Really, I just needed time to think.

"Samuel, you've got to understand, it was like suffering one of the biggest mind fucks of my entire life. I remember asking myself what exactly was going on. My family was murdered, the date of their death carved into some door fifty years earlier. It's been less than seventy-two hours but felt more like seventy-two days. I felt totally devastated, but at the same time, I was having this feeling." Steven paused, his face twisted but his eyes were bright as he tried to put his feelings into words.

"It's very hard to explain. Well, shit, Sammy, I've seen and spoken to my dead wife. Then there's this long-ago deceased relative who had comforted me and is supposed to be my guardian angel. And of course, there was the famous pictures which have not only confirmed her existence but have also transported me back in time to a little village where I knew everyone and knew that there were numbers carved into the doorway of a house, and those numbers added up to the date that my family was murdered. What's even freakier is that not only did I know what the numbers were but that I recognized the house and knew it inside and out. Perhaps to describe it as unequivocal insanity would be to admit that I was totally fucked up. I remember thinking back then that maybe good old Dr. Kimberly gave me more than just sedatives, bless her heart. Then again, I thought I could be completely sane and, in fact, had experienced all of it. Could it be? Was there, in fact, a message coming, and if there was, who would be messenger?

"Samuel, I was confused. The only thing I knew for sure was that they were dead, and somehow, I had to focus on that reality. What else can I tell you? The funerals were the next day, and the least I could do was appear to be in control as opposed to incoherent. I knew I needed to be strong, if not for myself then for my parents and everyone else. As with all the other stuff, I knew that I would have to deal with it later. I remember thinking a week or two or even a month or two. When? Didn't matter. All I knew for sure was that when the time was right, I would pick up the picture again, start from scratch, and see where it brought me. Perhaps back to 9612. So am I nuts? What do you think, Samuel? Want to get on the next bus home, or are you crazy enough to hear more?"

Samuel, appearing calm and sensitive to what Steven had just revealed, was, in truth, trembling with awe. Internally, he was about to burst. He believed Steven, and he believed every word of it! He knew the town and had seen it in his own dreams, but deciding that now was not the time to disclose this. Instead, he would silently celebrate his own sanity as, once again, he has been given affirmation of why he was here.

"Steven, I would like to hear more, and sometime soon, I think that the questions you ask yourself will all be answered. Why don't we stop for now and we'll carry on later?"

Steven's mind was going a mile a minute and really didn't want to stop but respected Samuel's judgment. Trembling ever so slightly, he put his hands down by his side to try and curb the emotion that was struggling to erupt. With Samuel's encouragement, the two men emerged from the den, and as they did, Samuel instantly felt the chill and shot up from his bed.

Disoriented at first, he found that the recollection of his dream was more easily remembered compared to the last time. Now as he stretched out in his own bed in his dimly lit bedroom at St. Pat's, he smiled at his memories of his latest experience. Forcing his stiff legs over to the edge of the bed, he again stretched and twisted his body, trying desperately to unkink his stiff muscles before collecting his journal and writing down all that he had remembered. Then as he began his morning prayer, he thanked the elders for trusting him with the mission.

* * *

As Samuel finished his prayers, his thoughts went back and beyond that day to six years earlier as he prepared to leave home and join the seminary. He remembered how distraught and disappointed his father was. They had argued for almost two years about his plans to become a priest. His father and his friends simply didn't understand. He couldn't blame them though. At first, he wondered himself what it was that was drawing him to the church. After all, it wasn't a deep belief in Catholicism or even God; it was just something he had to do.

Despite all the negativity that surrounded his decision, Samuel remained determined to stay the course and find out what it was that had him so intent on becoming a priest. To this day, he still maintains that it was not simply because his father and friends disapproved; it was, in fact, to follow his calling, but it wasn't until he met Steven Di Carlo that he knew what his calling was.

Samuel had stopped going to church after his mother had died, and even when he went, he never enjoyed it, but nevertheless, on the morning of his sixteenth birthday, and to his surprise, he awoke with the determination to join the church.

His father, a very successful real estate developer and self-made millionaire, humored him at first, but then became more and more incensed, and as time went by, Samuel didn't waver from his plans. His father tried bribing him with the rewards of having lots of money and, on his seventeenth birthday, bought him a brand-new Corvette and then told him he could only have it if he enrolled in college. When that failed, he took Samuel to Las Vegas, thinking that the lose slots and the even loser women would corrupt him. When this failed, he threatened to cut him off, and for two lonely months, his father wouldn't speak to him. It was on the eve of the day that Samuel would leave to pursue his destiny that John Stewart succumbed and embraced his son for what seemed an eternity.

When he spoke, John Stewart's bottom lip, tight against his teeth, his right eye twitching as it did whenever he was nervous or upset, had the tone of a defeated man, with his eyes welling up with tears he finally spoke, "Samuel, my son, I am so sorry. I had no right to treat you this way." Then barely audible and visibly shaken, he spoke the word Samuel longed to hear, "I love you, son. I don't have the right to tell you how to live your life. I didn't mean any harm. I just wanted what was best for you. Please forgive me." That day would mark the first time that Samuel had cried since the death of his mother.

They'd grown closer since then, and three years ago, his father moved Samuel to cry for a second time, which was when he came to St. Patrick's Cathedral to witness his final vows. He remembered looking back at his father who was seemingly comfortable in very unfamiliar surroundings, beaming that all too familiar smile he remembered so fondly, the one he used to shine when Samuel would sink a three-pointer from outside the paint during one of his high school basketball games. Now as Samuel looked out at the snowy streets of New York and remembering Steven's story of his father, he realized just how much he missed his own father and how he longed to hold him and tell him how much he loved him.

As Samuel thought of his father, a light rap on the door announced the arrival of Father Michael. Together for the next many hours, they discussed the recollection of their dreams and thought about where Steven's story would next take them.

CHAPTER 22

THE FUNERALS

WHILE SAMUEL STEWART was waking at St. Patrick's Cathedral, causing his connection to the nightmare to be severed, Steven Di Carlo, just a few miles away, was still in his hospital bed, still comatose, and still being bombarded by the relentless dreams of a reality that was yet to come. As his eyelids fluttered and a deep longing seeped into his soul, he breathed out heavily, startling Victoria, who was dosing off in the bedside chair next to him. Steven's hand had just slipped from her grip as the emotionally spent woman succumbed to the exhaustion of worrying and caring for the love of her life. A quick check of the monitors told her that nothing had changed, so she quickly closed her eyes, wishing for dreams of her own, dreams of a reality that was, a truth that was full of love and happiness and a promise of a bright future.

Deep beneath his subconscious at his cabin at Lake George, Steven and had just left the young priest, and now, instead of heading to his usual sanctuary which was the den, Steven instead headed upstairs to the master bedroom for some shut-eye. This would mark the first time since Victoria's death that he would lie on their bed, never mind trying to sleep on it.

While standing at the foot of the bed for what seemed an eternity, Steven wondered why being in this special room was so difficult. After all, it was Victoria's favorite room, so where better to remember her than right here. Closing his eyes, he willed the memories to come to him. He prayed for a smile and for the anger to leave him even if was just for brief moment. Then as though his prayers had been answered, there she was. He could see Victoria; she was all curled up asleep in their bed, embracing her pillow tight to her cheek, just as she did every night. Not unexpectedly, tears welled up in his eyes and the empty pit deep in his soul began to ache. When he opened his eyes, she was gone. All that remained was the moisture from his heartfelt tears and the need to blink repeatedly to clear his vision. Walking over to where she would have been sleeping, Steven lifted Victoria's pillow and crunched it up tight to his face, breathing in deep, trying to capture some of the remnants of her scent, a scent long ago gone. Still, his mind filled him with the aroma of her perfume and the sweet smell of her hair. Remembering her calmed his anxiety, and without any further apprehension, Steven lay down on their bed.

He dozed off, still clutching her pillow. No sooner did his eyes close than dread began circling his thoughts. In this dream inside a dream, he tossed and turned, trying to ward off the unwelcome nightmare. His head shook from side to side, his eyes were crunched together in tight closure, his fingers moved just as though he was typing a letter, and his mind continued to take him on that unwanted journey. As the nightmare deepened, he desperately tried to divert its direction to other times but to no avail. The nightmare's intention was to, once again, force Steven to revisit the day of the funerals, a day which, for him, was an emotional blur. Consciously, he didn't remember much of that day, but in his dream, the images of the coffins were all too real.

Then as though he were hovering above the proceedings, he saw himself sitting in the pew at the front of the church, and as he descended toward his body, the numbness he felt on that day returned. When he was fully sitting inside himself, he felt the convulsions that had imprisoned his body on that day and many others that followed. The overwhelming grief was back and the fear of the reality that was had him fix his eyes on his feet instead of looking at where his young family lay unmoving.

Emotionally, he had shut down and turned off the turmoil of his surrounding's content to be in his own universe, his own little world, consumed not only by grief but more so by self-pity. It wasn't until he heard the sounds of children that his will would release his tortured soul; and then through his broken heart, he thought he smiled as Tommy and Cathy's friends had walked up and honored them by placing team sweaters on their coffins, a Mighty Crunch jersey with Tommy's name and number ten on it and Cathy's soccer sweater. She wore the Blue Angels number seven.

Accepting condolences from each of them was a difficult reminder of what he would miss for the rest of his life. Then watching his mother hug and thank each child and listening to her as she asked them to always remember Tommy and Cathy had him wondering where she found her strength.

After the children had paid their respects and the sound of shuffling feet had stopped, a welcomed silence overtook the church. Beyond the odd sob, there was a lot of sniffling and the sounds of tissue paper wiping away tears. The slamming of the knee rests being returned to their slots occasionally interrupted the stillness inside the small cathedral.

The mass was a complete blur, but the number of friends and relatives who had come to pay their respects was crystal clear. Following the service, they all lined up to give their condolences. This, of course, was the most difficult part of the service. Rather than sharing the pain, which is usually the intent but for Steven, the pain and sorrow was intensified to the point of being unbearable.

The drive to the cemetery took them past their home, which, in Catholic belief, would release their souls. After a brief pause, as a neighbor opened the front door of the Di Carlo home, the procession continued to Forest Lawn Cemetery.

Still tossing and turning, his restlessness began to ease as his eyes beneath his lids showed him the path to where they were to be interned. One step after another Steven walked slowly behind the coffins, His hands locked together as his mother held on to his left elbow while his father clasped his right. Then as relentless as his dream was determined to be, it began to replay the burials just as they happened those many months before. Lying in his bed, his hands balled up into fists, his face began to twitch uncontrollably, and his breathing once again became very erratic. Unable to wake himself from the continuing nightmare, he was forced to watch the coffins being lowered into the ground. Suddenly, a feeling of suffocation gripped him just the same as it did back then, and just when the lack of air forced his lungs to gasp, his subconscious transported him to the week following the funerals.

He was alone; the crisp morning air felt cold against his tear-soaked cheeks. He stood silently, not praying, not even talking. He just stood, hands in his coat pockets, reading the tombstone over and over with total disbelief. The tombstone was of three angels; the middle angel held a tablet scroll which read,

Di Carlo/Weeks
A Wife and Mother
Son and Daughter
Together they were taken from us
Together they rest in this place
Together they will enter heaven
Together they will be loved forever.
Victoria 1975–2012
Tommy 2001–2012
Cathy 2003–2012

* * *

Back then, Steven's life had digressed; his desires had all been ripped away from him, and he could see no way of getting them back. His merciless dream inside a dream took him on a journey of his self-loathing and self-destruction. Back then, he simply didn't care about anything, especially his own well-being. It wasn't until his family and friends conducted an intervention that Steven began to, once again, think rationally. As Steven was now forced to relive it yet again, he remembered as though he had been abducted. Once again, hovering above himself, he watched as the Steven below him begged and pleaded for them to let him be, but to no avail. He watched as his family and friends showed absolutely no mercy, and as he slowly descended into his own body, he found himself looking up at his best friend and was reminded of how pathetic he had become.

"We are done feeling sorry for you, man. Give your head a shake!" Jimmy yelled angrily at Steven. He told him that was it. There would be no more codling, no more walking around on egg-shells and then repeated that there was no more feeling sorry for him because he was doing a really good job of it himself. The disgust in his voice as he spoke shook Steven in a painful way.

In this vision that may have been a dream or conscious memory, Steven remembered how his family and friends saved him.

"Shit, Steve, you've almost drowned in your own sorrow. Wake up, man. Look at what you're doing to yourself." Then it was Robby's turn to lay in on him; he asked Steven when it was that he became a quitter and what would Tommy think of him right now.

Stef and Tony were in the background, not saying too much, and when Steven looked at them for support, they just turned away. Then his mother asked him about the gun he had bought. Steven felt shocked that she knew about it. He lied and said that it was just for protection.

"Bullshit!" Roberto Di Carlo glared at his son. Steven had never seen his father so angry, his voice trembling with emotion, his eyes red with rage, and his fist balled up so tight that he looked like he was about to strike something. His words shocked Steven as he spoke.

"When did you become such a coward?" he yelled as he asked this and then cried. "You've never looked for the easy way out before, son. Why now? When did you become so fucking selfish? Do you think that blowing your brains out will ease your pain? What about our pain?" Then barely audible and full of heartbreaking hurt, he went on, "What about Victoria's message to you? Remember her message, son? She said if you take your own life you will never be able to be together with them again."

After he finished, the silence was unbearable; they just sat there waiting. The only sounds were those of Maria Di Carlo crying softly, trying to hide her distress.

Steven, eyes focused on his feet, knew that they were all looking at him, and he dared not return their gaze. To do so would mean that he would have to speak, so no one spoke. The air was so thick you needed a chainsaw to slice through the tension. Steven tried a couple of times to get up the courage and defend his actions, but the lump caught in his throat made anything he tried to say totally incomprehensible.

As the silence continued, he began to realize just how true and hard-hitting their words were. This realization had him feeling ashamed, wondering how he would ever be able to look them in the eyes again.

It seemed a long while before he had built up the courage to speak. After all, how do you respond to the closest people in your life thinking of you as a quitter, a coward, and a selfish asshole? And more so, how would you admit that they were bang on? Jimmy, frustrated with silence, decided to break it, and his words again rang true.

"Look, Steve," he began calmly at first and then progressively began to bulldoze him, "what would you do if you thought I was going to blow my brains out? What would you do?" His anger was telling, his concern was more consoling. "We know that you've suffered this huge loss in your life and that you need time to mourn, but you haven't been eating, you haven't been taking care of yourself. You're shutting everyone out, and now we find a gun and a fucking note telling us you're sorry for offing yourself. So you tell me, what would you do in our spot? What would you expect to hear from me if things were reversed because you know what, asshole? That's exactly what you should be saying to us. We need to know that we're getting through to you, understand?"

Steven, his head held high, his fists pushing down hard on the seat of his chair, gritted his teeth and told them that he did understand, and then as the crushing silence in the room completely overtook him, he brought his hands up to his face and began rubbing his eyes as though he were trying to wash away the guilt. "Yes," he said more subdued, "I understand." Then with as much emotion as any almost forty-year-old was willing to show, he asked for their help.

"I should have been there to protect them," he began. And then with his body quivering and his words stuttering, he told them about how he had been affected after hearing all the fucked-up shit that was in the autopsy report and that he had trouble dealing with what they had told him. With his top lip quivering and his mouth distorting in an unnatural way, he tried to maintain some control as he continued.

"When I close my eyes, it doesn't matter if I'm awake or asleep. All I see is their battered bodies lying dead in our home and then that fucking coroner's report. God, how could I have let this happen?" Then with more anger than tears, he revealed to them what the coroner's report had said.

"They were all beaten and raped repeatedly. They were tortured, abused, and violently molested for hours. Just thinking about the fear and terror they must have felt . . . " Steven paused as his voice was trying to find the strength to continue, and then with his stutter now reverberating and barely audible, he continued, "I can't sleep or even close my eyes without seeing it happen. The horrors they had to go through have left me with this enormous sense of guilt and despair. I hear their screams every minute of every hour, every day. I see their beaten bodies, their lifeless faces, and all that blood. God, it was everywhere. I can still smell that smell of death from that awful night." Again, Steven stopped, his chin pointing out at his family and friends as his lower jaw tightened in a painful way. His hands gripped the seat of his chair so hard that his arms were shaking, then as the anger gave strength to his voice, his stutter disappeared as he continued, "Then I asked myself why. Why would anybody do this? We have no enemies. There were no ransom demands. Fuck, this could not have been just for pleasure. There had to be a reason, and God knows I need to know why."

When he looked up, expecting some sort of answers, he noticed a look of shock in each of their faces and then realized that this was the first that they had heard of what was in the coroner's report. Then—BANG! Stefano had just put his fist right through the wall of the study.

Looking around the room, Steven saw that Jim and Rob were hovering around his parents and then realized that his mother was

142

having some sort of trouble. As he jumped up to see what was wrong, Robby was already on his cell phone, dialing 911, and Jimmy was helping his dad ease his mother to the floor. She appeared to be breathing but was unconscious. His father was starting to panic, and Jimmy kept reassuring everyone that she would be okay.

When the paramedics arrived, they quickly strapped Maria Di Carlo to a gurney and said she needed to be transported to the hospital immediately; it appeared to be a heart attack.

* * *

Steven's memories or dream, whatever it was, jumped to later that same night after his mom had been admitted to hospital and after they had returned home.

"Look, Stef, it's late. Say what you got to say, and then I'm going to bed," he heard himself say as the anxiety of the intense happenings just minutes before had not quite left him. Within Steven's dream inside a dream, there was no confusion, only anxiety. He knew the story and knew what was going to be said, so why did he have to live through it again? Why was Stefano so important in this damned message that refused to end? With no way of waking or shutting down the dream, Steven simply watched as Stefano's own anxiety force a crooked smile on his face, and then he watched as Stefano's comfort zone had him focused down on his own feet.

For Stefano, he was unsure how what he had to say would be received. After all, he wasn't sure he believed his own experiences. Still, raising his eyes from his feet, he stared across at Steven, full of conviction for his purpose; then leaning forward in his chair, he tried to sound confident as he spoke, "Listen, Steve, you're going to be going through some major shit in the next while, and I just want you to know that I'm here for you. It's hard to explain right now, but I've been getting ready for this for the past while. Soon, you'll know what I'm talking about, but in the meantime, when all this stuff gets real strange, come talk to me and I'll do my best to help you understand."

The word *understand* continued to echo in Steven's dream inside a dream; the echo became a scream, and the voice changed from Stefano's to Jimmy's, and then the echo stopped screaming and became an emotional plea. The trembling voice belonged to his father. As quickly as the dream inside a dream began playing out, it was over, and as if he had never left, Steven Di Carlo was once again lying in his bed back at Lake George, fully engulfed by his original dream.

CHAPTER 23

CHRISTMAS EVE MORNING

MARIA DI CARLO rushed into the hospital room, and upon seeing her daughter-in-law, she ran to her and embraced her with all her strength, holding on to her as if she hadn't seen her in a very long time. "Oh, my dear Victoria, how wonderful it is to hold you." Rocking back and forth with Victoria in her arms, Maria Di Carlo silently thanked whoever was listening, primarily the Lord, for making her horrible nightmare just that, a nightmare.

"What is it, Mother? Is everything okay? Are the kids all right?" Victoria, concerned about Maria's behavior, pulled back from the embrace to look her mother-in-law in the face. What she saw was a pale worried woman, not surprising. After all, her son was lying in a deep coma near death, so who could blame her? Taking her mother-in-law to Steven's bedside, they both watched as beneath his closed eyelids, his eyes continued to move from side to side while his face twitched, sometimes appearing to be in pain and other times appearing to smile.

* * *

Just outside Steven's room, down the corridor, the tall, thin man searched his consciousness for any danger of being detected. *Good, those two filthy pretenders are not here*, Gabriel thought this to himself as he tried to feel the presence of the prophets. Knowing he needed to act quickly, he began searching for a disguise, and where better to find one than in the staff lounge as he passed the big blue door marked Staff Only. *Hmmm, a doctor's smock, and oooh, a flowery surgeon's hat. I like that.* Gabriel grabbed the two items and quickly locked himself in the staff bathroom. He put the cap on first, then looked at himself in the mirror as a nod of approval looked back at him. Stroking his pencil-thin mustache beneath his prominent nose, a sinister smile creased the left side of his mouth. "I look rather fine," he said in a soft whisper. Then putting the jacket on, the disguise was complete.

* * *

Deep beneath the surface of his restless eyes, Steven Di Carlo's awakening continued. Still, somewhere deep in his subconscious, he knew that it was a dream but also knew that for him to finally awaken, the full chronicle needed to be told. So as he lay there oblivious to his surroundings, and with both his mother and his wife at his bedside, worried beyond comprehension, he had found Samuel and had, once again, began recounting his story to the young priest.

* * *

"I don't remember how I ended up there or, frankly, what it is that is finally giving me the courage to talk about it, but here goes." Steven paused as sweat broke out below his hairline, staining his forehead with a glistening bead of dampness. Then with the disbelief that he was about to tell someone this particular memory, he felt overwhelmed; then taking a deep breath and holding it, he leaned back in his chair, tilted his head back, and massaged his temples as he slowly exhaled. When he was done, there was sparkle in his eye that Sammy grew to know as a precursor to a fond memory. Still sitting straight up, shoulders squared to Samuel, he waved his finger at him as he continued, "I know that you claim to believe all the weird stories I've been telling you, but this one is as strange as they come. I hope you're ready for it my friend.

"Sammy, it was a couple of weeks ago. I was lying down on my bed and staring straight up at the heavens, trying to summon Victoria when, suddenly, my bedroom ceiling turns into this magnificent dark blue sky full of stars. My bed turned into a meadow of beautiful flowers, and as crazy as this sounds, my pillow turned into Victoria's lap. Sammy, she was stroking my head with her hand and speaking to me. She was telling me not to be afraid, that things would be fine, and that my purpose in all this would soon be revealed to me." Steven looked at Samuel in a questioning way, almost as though he was asking permission to continue. Samuel responded with a nod, encouraging Steven to go on, and so he did.

"Never in my entire life did I feel as much at peace as I did then. When I looked up into Victoria's eyes, they were somehow different, and as beautiful as they were before, there was no comparison to the depth of the color and the joy that was in them that night or day, or whatever it was. You see, I wasn't quite sure." Steven's eyes began to gloss over as he looked up at the ceiling, hoping to see that same sky. His mouth formed into a warm but embarrassing smile as the recollection of his experience had him wondering how he could possibly tell this amazingly personal story to a priest, then setting aside his feelings of discomfort, he continued.

"Sammy, the sky was sort of a night sky with the stars set in a deep dark blue, but somehow, the meadow was bright, just as it would be on warm summer afternoon. It was so beautiful that I was afraid to move. I thought that if I did, I might wake up and then it would all disappear; Victoria, the meadow, and the sky. Man, I wanted it to last forever."

Steven again paused as his gaze became distant. The memory of his experience had him in a temporary daydream. Samuel, looking at Steven, witnessed the inner peace that had taken over his appearance. For that all too brief moment, Samuel envied his tortured friend and then listened to his soft deep voice continue just as though he had never stopped telling his story. "Sammy, it was as though Victoria was reading my thoughts. You know what she told me? She told me that it would be okay to move, that we could sit up or even go for a walk if I liked. I asked her if it would be all right to just hold her for a while, and as I did, I can remember still debating in my mind whether it was a dream or some weird hallucination. I remember thinking about pinching myself and then thought better of it. At that point, I didn't care whether it was real or not. I just wanted to enjoy it. Anyway, if it wasn't real, why could I smell her hair and touch her skin? How could I feel the softness of her body? Shit, Samuel, I could even smell the flowers and the grass and feel the warm breeze on my bare arms and face.

"Looking at her and then looking around at the paradise that surrounded us, I said let's walk. I asked her where we were, and she said, 'You're with me. Does it matter where?' As we began to walk, it felt like I was walking on powder. Even though I was barefoot, all I felt on the bottom of my feet was this softness caressing them, better than powder sand and softer than most plush of carpets. As we walked, Victoria told me that everything would be all right and then asked me if I really understood that what happened had to happen. I remember answering in a sort of desperation. I told her no, I didn't understand why she had to die.

"I tried to explain to her that I just felt lost. I promised her that I would never take my own life and that I would live until it was my time to be there with them. That's when she held me, and we kissed. Samuel, it was an amazing kiss, so amazing that it was like taking all the love that we ever shared and then expressed it in a single kiss.

"I asked her about Tommy and Cathy and if I would be able to see them. She told me that it wasn't time yet, but she did want me to meet someone else. When I asked her who, she didn't answer. She simply held my hand and pulled me along. We walked for quite sometime. The meadow turned to thick beautiful green grass, and this time, I could feel the blades of grass between my toes, and the coolness of it reminded me of the times when we used to stroll the grounds at our home after a late-night swim. As I thought back to those incredible times, we were suddenly there, in Riverdale, every-thing as it was, except for the roses. The roses were so much more vibrant. The colors of all the flowers were incredible. I asked if we were we really home. Vic looked at me and smiled. She told me that she visits our home every day, then she said very playfully, 'Are you still shy?' With that, she let her clothes fall off and dove into the pool.

"As I looked around, I noticed there was nothing outside of our property. There were no neighbors, and in fact, there wasn't even a neighborhood. Simply nothing, no other houses, no streetlamps. I guess that was because there were no streets. There were just rows and rows of flowers. As far as the eye could see, there were just flowers. It was so hypnotic that it took Victoria calling me to snap me out of it. I looked at her and, very quickly, took off all my cloths and jumped in.

"The water was warm and felt velvety with an inviting strangeness to it. When I lifted my arms out of the water, they came out dry. When I came up after dunking my head, my hair remained dry. It felt like an incredible kind of weird. When I swam over to Victoria, we embraced. I asked her if it was okay. After all, this was heaven, wasn't it? She told me that in this place, everything is possible, especially where love was concerned, and we were in love.

"I looked up at the sky, maybe to say thank you, I don't know. But when I did, I noticed that it was changing from that deep blue to a magnificent orange. Things had now reversed as the ground had darkened and the sky had brightened. The bright orange sky produced this wonderful reflection on the water. The atmosphere was better than right, and the love of my life was in my arms. I told her that it felt like we were in our own universe and she said, 'Look around, baby. We are.' This time, when I looked . . . " Steven paused, trying to gauge Sammy's reaction to his unbelievable adventure, and when he saw the fascination in the young priest's eyes, he went on, "It truly was amazing, just as if we really were in space. There were planets and stars all around us.

"The stars would take turns shooting across the galaxy, and the planets. It was incredible, Sammy. The planets seemed close enough to touch, and they were surrounded by these amazing colors that were swirling around them like mini tornadoes. When we got out of the pool, I picked her up in my arms and carried her over to our special spot in between the rose gardens. There we found that our blanket had already been laid out. When on the blanket, we held each other so tight. Sammy, it was simply an incredible expression of love, so amazing that I prayed it would never end. Then, and I'll never forget the look on her face, my god, she was so hypnotic—her dark hair embracing her face, her skin was dark and smooth, her lips looked incredible, sort of plump and definitely moist, her breath had the aroma of sweet chocolate. Well, she cupped my face with both her hands and kissed me, then told me that it was time to go, that there was someone that I needed to meet. Sammy, I know you must think that I've really gone over the deep end, but, man, I'm telling you that this was no dream."

Samuel Stewart sat staring at his new friend with an embarrassing sort of awe. His cheeks did feel a little flushed, and in some sort of perverse way, he felt a bit jealous. Shaking off the longing for someone of his own to love, he reached out and held Steven by his shoulders as he began his assurances, "My friend, I promised not to judge you, and I won't. Things, crazy things, and all sorts of events in this world sometimes happen in weird ways and are designed to serve a special purpose, so go on. I am fascinated. Please continue."

"All right then," Steven continued, feeling a bit relieved and much more comfortable that the weirdness was out of the way. "Well, anyway, I don't remember getting dressed, but there we were, fully clothed, walking hand in hand down a cobblestoned street nonetheless. The sky was once again this brilliant dark blue and the moon was very bright and full. It cast a yellowish beam down the darkened street as if to guide us as we walked. I felt very strange at the silence during our walk. It had me feeling uneasy. Victoria, as if reading my thoughts, turned to me and told me not to worry and that everything would be all right.

"When we arrived at where we needed to be, she took both my hands and kissed them. She told me that our time together had been incredible and that she couldn't wait until the next time. Crying softly, she hugged me hard. I knew she didn't want to let me go. But then, she kissed my cheek, and she was gone. She just vanished. Suddenly, I was very alone and felt very frantic. Looking around, I saw nothing, no sign of anyone walking or, for that matter, even existing. I called to Victoria, but she didn't answer. There was this eerie silence that chilled me to the bone, and in fact, the only sound I heard was my own breathing. I was about to run, and only God knows to where, when I heard his voice. He said, 'Hello, old friend. It's been a long time, a very long time.'

"Startled, I called out, 'Who's there? Do I know you?' Then after some unbearable silence, he responded, 'You did, but it was long ago.' I think I heard his voice trembling. He sounded remorseful, anyway definitely emotional. 'It's good to see you, my dear Thaddeus.'

"Thaddeus! I remember asking myself, why do I know that name? After a bit of time, I challenged the voice. I must admit I was a little pissed at him for interrupting my time with Victoria. 'I'm afraid you have the advantage, so please tell me who you are and where you are.' I was a bit confused at the situation I was in, not being able to see the man or even recognize his voice, but then I did feel at ease despite the creepiness.

"All I could think of was, where was Victoria, and what happened to that wonderful feeling I had a few minutes ago? The sky had gone from being inviting to being menacing. It had become black with not even a glimpse of the moon, and without the moonlight, there was no way to see whoever it was who was talking to me. I remember the startled feeling I had and the hesitation in my heart as it skipped a beat when he spoke again. His voice, as melodic as a song, had the tone of a tenor. 'Come, join me. I'm right here.' Then just as if on cue, a streetlamp lit and its glow lit up a sidewalk café. Seated at the only table was a distinguished-looking old gentleman, perhaps in his seventies or eighties, wearing a black cape and what could only be described as a beret. 'Come,' he repeated and motioned me toward the only other chair.

"Accepting his invitation, I strained my memory to try and recognize him but couldn't. He wore a long white beard that was neatly kept, a burgundy silk scarf hung from his neck, and he wore white gloves. He held a cane firmly in front of him just as if it were there on display for me. The cane had a golden hawk gripping the round handle. What was crazy, Sammy, was that the cane was far more familiar to me than my host.

151

"I sat there staring at him, and he stared right back at me. He was smiling with an amused look on his face. Shit, I thought he was going to burst out laughing. Instead, he began to talk. He said that he understood my concerned curiosity and told me not to trouble myself in trying to remember who he was. He assured me that it would all come back to me in good time. Ignoring his advice, I again asked him who he was, and he again answered, 'All in good time, my dear old friend. I beg you for your patience as we have much to discuss and very little time to discuss it.'

"As if by magic, a drink of some sort materialized in front of him and an espresso for me. I asked him how he knew that I preferred espresso, and he said with a strong unrecognizable accent, 'Ah, one gets to know another after a few lifetimes.' And then with a very serious expression, he began to tell me things. Much of what he told me made no sense at the time, such things as my journey will take me to many cities and many places within those cities and that I must always be alert to see those things that are not meant to be seen. 'My dear friend, he continued, when the time is right, you must travel here to this village,' and as he motioned with his arm, night became day and the small village we were in was now visible.

"The streets were tiny, the buildings were joined to one another, the shrubbery was dry and sun worn, except for the cactus. They appeared to be everywhere. I recognized the fruit that grew on the plant as it is one of my mother's favorites. She always told that the best taste in the morning was to go to one of these plants and carefully pick the juicy fruit that was bloodred on the inside and prickly cactus on the outside.

"He asked me to walk with him. He showed me that the village was on the very top of a mountain. The view of the valley below was spectacular, and from where we stood, we could see two bodies of water. He pointed and said, 'There, the beautiful Ionian Sea,' and then looking to the other side, he pointed out the Adriatic. 'This is the place that you were last awake, and it is this place that will awaken you again.' As if I wasn't confused enough, he then hit me with a riddle. He told me that when I came to this place, I was to look for myself, and when I found myself, I would understand.

"'Wait, what are you talking about? How do I look for myself, and why do you need to talk in riddles? If this is so important, why don't you just tell me what I need to know?' The impatience in my voice drew a smile on his face, and as he put his hands together, as if in prayer, he riddled me yet again. 'What you need to know, dear one, is this: If you have a question, simply ask it and you will receive the answer. The answers will come to you in many ways, and with time, you will know where to look and how you should receive them. Very soon, you will awaken and, with the awakening, will come to the understanding of your destiny. Your cousin and dear friend Stefano will help you. Although there is a past with him, this will be his first purpose. When he returned, he was given the path of a warrior and positioned to learn the art of battle. He has acquainted himself with the others who share your destiny, and with all that he has learned, he will guide you to many of the answers that you seek.'

"'What do you know of my destiny, and why me? Why didn't you choose to destroy someone else's life?'

"'Oh my, my. It was you, my friend, who chose this path. I am only here to guide you as it was meant to be.'

"'Who are you? What do you mean by that? How could I have chosen this path? Tell me, are you one of the spirit guides that Victoria told me about? What am I to do? I'm not like Stefano. I am not a fighter.' With that, he just smiled at me and said, 'I am Augustus, and although we are of different paths, our goal is the same. Follow your anger, dear Thaddeus. In there lies your strength.'

"I was wondering why he had called me Thaddeus when, suddenly, the familiarity of that name began to shoot pains into the back of my neck, and then just as revealing as that was, the realization of who Augustus actually was had me filled with this incredible need to talk with him. I was so excited I called to him, but it was too late. He was gone. Instead, I was greeted with an incredible turbulence in the air. The sky had once again become dark. Only this time, it was filled with exploding thunder that crashed and roared all around me and violent spears of lightning shooting down to earth, barely missing me. It was so crazy I crouched down, covering my head and ears."

* * *

Back in the here and now, at the Mercy Medical Center, Gabriel was very quiet as he entered Steven's hospital room. When he spoke, he startled both Victoria and Maria Di Carlo. "I'm sorry to intrude," he said, his sinister smile still present but hidden by his right hand that was smoothing down his pencil-thin mustache.

"May I have a moment, ladies?"

"Who are you?" asked Victoria. "Where is Dr. Brunstrom?"

"Dr. Brunstrom is at home with his family," responded Gabriel, his right hand extended and accepted by Victoria. "I'm Victoria Di Carlo, this is my Mother-in-law Maria Di Carlo."

"I am Dr. Ricci," lied the tall, thin man. "And this must be Steven." He walked over to Steven's bedside, but as he did, his elbow brushed against Maria Di Carlo's shoulder, shooting electricity right through her. The encounter had the elder Di Carlo screaming with fright when, suddenly, she grabbed Gabriel's arm, shouting, "You are not welcome here! Leave now!" She then grabbed the nurses' call button, pressing it repeatedly, which chased the tall, thin man from the room and out of the hospital.

* * *

Unaware of the happening at his bedside, Steven Di Carlo's face began to darken; his eyes retreated into their sockets as his comatose nightmare continued. Samuel, sharing his nightmare, watched helplessly as Steven's eyes began to blink and the right side of his face spasmed. His hands seemed to not know what to do as they pulled at his earlobes, then move to rub the bottom of his nose, and then together, his hand forced their way through his hair. Fear had gripped Steven as he continued.

"Did you feel that? Was that my mom yelling?" exclaimed Steven, more as a statement than a question, as he continued without waiting for a response. "You know, I didn't remember this part of the story until just now." He went silent again and wrapped his arms around his shoulders in a sort of instinctive way of protecting himself before continuing, "I was there, crouched down, terrified that I was going to be hit by the lightning bolts when everything around me went out of focus, a bizarre type of blur. When it cleared up, I was back in Manhattan for the umpteenth time and, once again, just outside the New York Mutual Bank, Victoria's bank! In this version, everything was in black and white, just like an old movie. All the color was gone, the streets were deserted, there were no people, no cars, no buses. The only light appeared to be coming from the bank, and it was as though it was the only building in Manhattan.

"And just like in the other episodes, I suddenly felt this desperate need to get to the bank and again found myself running toward it. When I got there, the doors were still locked. So I cupped my hands around my eyes on the glass door to look inside, and there in the middle of the lobby, tied to a chair, was Victoria. She looked terrified.

"I know I told you about this vision before, but this time it was different. This time, there were five men circling her. It was crazy. I tried everything to get in, but it was as if the glass was three feet thick. I pounded the doors and yelled, but it was no good. In this new version of this old nightmare, the unthinkable began happening right before my very eyes. I watched helplessly as one of the men began to do unspeakable things to her. He was brutalizing her, and there was nothing I could do." Steven stopped again; his head hung down to his chest, his legs were pumping up and down in a nervous rhythm, and his body was shaking from side to side as he desperately tried to ward off the memories. Then with darkened eyes that were wet with tears and red with rage, he stared straight at the young priest.

"Sammy, I was screaming at them to let her go when one of them finally looked at me. His face was pure evil. Better still, it was like he had no face or features, just a horribly wicked grin. Instead of a gun, this time, he held a knife in his left hand, and without taking his eyes off me, he plunged it deep into Victoria's neck. The shock of what I had seen froze me. I couldn't breathe. Everything was spinning, then the bastard turns and walks toward me, comes right up to the glass door, laughing and mocking me. As hard as I tried, I couldn't get to him. It was like I was trying to break through steel doors. I yelled at him to come out. Instead, he just stood there laughing at my futility, and then all of a sudden, he stops laughing and just like that, his face turns into this frightening devil. I don't quite know how to explain it. It wasn't like he had a hideous ugly face that was scary. It was, instead, the evil that exuded from his face that was terrifying, just as though it was the devil himself looking at me.

"Still, as wicked as it was, it did show me some of his facial features, like brief glimpses of his nose and of his eyes. Sammy, the glimpses of his features, as frightening as they were, were also familiar to me. I've seen him somewhere before. I know it. And somehow, somewhere, I will figure it out and then maybe, just maybe, this horrible vision will lead me to the killers even if one of them is the devil himself

"Reenergized by the recognition, I began pounding the doors again and again. Only this time, the doors began to give a bit. Still, the bastard stayed his ground and kept mocking me. What he did next did momentarily stop me though. As if to further my anger, he brought the knife up to his mouth and licked off Victoria's blood. At that moment, as the shock of what he had just done wore off, my rage gave me the strength to continue battering the doors. When I finally broke through, the prick vanished, and suddenly, I was being grabbed from behind, and as I turned to strike the culprit, someone else had grabbed my arms, shouting at me to wake up, and just like that and far too early, I was back at home, looking into my father's terrified eyes as he struggled to hold me down. Sammy, it seemed so real, but instead, it was a horrible dream, or was it?"

Steven's eyes seemed to search the palms of his hands for answers as he unknowingly held them up, staring straight through them. "Sure, I was at home in my own bed. My father was securing my arms, but it was more than a simple nightmare," he continued, the tone of his voice becoming softer and less certain. Then moving forward in his chair and closer to Samuel, his face lightened and his eyes again sparkled. The frown lines had all but disappeared, and his hands became animated as he spoke. "Buddy, I gotta believe that there were messages being delivered to me, and with your help, maybe I can figure them out and understand what they mean."

"I know we can, Steven," Samuel responded with unquestioning certainty. Staring straight at Steven with determined eyes, his chin raised and pointing out while his mouth formed an unwavering smile. "There's no doubt in my mind. I know that all the episodes have got be leading somewhere, and as God is my witness, we're finding out where. Tell me, how did your father react?"

Steven, amazed at the conviction his new friend had shown him, sat back in his chair as relief replaced his fears. Maybe he wasn't going nuts after all, and now, he was not alone. Reaching for his coffee that had, long ago, gone cold, Steven continued with his story, "How did he react? He's my father. He was broken. Everything I was going through, he was feeling twice as hard." Steven's demeanor changed; a heartfelt sadness forced his face to sag. His eyes that, moments earlier, were red and dry began to moisten, and his hands trembled as the regret of what he was doing not only to his parents but also to everyone close to him had him feeling very selfish, but how would he control it? Would Samuel and the church really be able to help him? Keeping his questions to himself, he continued.

"He's the best, you know, my dad!" he said as though he had to clarify who he was talking about. Then after a short pause, he wiped the moisture from his eyes, cleared his throat twice, and then took up where he left off. "He loves me so much. Anyway, when I was able to get him to let me go, he simply broke down, sobbing. We held on to each other for I don't know how long. He just kept repeating that everything would be okay and that it was just a bad dream. I looked at him, Sammy, not realizing what I was doing to him and then made him worry even more. You see, the anger was still vibrating throughout my entire body, so I shook my head and mumbled, 'No, Dad! It couldn't have been a dream. It was too real.'

"I just wanted to be left alone, so after convincing him that I was okay, I was able to get him to leave. When I was finally alone, I tried to slow my heart as it was still racing. I tried to figure out what it was that I had just experienced. Samuel, somehow, deep down, I knew that it wasn't just a dream, but logic and common sense suggested that I was nuts. After all, what else could it have been?

"Anyway, I decided that I would write it all down—everything. And I remembered all of it. It was as if somehow, sometime during the night, I got up out of bed and traveled or, better still, teleported to wherever it was that I went. The experience was so real that I could still feel the anger I had at the bank, the dread that I felt watching the love of my life being brutalized and murdered, but along with that, I could still feel the softness of the ground under my feet and the scent of the warm breeze touching my skin when I was with Victoria. I could still feel her embrace and every spot on my body that she touched. Shit, I could still smell her.

"Samuel, I honestly felt as if I experienced all of it, and I mean all of it. Every sensation in my body told me that it happened. Everything that I remembered was so clear. Not only did I remember the smells that came with the warm breeze but also the enticing aroma of a bakery in the village. I can still feel the spot in the crook of my arm where Victoria held on to during our walk to that village. As unbelievable as it sounds, my heart tells me that it had to be real.

"What I remain confused about was recognizing Augustus and knowing why he called me Thaddeus but not remembering beyond that. I just know that my name was once Thaddeus and Augustus was once a friend, but that's it. The memory that I recollected when I met him has all but left me. Then even more confusing was the utter and complete horror that happened at the bank. Why the bank? Why do I always have this horrible vision of the bank? After all, and as I've told you before, I know that didn't happen there. It could have been those same faceless animals that were in the bank, but she wasn't killed in the bank. She was killed in our home. Maybe all this was to give me that momentary glimpse of recognition of who the killers were."

Steven then stopped, got up out of his seat, and went directly to the speed bag. The rhythm was masterful and smooth—left, left, right, left, left, right, then faster and faster as the rhythm of his fist hitting the bag sounded like a drummer dishing out a solo. When, finally, the rhythm slowed, Steven gave the bag one last pop, almost knocking it off its chain. Then after grabbing the bag to still it, he returned to his chair, a bead of sweat dripping down his face as he purposely avoided eye contact with the young prophet. They both sat there quietly and patiently waiting for the other to speak when, finally, Samuel gave in and asked Steven if he was okay.

"Yeah, I guess so. I'm just mixed up. It seems like I'm always hit with a good, happy vision that always ends in sadness, anger, and disbelief. Just wish I could get a better grasp of the messages." Looking at Samuel, Steven began to stir in his seat and was tempted to go back to the speed bag. Instead, he got up and began pacing the room, with his hand cupped behind his neck and his elbows stretching back. He looked up at the ceiling as though he was speaking to it. "You think my world couldn't get any crazier?" he asked as he continued with his story. "Believe me or not when I say this doesn't really matter because I was totally awake when it happened. But when I finished writing down all my notes, I went to take a shower in the hopes of rejoining the world of the living. Well, while I was in the shower, as hot as the water was, I suddenly felt an intense cold. Then I thought my mind was playing tricks on me because I could hear Victoria whispering in my ear, and I could feel her breath tickle the nape of my neck as she spoke. You know what she said? She said, 'Honey, it was real, and it was wonderful.' I called to her, but she didn't answer.

"I reluctantly got out of the shower, worried that she would come back and I would miss her, but as I was about to shave, I felt that same chill again, and as the cold intensified, I could see my breath just like you could on a winter's day. Samuel, it was so cold that a thin layer of ice had formed from the steam on the mirror, and when I went to touch it to see if it was really ice, a heart materialized right before my eyes, just as it did that day in the hospital. Sammy, it was the best. It was the most awesome feeling. In fact, it was that precise moment that convinced me that it was no dream. It really did happen. You see, it's not that I don't believe. It's that all this is so crazy that everyone thinks I'm nuts. Not being able to share this amazing experience has, instead, made it a curse, that is, until now."

Steven paused at that point, trying to read Samuel's thoughts. When he looked at the younger man, instead of seeing disbelief, he noticed that his eyes were moist and that there was a longing deep inside his trance that appeared to be distant but heartfelt. "You okay, buddy?" Steven nudged Samuel, bringing him out of his temporary stupor. Staring back at Steven, Samuel responded, "Yeah, yeah. It's just that I can relate. For years now, I have had these dreams, dreams about what we're going through right now. For as long as I can remember, my dreams have been preparing me to meet you. Can you believe it? And you know what, it wasn't until just now that I realized it." Then he paused and looked at Steven straight in his eyes and blurted, "This is awesome. I feel like, wow, I feel vindicated. Shit, I used to tell my dad and my friends about my dreams, and they would all look at me like I was nuts too. So I can relate. Wow, I feel euphoric right now. I can't explain it, but wow."

"Then you truly do know how I feel and how I felt when I saw the heart for a second time. Shit, I felt alive again, like you just said, wow! It was like a thousand tons had been lifted from my shoulders. Best of all, Sammy, maybe I wasn't going nuts, and somehow, someway, somewhere, they still existed and if the place I visited was where they existed, then they were in a pretty cool place. Funny but that morning as I sat back and thought about it all, I felt so incredible, perhaps even enlightened. Maybe I felt the way you're feeling right now, and you know why, my friend?"

"Yes, Steven, I think I do, but please you tell me."

"Because, Sammy, the realization that there was something beyond this world, beyond this life and this reality was something so incredibly wonderful that I was filled with awe. I think I whistled as I skipped down the stairs. My father, worried at first, smiled as he watched me come down and then laughed at me and said, "Welcome back, son."

"When we picked up my mom from the hospital, I was relieved to see that she not only felt better. She also looked a whole lot better. When we arrived home, I reassured her that the doom and gloom attitude was gone and that I now realized and sort of understood the messages that I had been receiving. I told her about my experience, and in her wisdom as a mother, she explained to me that this happens to everyone all the time, but it's only the blessed or the dammed who remember. For a long time, I remember wondering which category I was in."

* * *

Back at Steven's bedside, and though he was oblivious to what had just happened, Maria Di Carlo, pacing back and forth, was in a furor. Who was that man pretending to be a doctor and why had he come to Steven's room? When she finally stopped pacing, the answers came flooding to her. Her realization stopped her dead in her tracks; her face was transforming from the red hues of anger to a pale ashen look of despair. Teetering on the brink of falling, she braced herself against the chair and slowly lowered herself down to sit; her eyes were wide-open but staring blankly, her hands were both covering her mouth as if frozen in time. *It was the devil himself!* she whispered within her own thoughts. *It was pure evil. I felt it,* she continued to tell herself. "But why?" she said aloud, drawing the attention of Victoria and the duty nurse. Ignoring their brief attention to her, she continued with her internal debate. *Did it have anything to do with that terrible dream I had last night?* she wondered. It wasn't until she felt Victoria's warm touch that she was brought out of her trance. Victoria had knelt in front of her mother-in-law, taking her hands down away from her mouth and began to stroke them in a comforting gesture, her own eyes red and moist from exhaustion, her beautiful black hair completely disheveled from moments earlier when she continually ran her hands through it, trying to understand what had just happened. "Mom, Dr. Brunstrom and the hospital security are here."

Two blocks away, sitting in his black Mercedes sedan, Gabriel was cursing himself. "What the fuck happened?" he yelled at his driver. Then pounding the seat in front of him with his fist first, then with his forehead, he cursed again and again. "She must be an enlightened soul," he decided. "But why couldn't I feel her presence? Could it have been a lucky guess? Did I give myself away?" The tall, thin man continued to berate himself repeatedly, but still, he could come up with no plausible explanation of how she knew.

Back in Steven's hospital room, Dr. Brunstrom was reassuring the Di Carlo women that they were doing everything possible to find the intruder. The security guard added that they were looking at the surveillance tapes and would inform the NYPD. In the meantime, a nurse would be stationed inside the room with them, and if necessary, a security guard would be posted outside the room.

A few miles away at St. Patrick's Cathedral, Father Michael sat at his desk, trying to uncover the whereabouts of the evil entity. Through his connection to Maria Di Carlo, he felt the malevolence of the intruder as he neared the executioner, then with danger looming and alarm bells sounding deep within his soul, he enlisted her unknowing help and had managed to ward off the evil that had somehow gained the knowledge of the awakening. He now prayed to the elders for the strength to fight off the wickedness.

CHAPTER 24

9612

S AMUEL SAT SILENTLY as he waited for Steven to continue with his story. Sitting opposite his new friend, he fidgeted with his ears and then his nose, then dry washing his face, he finally went back to his nose and clamped his index finger and his thumb to the bridge of it as a small undetectable smile formed beneath his cupped hand. The knowledge that he was sharing a dream with Steven taking place in the future had him full of wonderment. It seemed so real, he thought, then crunching up his forehead in sort of a brain cramp, he wondered too, was it he who was blessed or was he damned?

"Sure, you know I've got to say my mom was right." Steven's sudden return to the story startled Samuel. "I do feel better talking about it. So where did we leave off?" Composing himself and trying not to let Steven see his smile, he leaned back and brought up his hands as though in prayer but more to cover his unrelenting smile as he answered.

"You were trying to decide if you had been blessed or if you had been damned," Samuel chuckled and then unintentionally snorted as he spoke, which caused them both to laugh.

"Right, think it's funny, do you?" Steven said and then, not waiting for a response, tried to bring the seriousness back in to the conversation, he went on.

"Well, that afternoon, I ventured back into my father's den and fired up the old computer. As it was loading, I took the old photograph out of the scanner where it had laid for a couple of week and held it up like some kind of clairvoyant expecting a vision. None came, no feeling, no carved numbers, and no walk down the memory lane of some small town.

"I thought at the time that maybe I was trying too hard, or maybe you just get one shot with each message. I turned to load the image on to the screen, and yeah, I was a bit disappointed at not feel anything. But as I was about to grab the mouse, the keyboard suddenly beeped and you had to see it to believe it, but someone or something was typing the number nine on to the screen. Now I didn't actually see the keys being pressed. The numbers just appeared one at a time, just as if someone was typing them. Then all at once, just like the bathroom did earlier, the den turned ice-cold, so cold that I had to embrace myself for some warmth." Steven paused as he gauged the reaction of his new friend. When he saw none, he jumped up as if to add enthusiasm to his story. "Sammy, it was unbelievable. Seeing all this again made me freak a bit but also made me feel good, and then just like that, it became even more magical as the entire computer screen filled with numbers and letters: 'hahaha9612hahaha96129612hahaha.' Whoever it was was laughing with me, and it felt nuts. Then just as suddenly as the writing appeared, it disappeared, and the screen was, once again, blank.

"Well, I got to tell you, it took me a few minutes to compose myself, but again, I had this feeling of some sort of enlightenment, a feeling of wonder, excitement, and anticipation. I felt in awe of everything that was happening. Somehow, it was hard to comprehend, but at the same time, it was as clear as a bell.

"I continued to scan the picture and went to grab a cup of tea while it was loading. When I returned, the picture was on the screen and the cursor was flashing right on the picture within the picture, the one of my mother as a young girl was holding to her chest. Perfect place to start, I thought, so I zoomed in on the photograph of the young boy and enlarged it as much as I could. Looking at it, I still felt and sensed this familiarity. It was uncanny. It was as if this kid had been connected to my life in some way, and I knew that finding out the connection would help me understand the so-called purpose.

"I decided that I would ask my mother about it later. Meanwhile, I dragged the cursor to the door and zoomed in on the top center panel where the address was, and sure enough, just as in my vision on the day of the funerals, next to the address, which was 9, there was 612. They were hand carved. The same numbers that, just minutes earlier, filled the computer screen were right there on the door."

Steven again paused. He had funny smirk on his face. His brows were raised, and when he noticed Samuel looking, he tried to cover his smile with his hand. Samuel, following Steven's gaze to a picture of him and his cousin Stefano, said, "What's up?"

"Nothing," responded Steven. "I just remember that when I told my cousin Stefano about this, he laughed at me. I was pretty angry at him, but actually he was laughing in relief. He's a bit like you. He also believes that there are messages being sent."

"Anyway, Sammy, looking at the numbers in the picture, I instinctively touched them, and you know what? I could feel that same sensation I had in my vision when I ran my fingers over the carved numbers on the actual door." Steven paused as he tried to organize his memories of that day in front of his computer, a picture that was inside a picture speaking loudly to him.

"Look, Steve, I think that you're getting messages from a whole lot of places and they're all connected somehow. I think we should talk this through and try and figure it out." At that point, Samuel walked over to the desk and grabbed a notebook and pen, then sat back down once again, facing Steven. "Let's do this!" he said. His eyes were bright and filled with excitement; his pen was ready and the notebook was open.

"Well, Sammy, thank God you're here. I feel that I'm finally closing in on all this and you're making it happen. I think the message has nothing really to do with the numbers but more with what you can create by putting the 9 and 6 together."

"Huh?" was the only word that came out of Samuel's mouth.

"I know it sound crazy, but hear me out. When you put the 6 and 9 together, you get circles, and as you build them, you get more circles surrounded by circles. Listen, Sammy, in one of my other dreams, I'm holding a box. On the lid of the box, there is a carved emblem of a big circle, and inside the circle were more circles inside of circles almost endlessly." As Steven was telling his story, Samuel suddenly became disoriented. The cottage had disappeared, Steven was no longer in front of him. He had been replaced by images flashing through his mind; a young boy, an ornate box, a magical door carved with an emblem of circles within circles, St. Patrick laughing, Father Michael smiling, and in a distance Steven's voice echoing circles within circles, this continued to resonate in the young priest's mind until the darkness took away the light and the flashing of images abruptly stopped.

When Samuel looked up, Steven was still talking about the box and carrying it down many passageways and stopping at a wall with the same design. When Samuel looked down at his notepad, he saw the drawing.

Samuel, bewildered at the last few seconds, could not remember drawing the emblem when he heard Steven say, "Along with all this, I keep remembering a single word, *KHokeum*." Startled, Samuel wrote down the word *Namzu Anunnaki* and showed the notebook to Steven.

"I've seen these too!"

Putting down the notebook, his hands trembled as he tried to find something to hold on to or some way of letting out his anxiety; they moved involuntarily from his chair to his chin and then, finally, through his hair as he attempted to restrain his need for answers. With both his eyes twitching, he looked at Steven and wondered what kind of power his friend really held and what kind of danger would be lurking. Would it come in the form of a dream, or would his dreams finally catch up to his reality? Samuel, compelled to continue to allow the discovery as instructed by Father Michael, would not ask the hard questions he so desperately needed answers to. He would, instead, continue to probe and bring out the full story as it was meant to be told.

Now with what could only be described as a dazed look, he watched his friend whose stare was returned equally with shock and wonderment. *You've seen these too?* Steven, who, days earlier, felt like he had the weight of the world placed squarely on his shoulders, was speechless. *I'm not alone* were his only thoughts and hesitantly decided that it was necessary to continue. The topic would be something that had been completely avoided until now, so with all the courage he could summon, he whispered, "Mom."

CHAPTER 25

AMATO (CLAUDIO)

MARIA DI CARLO accepted Dr. Brunstrom's help and advice and lay quietly on the cot that was set out for Victoria, who stayed all day and all night, hoping that Steven would wake. Closing her eyes, she could hear Steven calling to her, and suddenly she was back at the Lake George cottage, looking down the hall toward the den.

Steven sat there silently, contemplating his question. For months now, he wanted to approach his mother about the boy in the picture, and for reasons that were beyond him, he kept putting it off. Now as the story was beginning to show itself, it was time to begin stitching in all the other pieces.

"Hey, Steve, you've never told me what your mom said about the kid in the picture."

Looking at his feet, Steven, almost too quietly, responded, "I've never asked her."

"What!" Samuel almost hollered at him.

"Look, Sammy, I don't know why and I don't know what it is about this kid, but it's like I'm afraid to ask. It's almost like I know that whatever my mom tells me about him, it's gonna hurt. So I've never asked her."

Steven, sitting on his hands, rocking ever so slightly, looked at Samuel but was unable to speak. He stared back at him with a puzzled look that seemed to be screaming, "AND?" So Steven quickly added, "But you know what, I think now would be a good time to go ask her and you should come with me."

After Steven's words had sunk in, they headed off to the kitchen where they knew they would find Steven's mother.

"He was my cousin," she proclaimed even before they had a chance to ask, and with that, they all sat down to listen as Maria Di Carlo began to tell them about the young boy that was in the picture within a picture.

"He was my aunt Rosa's son. Dio bene'dice la anima." She was making the sign of the cross as she prayed for God to bless their souls. "As fate would have it, they both died on the same day that photograph was taken. He was murdered, my poor little Claudio, and she, la buon' anima di Zia Rosa, she died trying to save him."

At that point, she stopped as the memory from the past still held a lot of pain. Her hands covered her face as mild tremors shook her body as Maria Di Carlo tried desperately to shake away the sadness that had invaded her thoughts. Finally able to compose herself and with a slight rasp in her voice, she continued.

"Yes!" she said, just as if answering a question that had yet to be asked. "Claudio, my dear little cousin, was only twelve years old when they killed him. Those bastards. May they all perish in hell!" She was crying softly, remembering what it was that had happened back then. Steven, looking at his mother, was certain that some of those tears were for Tommy and Cathy.

When she settled down, Steven asked her if she was up to it, and nodding her head slowly, she continued. Samuel and Steven sat back, unaware of the amazing story they were about to hear.

"Claudio was an enterprising young boy," she began. "If there was money to be made, he knew how to make it. He mostly delivered things and ran errands for the elders. Everyone in town loved him. If they needed a liter of wine or a loaf of bread, they would call on him to go and fetch it. He was a good boy. Each day he would earn his lire and bring it home to help the family. Zia Rosa and Zio Giuseppe were so proud of their young entrepreneur that when they spoke of him, their eyes would sparkle with that pride only a parent could show.

"Claudio's favorite work was with our town doctor who not only had Claudio deliver his medicine but also took him under his wing and was teaching him mathematics, science, and even some medicine. My sweet Claudio, he would have been a great man. You know, he dreamed to, one day, be a doctor himself and follow in the footsteps of Signore Salvatore Donato. Dr. Donato had no children of his own, so he was very proud and pleased with this, so much so that he promised to help him with his schooling. Each day, Claudio would be with the doctor to learn his lesson and to help tend to his patients.

"I remember when I was sixteen, I became very sick. My stomach felt as if it would burst. With the doctor tending to the pope in Rome, Claudio took it upon himself to cure me. He went to the doctor's home and mixed up this medicine, and then he forced me to drink the awful-tasting stuff. I can still remember how terrible it smelled. Well, he tended to me for two days until the doctor returned, and you know what he said? He said that Claudio cured me of a sour stomach that was probably caused by bad milk. He said that Claudio's quick and correct diagnosis probably saved me a lot of discomfort, perhaps even death."

"Wait a minute, Mom. You're saying that this guy from your tiny village was the pope's doctor?"

"Oh yes, my dear."

With her eyes sparkling in recollection and with a bit of excitement in her voice, she seemed particularly proud as she continued, "Steven, I have to tell you that Salvatore Donato was the region's pride and joy and was one of the most revered physicians in all of Europe. My dear, he not only treated the pope. He also took care of many of Europe's aristocrats, including the government leaders of Germany and Austria. They would sometimes come to Amato to see him or they would summon him, and he would go to see them, but he would always come back home to what he called his favorite town in the whole world.

"I was very young when my papa, your nonno, talked about the war and don't remember much of it, but it was said that during the war, Dr. Donato saved our beloved Mussolini from a very serious illness, and so he became the doctor for all the generals, even some of the German commandants. His reputation grew and grew so that after the war, the pope summoned him to Rome, as the story goes."

Maria Di Carlo did not look directly at Steven and Samuel as she spoke. Instead, she stared at the tablecloth that she held between her thumbs and forefingers, moving them along as if silently counting the stitching in the fabric. "The pope," she continued, "was suffering from a very serious liver disease and was on his deathbed. Well, they said that Dr. Donato saved his life, and from then on, he became the pope's exclusive physician, and he would go to Rome each month to treat him. It was even said that on his visits to the Vatican, our Dr. Donato would spend the night right in the papal home, even played cards with the pope. Can you believe it?"

Maria Di Carlo, making the sign of the cross as she spoke of the pope, smiled as she reflected on those very special memories. Then when she continued, she touched the palms of her hands to the table and brought them up to her chest, as if to embrace them as she spoke, "When he came back to Amato, he would bring blessings from the pope. All the children would gather in the piazza to hear the stories about his adventures. The one who would sit right next to the doctor was little Claudio. It was obvious that Claudio was the doctor's favorite, but then Claudio was everybody's favorite."

And as quickly as the fond memories arrived, she became solemn again; her hands were cupping her face, slowly rubbing her eyes. Then without looking at the two men who had her undivided attention, she nodded in her own quiet understanding.

"Unfortunately, I think that it was this charm that he had and, of course, his love for Dr. Donato that ultimately caused his death. You see, *mei cari figli*, along with all the doctor's notoriety came the misfortune of the Black Hand. They were the terrorists for all of Italy, and to our embarrassment, they were from our region, the south. Their capo was this bastard they called Don Luciano Lo Sciavo of Palermo, Sicily." She imitated spitting on the floor as she spoke his name. "They say he was a murderer and that he would demand money and goods from the poor. If they refused, he would burn down their house or even send his bandits to kill them. What was worse was that he had control of our government. This was because they feared him so.

"Don Lo Sciavo used to visit the doctor regularly. At first he was very nice and was kind to us. He always brought candy and toys for all the children and beautiful fabric for the women. He even took us for rides in his car, which was a real treat since no other person in town other than Dr. Donato owned a car. Then one summer, things began to go very wrong. The doctor told us that we should hide whenever the don and his men would come to town, and he asked us not to accept any more gifts. He seemed to be very fearful of these men when, on one very hot day in July 1959, the very brave Don Lo Sciavo had his men beat the doctor in the piazza right in front of us.

"I remember it was so terrifying, especially when Claudio charged one of the men. He was very brave but also very foolish as they gave him a beating as well. When my Zio went to rescue him, they forced him down to his knees and, with a knife, sliced his face down on the left cheek. They announced that this was the symbol of the Black Hand, and the next time that Don Lo Sciavo was disobeyed, the knife would continue down to the heart. Then the bastards grabbed Dr. Donato and, with the same knife, left the same symbol. Those pigs stayed in our village for the rest of the afternoon, forcing everyone in town to kiss the don's hand and swear loyalty to him. Of course, no one refused because everyone was so afraid. Your nonno, bless his soul, decided on that day that we would leave Amato and never return. Unfortunately, we didn't leave soon enough."

Once again, Maria Di Carlo, shaken by the memories, trembled with anger as she cried. She was talking in Italian to herself and, on more than a couple of occasions, said the words *padre mio* as she thought back to her father. Steven had never known his grandparents as they had both died long ago. His grandmother died giving birth to his mother, and to the best of Steven's recollection, they had never spoken of how his grandfather died. He had always assumed that it was from natural causes.

As his thoughts went back to his grandparents, he remembered visiting their graves. And although he was very young at the time, he did remember his mother telling him all about his grandfather, except, of course, how he died. Now, so many years later, along with a never-mentioned tragedy awakened by a present-day tragedy, Steven had the feeling that he was about to find out just how it happened.

"Are you all right, Mom? It's okay if you want to rest. You can continue later if you want."

"I'm okay, *caro mio*. I was just thinking about your grandfather. Oh, how I miss him. I remember him so clearly. Not a day goes by that he is not in my thoughts."

Maria Di Carlo smiled at them. She did so, making very brief eye contact with each of them, then almost clapping her hands together, not for celebrating but more for courage, she continued, "Well, after that day in the piazza, the Black Hand continued to visit the doctor regularly, bullying him, threatening him, and just simply making his life miserable. Then one day in August . . . " Pausing, she seemed to stare questioningly past Samuel, out the window and toward the lake. "I remember it like it was yesterday. My father and the other men were talking about a very prominent patient of Dr. Donato's. They were saying that he had died very suddenly, and the doctor had taken this very hard. In fact, he was refusing to see any more of his patients, even the pope.

"Strangely, the next time that Don Lo Sciavo came to Amato, he treated the doctor with this sarcastic respect. He even paraded with him through the village arm in arm to show us all that everything was just the way he wanted it to be. He wanted us to know that he had defeated our doctor, and in doing so, he had defeated us. Then just a couple of weeks later, everything went from bad to worse."

Again, Maria Di Carlo paused, almost as if to put her thoughts straight in her mind. A tear escaped her eye and ran down the left edge of her nose. Wiping the tear away with her trembling hand, she went on, "I remember it was September 7, 1959, and all that we held so dear was about to be taken from us. We spotted them from the hills as they made their way up to our village. This allowed us about an hour to get to Dr. Donato to protect him. Your grandfather and some of the others accompanied the doctor to a place just outside of town where they would hide him until the don and his men left. You see, they knew why the doctor was being terrorized all these months, and they swore to protect him at whatever cost. We, children, only found out later the reasons for the atrocities that fell on our families and our village."

Maria Di Carlo again fell silent as she remembered the terrible things that had happened. It was strange, but as she told them the story, Steven could visualize the events. He could see her story unfold before she told it. It was as if he had his own memories of the town his parents left forty-seven years earlier, four years before Steven would be born.

The fact that these things he remembered happened nine years before he was born was a bit disturbing, but with everything else that he had experienced over the last little while, it didn't surprise him. He knew that the pressure on the doctor was to kill the pope and that he had refused. He also knew that the prominent patient that had died in his care was a Sicilian judge who was creating a lot trouble for the Black Hand.

As Steven closed his eyes, he seemed to be transported back in time. When he opened them, he was observing a conversation between two men, one he assumed to be the doctor, the other he thought might be his grandfather. The doctor was saying that if he didn't kill the Sicilian judge, they would have killed Claudio. Shaking his head in resignation, he said he had no choice. Steven could see all this. It was as if he was eavesdropping from inside another room and peering through a tiny opening in a doorway.

The conversation continued from there, and the doctor told the other man that the don threatened to kill five villagers each week, beginning with Claudio, if he didn't meet his latest demand. That demand was to kill the pope. At that moment, Steven felt a hand on his shoulder, and when he turned, he was looking into the eyes of a terrified woman. His heart stopped as he realized that this woman was the same woman who was with him at his home and then at the hospital. It was Aunt Rosa. She was yelling at him in Italian; she called him Peppino and was in a complete state of panic.

"Hurry," she said. There was a fire. The doctor's house was on fire, and then she ran into the next room, calling Dottore. and upon seeing Steven's grandfather, called him Giovanni, which confirmed to Steven who he was. As they ran by him, he was yet in another state of amazement. This was his grandfather, and he could feel him grab his arm as he ran by, then he stopped and turned to him and said, "Forza Giuseppe, andiamo."

He called Steven Giuseppe, and when he realized whose eyes he was looking through, he felt a wave of nausea hit his entire body. Steven felt as though he was about to black out when, suddenly, he was grabbed from behind. This time, when he turned to look, it was Samuel's eyes he was looking at, asking him if he was okay.

In a surreal type of euphoria, Steven's eyes darted from his mother to his friend and back, then, with a bit of eagerness, almost yelled, "I'm okay!" Then looking at his mother and controlling his anticipation, he said, "Tell me about the fire." She looked at Steven in utter disbelief. Her expression twisted her face into a mask of confusion.

"How did you know about the fire?"

With apprehension gripping her imagination and her faith calming her fears, she repeated, "How did you know?" With her eyes wide with anticipation and her heart thumping hard in her chest, she reached over and cupped Steven's face with both her hands. "My son, your face is glowing. Please, Steven, tell us what you just saw. I need to hear it. I need to know if this was one of your visions."

After Steven described the fifty-year-old scene, Maria Di Carlo did the sign of the cross, then bowed her head in a whispering prayer. Samuel, copying the elder Di Carlo, did the same. Steven simply looked on and shook his head at both of them, eager to hear more of his mother's story. After her prayer, Maria got up and walked over to her bedroom and, from her suitcase, pulled out an old photo album and brought it back to the kitchen table.

Along with the old photographs was a handful of letters; these letters, dated 1960 through 1962, were from Steven's father addressed to his mother while they were courting. The pictures were of an Italy long ago with many faces that were familiar to Steven, and some of the faces were faces that he had just seen in his latest revelation.

One of the pictures Steven knew to be that of the doctor's home after the fire. There were men standing around what remained of the small structure; their faces told a story of the defeat. Their expressions were full of hate and fear. Among the men, Steven recognized his grandfather; he was dressed as he was in his vision. With him, his mother confirmed, was Dr. Donato; he looked distraught and, in the picture, appeared to be reaching out for another man whose back was turned.

Steven could remember the embrace; he could feel him tremble, and the tears, oh, those tears. He could still feel the wetness against his cheek and hear his sobs.

There was no vision this time. He just knew; he knew who he was and he knew what had happened and how it had happened. There remained no doubt, no confusion, just clarity. Steven Di Carlo was Giuseppe D'Amato; he was married to Rosa, and he was Claudio's father. He also knew that just after the picture was taken, Claudio was brutally murdered by Don Lo Sciavo.

Steven, reliving that day, remembered that after the fire was put out, they took the women and children to a secret cave just outside of town. Dr. Donato remained behind to look for Claudio; he had not been seen all afternoon. As it turned out, Lo Sciavo's men were holding him. Apparently, he had witnessed the fire being started and tried to stop them, but instead, he was held and beaten by Lo Sciavo and his men.

As Steven was thinking back to those days, he was overwhelmed by all the memories. Faces upon faces flashed through his mind, among them were of Victoria, Tommy, Cathy, Claudio, Rosa, and numerous other faces that he recognized but did not know.

In the middle of all the flashbacks, there was a book, a manuscript. Steven could see the pages that were full of notations. The book appeared to be large and ancient, the kind that you would see in a museum. Bound in leather, it seemed to him to be of great importance. He did not know how or why, but he was sure it existed, and he knew that, one day, he would have to find it and eventually he would know where to look.

Steven's mother interrupted his flashbacks when she began telling them all about the picture.

"Steven, are you listening? You asked about the fire. Well, this picture was taken that afternoon. The Black Hand, those bastards, burned down the doctor's home while everyone in town was having lunch, everyone, except for poor Claudio. We heard the bell as we were finishing our pranzo. I remember Zia Rosa running to call everyone. She was out looking for Claudio and instead found the fire. All the men in the village did their best to save the doctor's home, but the fire was too powerful.

"After the fire had been put out, Papa took charge and suggested that all the women and children go to the cave where we would be safe. The cave. The town used it as a shelter during the war, and Papa was certain that Don Lo Sciavo did not know of our secret place. It was at the top of Amato, behind the graveyard. It overlooked the Ionian Sea but was impossible for anyone to spot.

"Inside the cave, we had stored supplies, including weapons. Under my father's and Zio Peppino's direction, we were preparing for battle. Unfortunately, there was to be no battle that day, only sadness. That day was the day the heart was torn out of our little village and none of us would ever be the same again. When the men returned to the village, prepared to put an end to the Black Hand once and for all, they found Dr. Donato on the street, weeping uncontrollably as he held the lifeless body of my little cousin Claudio. Upon seeing this, Zio Peppino went crazy with rage. He looked everywhere for those animals, but they were gone. They had run off like the cowards that they truly were."

Steven could hear his mother's words trail off as, once again, he was thrust back in time and into a past identity. As sure as he was Steven Di Carlo, he was also sure that he was once Giuseppe D'Amato. He could hear someone sobbing, and it wasn't until he wiped his eyes that he realized that is was him who was making those lonely sounds. He was looking down into what was left of his little Claudio's face. He was still warm but was cooling fast as the blood left his body like water from an open tap. He buried his head into his lap and cried; his body, full of tremors, was uncontrollable as the rage filled his very being.

The anger was familiar to Steven, unsure of why, just familiar. When he looked up, Dr. Donato was on his knees, praying and sobbing, calling Claudio's name; he repeated this over and over. When he gained some control, Steven felt Giovanni's arm around his shoulder, and as he tried to control his own emotions, he was telling Steven that vengeance would be theirs and that nothing would stop them.

Bringing the doctor into their embrace as they held on to what remained of Claudio, the doctor began to tell them of the events that happened while they were in the cave. His voice, cracking with pain and trembling as if he were in icy water, made his teeth chatter as he spoke. The words he spoke would only come out in kind of waves, sometimes a couple at a time and then others would come out as groans. At times, his words were loud and then barely audible. His face, smeared with Claudio's blood, was creased with immense pain. His eyes appeared as slits, barely open, as the weight of what had happened forced them almost shut. The only visible sign was the red beneath the lids and the tears flowing out like a dripping faucet. Steven felt his pain and wanted to reach out to him, but then, he would be overcome with his own grief and would barely remember that he was even there speaking to him.

"There were four of them," he said. "Those bastards. They drove up to me in the piazza and dragged little Claudio out of the car." The doctor's pain was stenciled on his face; a noticeable throb distorted his left temple while his hands were clenched into balls of hatred. His throat sounded raw as he spoke, and his body convulsed as fierce spasms forced him to pause after every couple of words. "It took two of the bastards to hold him, one on each side. They held him by his arms. When I demanded that they let him go, Lo Sciavo just walked up to me. He had an evil look on his face, and then laughing, he slapped me across the face and even spit on me. He told me that we were insolent and that the whole village was to blame for what was about to happen." Dr. Donato, burying his face in his hands, paused as the grievous pain took hold of his body.

Steven felt helpless as his two identities confused him, leaving him unable to console the poor man. Finally, as he was about to reach out to him, the doctor continued angrily.

"Did we really believe that we could deny the Black Hand?" he asked me. "The pig! He called us stupid and ignorant and said we should stick to tending our sheep instead of plotting against him. Then he asked me why the pope was still alive, did I not understand the consequences, and did I not believe him when he said that villagers would die if he were disobeyed. This was my fault. It is because of me that Claudio is dead." Again, the doctor broke down, seeming unable to continue. And with grief gripping the three men, there was no one left to console him. Still, the doctor reached deep within himself to continue.

"The pig, he said to me, 'Dottore Donato, I leave you to tell these peasants what happened here today in your beloved little town. Never again forget the power I have and never again question my orders.' It was then that the animal walked up to Claudio, lifted a gun to his face, and just pulled the trigger." The doctor appeared as if the recounting of the events would certainly kill him as he held his chest tightly, gasping for air. When, once again, he seemed to get control of his emotions, he went on, "After shooting him, the pig turned around and spoke to me like he was regretful, 'Let them know that this dear young boy has just paid for their sins.' Then as they were about to leave, he told me to kill the pope or the next time he wouldn't be so lenient."

They all fell silent in their sorrow; the crying that they were all doing was barely audible. Steven felt an incredible numbness and a feeling of detachment as he seemed to separate from his surroundings. He felt a hand stroking his hair, and when he looked up, there was a woman; she was smiling at him and telling him that everything would be all right. She spoke in a language different from his, but he understood her nonetheless. Her complexion was that of porcelain; her hair was very long and as red as fire. She gave him this feeling of calmness, almost a feeling of awe. He was thinking that this woman must be an angel and that she had come to take his Claudio to some better place. Now as he looked at her, he was afraid to admit it to himself, but he was awestruck by her beauty. Somehow, he knew her and his knowledge of her was more of an intimate recognition than angelic, but from where?

CHAPTER 26

ROSA

DESPITE THE IDENTITY crisis overwhelming him and the fact that he was comatose in a hospital bed, Steven knew who he was. He was also fully aware that, somehow and as incredible as it sounds, he was reliving a past life as Giuseppe D'Amato and he was doing so in a dream that seemed to never end. In his confused state, he knew that he belonged in the future, and in that future, he remembered living this same horror, feeling this same incredible anger, and suffering the same unbearable loss. Why was this all happening to him? Why was he reliving events that happened more than fifty years ago? Why, in his past life, was he, his mother's uncle, married to his aunt Rosa? And why have his children been murdered in the past as well as in the future? As many questions as he had, he knew the answers to each of them, and as bewildering as it all seemed, his mind began to clear.

It was Rachel who stood with him now, giving him strength and reassurance, just as Rosa did when Vic, Tommy, and Cathy were taken. Rachel was his wife. They were married long ago, and to Steven's astonishment, he remembers it as clearly as he remembered the day that he married Victoria and the festival that surrounded his marriage to Rosa.

It was May 31, 1775, at St. Francis Cathedral in Inverness, Scotland. He had just turned twenty, and Rachel was barely seventeen. They had two children; both were taken and murdered by their enemies back in 1789.

Charles Francis Mackenzie was barely twelve and Elaine Rachel Mackenzie was a mere ten when they disappeared. As much as they tried, they were unable to find them, but they did find those responsible, and the clan Mackenzie killed every last one of them. Still, the pain of losing their children was too much to bear, and Rachel died of a shattered heart two years later.

With further reason for vengeance, Francis Mackenzie and his men went on seeking and killing those that would dare try to destroy the order of the way things were intended to be. Their wrath was felt as far away as the shores of Africa and as near as the docks of Inverness.

Even as all the memories of past lives flooded Steven's very being, he held on to the lifeless body of Claudio, and as he looked into his empty eyes, he again began to weep. Giovanni and Dr. Donato remained at his side, sharing in his despair. Their weeping turned into whimpers as they searched around for some sort of comfort or explanation and then back to uncontrollable outbursts when they found none.

Steven chose not to acknowledge Rachel, knowing that doing so would confirm the reality. But then as the word spread throughout the village and as the entire townsfolk began to return from the cave, he could hear the immense pain that only a mother could suffer, and the reality of this horrific day seized his heart and took hold of his pitiful existence.

All he could think of was his dear sweet Rosa, her only child murdered, her pride and joy so brutally taken away. How will she ever survive? How will either of them survive? Rachel, looking down at him and reading his thoughts said, "With vengeance, my darling. With hate and with vengeance." Even as he silently understood why this had to happen and what was expected of him, the pain of losing one's child was too horrible of a way to achieve what was necessary. Angry at his predicament, Steven was ready to succumb. He was living two lives simultaneously and knew exactly what was about to happen in 1959 while not knowing at all what he was up against in

2012. When would he come out of this torturous journey to the past, when would his mother or, for that matter, Samuel notice his trance and wake him? He so desperately wanted to leave this time that should have remained in the past. He needed to rid himself of this pain that Giuseppe was enduring and return to his life as Steven Di Carlo.

He knew that as Steven, he would still have an incredibly dangerous journey and that it wouldn't be much different than the one that he had while he was Francis Mackenzie or for that which he dreaded he was about to relive as Giuseppe D'Amato. Still, there was no relief. He remained in the piazza with his dead son in his arms and his dear friends at his side. His wife from a time long ago offered support, support that only he could see or hear, and Rosa, so distraught and only minutes away from seeing what her brain would not allow her to believe. How could he face her? How would he tell her that while he was protecting everyone else, he allowed her only son to be slaughtered?

With Steven fading from his memory, Giuseppe wondered how he would live out this nightmare. Would he ever be able to hold his head high again, and would he ever be able to face his family or friends? What worried him most of all, though, was how would he ever be able to live without his Claudio.

Giuseppe knew that these thoughts were simply self-pity and that, in fact, when this business was all over and done with, he would be called a hero. But he asked himself, what kind of hero required that his children be murdered, to be motivated enough to commit murder himself?

To Giuseppe, it seemed like an eternity before Rosa would arrive. He could hear her wails and her distress as she approached, and then in utter horror, he watched as she tripped over an embankment and tumbled down the steep slope to the rocks below. From one hundred meters away, he could hear the thud of her head hitting a large rock, and as he watched in disbelief, he could see the rock that she hit change color from white to crimson, and even though Dr. Donato was rushing to her aid, he knew that his dear Rosa, in her haste to try and save her only son, would instead join him.

Embracing Claudio's limp body in his arms, he ran toward the embankment with Giovanni matching him step for step. When they arrived, Giuseppe reluctantly gave Claudio to Giovanni and rushed to Rosa's side. She was still alive, but the somber look on the doctor's face told all. He knelt beside her and cradled her in his arms, unable to speak a single intelligible word. So he held her tight to his chest and rocked her back and forth in an attempt to comfort her.

In his anguish, he stared at Rosa as she struggled to breathe and then at Claudio, whose lifeless body could not be willed to breathe. In that moment, with despair smothering his very being, Giuseppe D'Amato embraced the hope of at least saving his Rosa. So he picked her up in his arms, then carefully carried her home to her bed. Giovanni, not knowing what to say, followed him closely with Claudio held tightly to his chest. Dr. Donato, unable to move, sunk to his knees in a painful kind of misery, then, with the help of some of the villagers, found some strength and made his way to Rosa's side to try and comfort her in her final hour.

That evening, Amato was in mourning. The villagers, all of them, were outside the D'Amato home as they prayed for Rosa's recovery. The crying and praying was constant. Giuseppe was certain that the sounds of despair carried from village to village because, by morning, well-wishers were arriving from as far away as Catanzaro.

Kneeling beside her, he gently embraced her, then resting his head on her chest, he quietly cried and challenged God to show himself and save his beloved. He felt her hand first as she stroked his head, then heard her voice as she tried to comfort him. "Caro Peppino, you must be strong and not lose your faith. Pray for us, my dear husband. God believes you are special, so he does listen to you. Dear husband, bring me my Claudio so that we can travel together to heaven. Surely they would not turn away the mother of such an angel."

Rosa, resigned to the fact that she would die that day, continued to comfort Giuseppe. She spoke words of faith and devotion to God and about the purpose they all needed to serve. Unnoticed, a strange priest entered their home, the priest who, they were later told, came all the way from Nicastro, knelt next to Rosa.

"My dear wonderful lady, you have been a true instrument of our path, and you have served all of us valiantly. Heaven awaits you and your courageous son as you both have fulfilled your purpose here on earth. The two of you will now guide us to fulfill ours."

Throughout this, Rosa was strong as she held on despite the inevitability. Thanking the priest for his blessing, she turned her attention to Giuseppe.

"My dear husband, you must let your anger guide you through your journey against evil. Promise me that you will avenge Claudio's death with all the fury that God will give you." Then she spoke of Rachel and told him that she too could see her.

Rosa, looking into his eyes, reached up with both her hands and cradled his face. She spoke soothingly as she massaged his eyelids with her thumbs, and then with conviction, she drew him close and whispered, "Dear husband, you must recover the manuscript. Rachel will guide you, my love. We will both guide you."

When he asked of the manuscript, Rosa told him that once he had read it, he would understand. Those were her last living words to him, but she would keep her promise and guide him through his revenge.

As was Rosa's wish, and with everyone's help and support, she was buried with Claudio. Father Michael asked permission to participate in the service and conducted a moving mass. He spoke of destiny and of sacrifice; he told the villagers that they were all about to play a very important role in the salvation and survival of our species. He said that there were evil forces that would destroy the hopes and dreams of man if we allowed them and that these evil forces must be stopped. He told them that his purpose in all this was to bless their mission, just as he has done time and again throughout the ages.

"Yes," he said as he slammed his fist down on pulpit, startling the mourners. "We have battled for our survival since the beginning of time, and we will again prevail because it is our purpose to do so, which makes it our destiny." He went on to say that the men who did this and the others like them also have a purpose and that their purpose is to destroy all that mankind held dear and then claim this existence as their own.

Causing a flurry of whispering, Father Michael walked up to Giuseppe, and then bending down on one knee, he pledged his faith and his loyalty to the one he called the executioner, then looking directly at Giuseppe, he bowed his head and prayed and then blessed the mission ahead.

Later that day, the men of the village came to the executioner and, one by one, pledged their loyalty. Giovanni, as their spokesman, told Giuseppe of their plan to lay an ambush for Lo Sciavo and his men. His words drew an eerie silence over the room, and although he could see Giovanni's lips move, Giuseppe could no longer hear him speak. Instead, it was Rachel's voice that he heard, and looking across the room, he could see her. She smiled at him; neither Rosa nor Claudio were with her. She told him that, indeed, vengeance would be realized, but first he needed the manuscript and that he should leave immediately and travel to Inverness to retrieve it.

CHAPTER 27

THE MANUSCRIPT

VICTORIA DI CARLO, stretching her tired body, decided to venture to the hospital cafeteria and grab a cup of bitter coffee. Her mother-in-law had quickly fallen asleep in the spare cot, and Victoria needed a break from her bleak despair. When she returned to the room, the duty nurse was watching both mother and son. "This is amazingly weird," the nurse said in a hushed voice to Victoria without turning around to see that it was indeed her.

"I just called Dr. Brunstrom. He's going to want to see this," she whispered. Victoria hesitantly approached the tall, stout nurse, then followed her eyes as they moved between the elder and younger Di Carlo.

"Somehow, they're communicating with each other," she quietly exclaimed, afraid of disrupting an unbelievable occurrence.

"Watch, look!" she said excitedly as though Victoria didn't believe her, her eyes round with astonishment, her mouth agape with disbelief. "Look," she repeated. "See, first your mother's lips move, and watch when she stops, then your husband's move. They are talking to each other, and they've been doing this for at least the last ten minutes. That's when I first noticed them." She brought her hands together as though in prayer and then raised them, lightly touching her smiling lips as though she was witnessing a miracle. "It's fascinating!" she said through her cupped hands.

"My God, they are!" Victoria said in utter disbelief. "This is crazy. Have you heard any words?"

"They were talking about a fire. Couldn't quite make it out except that someone's house was destroyed by fire."

* * *

Back inside Steve's comatose nightmare where both Samuel, who was asleep miles away in his bed at St. Patrick's Cathedral, and Maria Di Carlo, who was asleep just a few feet away from him, were willing participants as Steven's awakening had taken him down the road of dark memories and then back to disbelief.

"Steven dear, are you listening to me? Steven . . . Steven . . . ?"

Giuseppe could hear the familiar voice as it echoed through his mind. Intent on trying to recognize whose pleas they were, he focused on listening to the woman who was calling to him, but dozens of faces flashed through his mind, confusing him further. He strained his psyche, reaching out for Rachel as she slowly disappeared. He grasped at empty air, trying to find Rosa. Panicking, he turned to beg Giovanni and Father Michael for some kind of understanding only to find that they were not there. Confused and broken, he rolled himself up into a ball and surrendered.

When he awoke, it felt as if his head were about to split open, and his eyes, large and round, darted around the room in a total state of confusion. Where was he, and who were these strange people? Feeling detached from everything around him, it took him awhile to figure it all out. In absolute bewilderment, he could see and hear them but was unable to comprehend what they were saying. Then as familiarity of the surroundings began to comfort his apprehension, he thought he recognized the two faces looking down at him, but at the same time, he was wondering who they were.

He heard himself babbling in Italian when it struck him that he barely spoke the language. With this revelation, his mind began to clear, and as it did, he once again became Steven and was finally able to recognize the concerned faces staring down at him.

Steven quickly acknowledged his mother and then Samuel. They looked longingly at him for an explanation. Instead, he excused himself and hurried upstairs to his bedroom; he needed to clear his head, but mostly, he needed to regain his identity as Steven Di Carlo.

Samuel, with a sharp poke in the ribs from Mrs. Di Carlo, followed Steven up the stairs and uncomfortably poked his head inside Steven's bedroom. "You okay? You know, we could go for a walk if you like. It'll clear your head."

"Yes, Steven." The sound of Maria Di Carlo startled Samuel as he didn't hear her follow him up, and she was inches away from him, peering at Steven as she continued, "You should listen to Father Stewart. The fresh air will do you good."

Maria Di Carlo was visibly concerned, yet there was a twinkle in her eye that begged to know what it was that Steven had experienced. When he sharply refused and asked to be left alone, she set a cup of chamomile tea down on his nightstand and then locked elbows with Samuel as they both turned to leave. "Wait a minute," Steven called out, his face sporting tinges of red from the guilt of his rudeness.

"Mom, Sammy, I'm fine and I'm sorry. I'll tell you all about it later, I promise. I just need a few minutes to figure some things out." Then looking at his watch and scratching his head in bewilderment, he called to them again, "Hey, Mom, tell me, how long was I out?"

Her reply startled him. "Just a few minutes, my dear. We let you be when we noticed that you were asleep, and when we came back from making the tea, you were waking, probably no more than twenty minutes."

Disbelief battled Steven's acceptance of his mother's words. *How could it be?* he thought as he watched his bedroom door close, leaving him on his own. "Days had passed. It's nuts," he said aloud and to himself. As acceptance slowly crept its way through his disbelief, he became amazed at what he had experienced in just a few minutes. With his head spinning, he sat on the edge of his bed, his eyes open but staring into the darkness of his hands that were covering his face. Images of Claudio's lifeless body replaced the darkness in his hands, and then images of Rosa tumbling down the hillside overwhelmed him, but it was the thud of her head hitting the rock that completed the horror that he had just lived through. The uncontrollable convulsions are what he felt first. The lack of air had him struggling to breathe and the dismissal of self-control had him weeping for his families, the ones from the past and the ones that he just lost.

Sometime later, Steven summoned the courage to journalize this latest episode, so he went to his computer to enter all that he could remember into his diary. One day soon, he would need to transfer all of it to the manuscript once it had been recovered.

Sitting at his desk, Steven found himself weak and emotional at the memories of his past, angry and lonely at the reality of the present, and concerned about the prospects for the future. As drained as he was, he continued to type everything down, being careful not to miss a single thought.

The manuscript was the key; he needed to retrieve it from the cave in Amato just as Giuseppe had done in 1959 in Inverness. Steven didn't know how, but he remembered his journey as if it were yesterday. He could remember Giuseppe reading the manuscript. Steven found it difficult to speak of Giuseppe as himself, and in his mind, he chose to think of him and, for that matter, Francis Mackenzie as other people with whom he simply shared memories.

Francis Mackenzie, at the end of his journey, hid the manuscript in a crypt in the bowels of St. Francis Cathedral. The tomb inside the crypt was an empty memorial dedicated to his children, Charles and Elaine, which lay in state alongside all the bishops and priests that were buried there.

Giuseppe, with the help of Father Michael and the guidance of Rachel, knew exactly where to look. Retrieving it was a little more difficult. They had to enlist the help of the rectory matron who, for a few shillings, turned a blind eye one Sunday morning while, during Sunday mass, they entered the crypt and removed the heavy granite lid to recover the ancient book.

The book was bound in a crude-cured hide and was filled with pages that were made of a thick parchment. The cover of the manuscript had a crest of a mighty hawk with its wings spread, and in its talons, the hawk held the sun. The sun was emblazoned with many suns within it and many others within them. *Circles within circles, within circles*, he thought.

The pages were written in Latin, and although Giuseppe was never taught Latin, he was somehow able to read them. The first page was dated AD 999 and told the story of a Greek merchant who, like Francis, Giuseppe, and now Steven, suffered the same pain of losing his family.

Thadeus Kadoplois also had similar experiences with the so-called supernatural and their messages from beyond. To explain this, he told of his calling and the overwhelming challenge of victory, and then he told of the consequences of failure and the importance of the *Namzu Anunnaki*, which will either save mankind or, if mankind was undeserving, will destroy it.

How Steven knew all this puzzled him. He knew that he had experienced all that had happened in the small village, and he also knew that those experiences ended with Giuseppe never having left Amato. He recalled little else of the manuscript except for its current hiding place, which was in the cave below the cemetery, in Amato.

What Steven did recall was the vengeance that the men of Amato had taken against Lo Sciavo and his gang of thugs. Entering those memories into his diary had him feeling spent; his left eye began to twitch as a throbbing pain quickly shot through and continued through his forehead. His skin, wet with perspiration, felt cold as droplets of sweat found their way from his temple down the side of his face to his neck, forcing involuntary shivers. His entire body tingled with unknown anticipation, forcing the hair on the back of his neck to rise, while his breathing slowed to a dangerous level. Panicked and confused, he tried to call for help, but his plea was inaudible. Forcing himself up from his chair, he fell to his knees on the floor. Rolling over and lying on his back, he struggled to understand what was happening to him. His eyes were squeezed shut, his teeth clenched like a vice as the unbearable continued with no relief. With both his hand, he pressed his temples, trying to gain some control. Instead, his vision began to blur and white spots dance around in his eyes. Trying desperately to breathe he gasped for some air, but still there was no reprieve from the wickedness that had clamped on to his psyche and cut off his ability to breathe, think, or see. Then with no other choice, he gave up and succumbed to the blanket of darkness that overtook his consciousness. When, once again, air traveled through his lungs, it was crisp and cool. Relieved, he breathed in deep, then feeling content, he opened his eyes. The shock hit him immediately as he cried out in disbelief. He was back in 1959 once again in the shadows of a murdered son and dead wife.

CHAPTER 28

A DAY OF RECKONING

D R. THOMAS BRUNSTROM had entered Steven's room just
as Victoria was expressing disbelief in what she was witnessing. The doctor stood there silently, his much-too-big hospital jacket
hanging loosely over his shoulders, glass resting low on his nose, and
his right hand cupping his chin and mouth, as he tried to make sense
of what he was looking at when, suddenly, Maria Di Carlo awoke
with a start, almost jumping out of the small cot.

When her vision cleared and she had adjusted her mind to
where she was, she wondered why everyone was staring at her when,
in the echoing vestiges of her dream, she heard her son's voice calling
out to her. "I'm here, Steven," she said aloud. Still, the audience of
three just stared at her, not hearing what she had heard when Victoria
asked, "Mom, can you tell us about your dream?" Maria Di Carlo
just looked at them, walked over to her son, and kissed him on the
forehead, then walked over to Victoria and kissed her on the cheek
and, with a nod and smile to Dr. Brunstrom and the duty nurse,
quietly left the hospital room.

* * *

Steven, completely oblivious to goings-on at his bedside was,
once again, experiencing a dream inside a dream, or perhaps a night-

mare inside his dream, a dream that had thrust him on an unwanted journey back to 1959, back into the life of Giuseppe D'Amato. When the crushing pain in his head finally subsided and he was able to unclench his eyes, he found himself all alone in the small house in Amato. The small empty house that was once crowded and full of life, the house with the number nine on the wooden door, the forsaken house with only the remnants of a wonderful life, a son that was the center of that life and a wife who so incredible that he was the envy of all the other men.

He found himself sitting on the floor of his tiny house, the memories of a life so long ago ripping away his identity as Steven Di Carlo. The confusion between past and present was pushing him back to relive a vengeance he sought all those years ago.

With clarity replacing bewilderment, his identity as Steven Di Carlo was forced to the outer edges of his consciousness, allowing the tortured life of Giuseppe D'Amato to emerge strong, determined, and full of rage. His desire for vengeance was so intense that his normally soft face contorted into a malevolent mask full of hate. A frightening sneer pursed his lip tightly to the left side of his face while his eyes were mere slits, staring beyond the walls of the small house and deeply into the lust for blood, blood he could taste and a hunger for it that ached so deep in the pit of his stomach that bile threatened to exit his tightly clenched mouth.

The day of reckoning was close at hand. He knew this as the reminiscences of a past life mingled with a reality that wasn't. Distant thoughts emanating from the memories of an identity that was pushed aside, so distant that the origins of those memories were being filtered from Steven's hospital room in the present to his nightmares of the future and then all the way back to a past life as Giuseppe DAmato. A premonition is what Giuseppe thought, a message of warning, perhaps from his dear beloved Rosa or his very brave son, Claudio. "Yes, it is a message," he whispered to himself. "Today, I will have my retribution!" he shouted at the ceiling of his small empty house.

In October 1959, the protectors of Amato, led by Giuseppe, had planned and set a trap for Don Luciano Lo Sciavo, and the architect of the ambush was none other than Steven's grandfather, Giovanni Calla. And just as Giovanni had suggested, a message had been sent to Lo Sciavo that Dr. Donato was a broken man and was afraid of any further violence against the villagers. With this message, Lo Sciavo would most certainly think that the good doctor was ready to do his bidding and kill the pope. What he didn't know was that a painful destiny awaited him and his men on their return to Amato.

The day of judgment for the Black Hand came as Giuseppe envisioned in his premonition. It was a very chilly autumn afternoon, three weeks after the murder of Claudio and the resulting accident that caused the death of Rosa. It wasn't until Giuseppe heard the bells that he raised himself off the floor of his empty house, his sneer now a smirk as his face unclenched and his jaw muscles began to relax. It was just after twelve in the afternoon when the lookout sounded the alarm. The people of Amato were just about to settle in for their lunch, but instead, the women, the children, and the elderly were immediately taken to the cave to be out of harm's way. Some of the teenage boys were shown how to use the rifles and were given the responsibilities of protecting those in the cave in case Giuseppe and his men failed.

The protectors of the small village began to set up the ambush, and as they checked and rechecked their weapons and positions, anxiety crept into all of them. The wait was excruciating as it seemed as though it would take forever for the two large Mercedes to reach the village. The anticipation, mixed with fear, ran through the very being of each of the men as they waited to kill or be killed. Of all those who volunteered to follow Giuseppe, only twenty-three were chosen, each of them blessed by Father Michael and trained by Giovanni, who, as a former *sergente maggiore*, fought in the deserts of Libya for the Italian Army. Having had the highest rank in the village made him a natural choice to train the men and lay out the deadly plan. He worked them very hard for two weeks, and like any good general, Giovanni worried for his men even though he had set a plan that would, for the most part, keep them out of harm's way.

There was only one road winding up the steep terrain that led to Amato. The road, which was barley wide enough for one vehicle, was completely visible from the lookout spot and all the way down the five kilometers to the bottom. When the enemy let two of their men out to follow on foot and protect them from an ambush, it was immediately signaled to the five men stationed at the various spots along the road.

When the two cars were far enough up the hill, Giuseppe's men swiftly disarmed and captured the two before they could do any harm or expose the ambush. Francesco Grande, who was a commando stationed with Giovanni in Libya, oversaw the group assigned to protect the rear. Very quietly, Francesco snuck up on the larger of the two men and very swiftly placed his left hand over the assassin's mouth while his right hand held a large butcher's knife to his throat. The second man was neutralized with a quick blow to the head using the butt end of a rifle. Armando Castellano, who had no combat experience, delivered the blow as precise and as effectively as a seasoned commando would, and although the man yelled in agony, a second blow to his windpipe assured his silence.

Both men were securely bound to large cactus plants with thorns as sharp as razors. Every little struggle would result in painfully deep wounds. They were bound in such a way that they faced the cactus; they were forced to strip completely and then pulled in by their arms to embrace the cactus. With their forehead and necks tied securely against the unforgiving plant, their arms were then wrapped completely around and tied so that each arm was pulled toward the opposite side and secured from wrist to wrist. Their legs also wrapped the cactus and secured so tightly that their crotch was forced into the razor-like needles. Their mouths were filled with cactus pears too large to swallow and too hard to crush and then bound with what remained of their shirts. These two would be dealt with later. The information that they would be forced to provide would end up crushing the Black Hand and ending their reign of terror throughout Europe.

Back in the little town that would become a killing field, Giuseppe and Giovanni waited in the open piazza with Dr. Donato. Hidden from the enemy were four men on the rooftops of the buildings that surrounded the only street that entered the quaint little village. Four more men lay in covered trenches alongside the roadside.

The entrance to Amato was lined with olive trees and fig trees; two ancient buildings stood guard at where the dirt road changed to cobblestones. In these buildings, waiting anxiously were two more men armed with shotguns and crossbows. The final five men were positioned strategically around the town; two were seated at the coffee shop while another was behind the counter. The final two villagers that became warriors appeared to be fixing a building at the far end of the square.

Wherever the cars stopped, if not at the square where Dr. Donato made himself very visible, there would be someone close by with a weapon loaded and ready. Special holders were constructed under the stone benches where Giuseppe, Giovanni, and the doctor sat, each sporting a rifle. All three men also had handguns concealed in their belts and covered by their jackets. The men at the coffee shop, brothers Vincenzo and Pietro Guzzi, each had German-made Lugers that held eight shots while the man at the counter, Silvio Avelo, had an American-made automatic rifle that held twelve shots. The two would-be repairmen, Vittorio Galucci and Damiano Belmonte, each had shotguns in holsters that were strapped to their waist; the barrels were sawed off for easier concealment.

The protectors of Amato were expecting Lo Sciavo to show up with ten men. Instead, he came with nine. The instructions were to wait until all of them were out of the cars and into the sights of the men on the rooftops. The plan was to give Lo Sciavo and his bandits that secure feeling of being conquerors. The doctor would even bow to him, kiss his hand, and beg for peace and forgiveness. Giuseppe, when the time was right, would give the command to open fire; he would do this by simply dropping to one knee. The instructions were to shoot to kill, except for Lo Sciavo; a crueler fate than a bullet would await the eternal enemy.

The four men hidden in the trenches would quietly follow behind the cars as they passed; two of them had explosives that they would attach to the bottom of the second Mercedes. Six sticks of homemade dynamite bound with oiled rags and set with a short fuse would ensure that the cars would never leave Amato. The dynamite would be attached to the car with a wire hook that wrapped the deadly sticks; this was the most difficult part of Giovanni's plan. The men had to be swift and agile while, at the same time, being completely unheard and unseen. The ones selected for the task were two cousins Gino Totti and Luca Anselmo, who were considered to be the town's best athletes.

During the past two weeks, they were given the assignment of hooking wine skins to the seats of bicycles and to the backs of vendor carts without being noticed or heard. This they did with surprising ease and, in the end, proved to be the right choice as the explosives were, in fact, attached to the second car, completely unnoticed as it passed through the gates of Amato.

In the town hall at the entrance to the village, Marco and Dante Quarto waited patiently with their crossbows, the tips of their arrows wrapped with oil- soaked rags waiting to be lit. The two brothers had the responsibility of sending their arrows under the car and, with a bit of luck, lighting the dynamite. Of course, this would only be done if the Black Hand attempted to escape.

As the cars approached the piazza, Giuseppe turned to his dear friends, thanked them for their loyalty, and, with a sly smile, gave them a symbolic toast, "Amici grazie, forza a tutti."

"Per Claudio e per Rosa," responded Giovanni, whose eyes let a single tear escape, running down the length of his cheek as he thought of his sister and nephew brutally killed by these bastards. The doctor echoed the toast, and concealing a sinister smile, he said, "Vengeance will be ours."

The two large cars drove up and stopped right in front of the statue of the Madonna that guarded the piazza. The doctor's relief was visible as this was where they had hoped they would stop. Of course, this meant that Lo Sciavo and his men were a direct and easy target from all the strategic vantage points. Giovanni's plan had, so far, fallen into place.

The first to exit the second car was a hulk of a man, not so much tall as he was wide; he had no neck, and his cheeks were so enormous that they hung like jowls, forcing his bottom lip to fold in the middle. He held a shotgun in the crook of his left arm, and with his right hand, he signaled to the doctor not to move.

Without taking his eyes off the trio, he positioned himself to the left with his back to the coffee shop. As he did this, thug number two got out and stood directly behind him. He too carried a shotgun; his was in the ready position with his left hand on the bottom of the stock while his right hand was firm on the trigger.

The third man to exit was the one who captured and beat Claudio, then held him up for Lo Sciavo when the bastard pulled the trigger, the sight of him caused the doctor to tense up, tremors visibly shot through him as his anger welled. Seeing this, Giovanni put a hand on the doctor's shoulder as if to say, "All in good time, my friend, all in good time." Lo Sciavo's accomplice in the murder of Claudio had an enormous forehead that slanted upward; his shoulders were broad, and his waist was thin. He took up the right flank and had his back to the town hall; he sported an evil grin under his pencil mustache to show the arrogance of being recognized. His confidence was so great that he carried no visible weapons. He was tall and lean, perhaps in his thirties, with a scar down his left cheek.

As Giuseppe noticed the scar, he also noticed the resemblance to the scars that both he and the doctor had, compliments of Don Lo Sciavo. With his left thumb, Giuseppe traced his scar from top to bottom. As he did this, he looked deep into the eyes of number three, and without saying a word, he sensed the confidence turning into concern and there was fear in the assassin's eyes.

The last two to leave the second Mercedes were older than the previous three; both were heavyset and dressed in expensive dark suits. They openly displayed their pistols that were tucked into the front of their pants; they did this by unbuttoning the fronts of their jackets and placing their right hands on the grips. They took position at the tail end of the lead car, just behind the rear doors.

Lo Sciavo sat alone in the back seat of the big Mercedes while in the front seat, his two remaining men were both leaning over the seat in deep conversation with him, obviously receiving some last-minute instruction before the don left the vehicle to approach the doctor.

Meanwhile, the brave men of Amato began to position their trap; Giovanni's plan was simple and direct. The men were to quietly surround the vehicles from predesignated vantage points. The vehicles would be considered the center of the targets as it was correctly assumed that the intruders would not stray too far from the security of their cars should they need to counter any ambush.

Beginning with the right rear of the farthest vehicle to the doctor, each of Lo Sciavo's men would be given a number going from right to left. The closet man was number one, the next was number two, and then number three, and so on. Each of Giuseppe's men would, in turn, also have a number, and that man would be his target. Now since the men of Amato outnumbered the intruders sixteen to seven, the man who had number eight as a target would double up on number one, number nine would share target number two, and so on.

If everything worked as it should, each target would have two shooters, leaving numbers fifteen and sixteen, Vittorrio and Damiano, as the cleanup men; they would guard against any of the bastards trying to take refuge in one of the buildings.

When the time came, Giuseppe would give the signal by dropping to one knee. The second set of shooters would wait only an instant for the first volley of bullets. This would allow time to adjust for a missed target. When it's all over and done with, Lo Sciavo should be alone and alive with Giovanni holding a pistol to his head.

The moment had arrived as Don Luciano Lo Sciavo finally exited the Mercedes. He was dressed as always, wearing a very expensive dark suit, with a long wool overcoat that hung from his shoulders; his arms were folded together under the coat, no doubt concealing a weapon. The look on his face was that of a man who seemed to be full of remorse and concern. In fact, as he looked at Giuseppe, he hung his head as if in shame, then waited by the Mercedes until the last man to leave the car was in position directly behind him, protecting his back, while the driver remained in the car.

The don, still looking grave, approached Giuseppe instead of Dr. Donato; this was not expected nor was the apology that followed.

"Con lacrima nell occhio so retornato a Amato (It is with tears in my eyes that I return to Amato). What happened to your boy and your dear wife should not have happened." Clasping his hands together and pointing them toward the heavens, he closed his eyes, nodding his head in a type of self-resignation. "This shame of murdering your little boy will follow me the rest of my life." He paused as an incredible anger brewed within him, his top lip curled unnaturally, creating a frightening mask, and then with a venomous glare, he snapped at all three of them, "If only this saint of a doctor would have followed my orders. It was simple. All he had to do was kill that bastard of a pope, and today we would be amici instead of enemies. Your child would have been running around, earning his lire, your wife would have been preparing a delicious lunch, and everything would have been as it should have been."

Lo Sciavo became quiet; staring at the ground, he seemed to be composing himself. When he raised his head, he did so slowly and tilted it in sinister pose. Then angling his stare to capture each of their eyes, he shook his head as though he was disgusted with them. Gritting his teeth, he spoke quietly, "Make no mistake, my friends. The pope still must die, and the dear doctor must not let us down again because if he should, then the pain you feel now will be nothing compared to what this whole town will feel when I take my vengeance for being disobeyed again. Yes." Don Lo Sciavo paused, nodding his head, as if agreeing with himself, and then taking a deep breath, his manner seemed to soften.

"Yes, yes. I will suffer along with all of you, and yes, it would trouble me terribly. After all, I am not a man without a conscience, or feelings for that matter. You must believe that my heart aches for your family, but what must be done must be done."

His rambling went on for quite sometime, and as Steven's memories began to surface and he could no longer separate himself from Giuseppe, he remembered the anger he felt as the murderer of his only son continued to mock them and their intelligence. Trying to contain the tremors of anger reverberating through his body, Steven, or what was left of his consciousness, embraced what Giuseppe went through on that fateful day. With full acceptance of his dual identity with Giuseppe D'Amato, he hungered for what was about to happen and welcomed the reality that he was indeed back in 1959 and about to relive a moment in time that, once again, put the advantage into the hands of the path according to Constantine.

As his transformation completed, he could smell the ripe cactus pears that grew everywhere on this mountain, and the scent of the grapes that had been crushed and discarded filled his thoughts of past times where, instead of hatred, there would be a festival celebrating the new wine. Giuseppe could feel the ocean breeze that was mingled with the cool mountain air as it rushed over him, raising the hairs on the back of his neck and sending a chill down his spine. He could feel the anticipation of battle and the excitement of revenge as it entered every pore of his body. He could sense the resolve and determination of his friends, and as he looked into their eyes, he could see no fear. He could only see the loyalty and the trust that they had for him, whoever he was.

This trust and loyalty showed on their faces. Whatever it was that they were fighting for was much greater than just simple vengeance or the protection of this little town. They believed Father Michael and, in doing so, truly believed that they were fighting for the very survival of their beloved earth and the future of human existence.

Who were these men that would have the wrath of spirits come down on them? Where did they originate, and did they have spirit guides from another dimension guiding them? Was their purpose to commit evil on earth, or was it to claim earth for their own existence? Giuseppe, unknowingly feeling Steven's presence, knew that all the answers would be in the manuscript and that, as Steven Di Carlo, he would interpret them in the future, but as Giuseppe D'Amato, he had to ensure that there was a future.

CHAPTER 29

GIOVANNI'S PLAN

T HE END OF Lo Sciavo's rambling brought Giuseppe out of his confused state caused by his identity crises. Now completely free of his trance, Giuseppe watched as Lo Sciavo turned to Donato and, without any kind of warning, slapped the doctor hard across the face and began to yell at him like a lunatic who was out of control. His eyes were wild as his body shook with forced anger.

"This is on your head, Donato," he said, spitting. "I should kill you right here where you stand for all the trouble you have caused me. Why couldn't you do as I asked? Did you think I was not a man of my word? Did you think that I would feel pity for these peasants? Do you feel courageous now that you forced my hand and your loved ones are dead? You disgust me."

"No mio signore perdona mi, forgive my insolence," the doctor said, taking Lo Sciavo's hand and kneeling before him. "I give you my life, Signore Lo Sciavo. I will honor your wishes. Do with me as you will. I am your servant."

This startled Lo Sciavo but pleased him as well.

"*Finalmente*, at last these peasants understand. Listen to their fear," Lo Sciavo shouted to his men as he roared with laughter. "Look at them! Are they not pathetic? Such fear, such sad faces."

Turning to look at his men, he continued with a soft disgust, "I told you they would not cause us any trouble. They are a peaceful people. They tend to their grapes, their olives, and their sheep. They live a peaceful life. They were born to be followers, and just like their parents before them, they were raised to be cowards."

Lo Sciavo continued to mock them. Giovanni watched helplessly as the tall, thin man with the pencil mustache approached Giuseppe and spat in his face. He groaned as his brother-in-law began to clench his fist, and then in the nick of time, he watched as the good doctor flashed Giuseppe a stern look. Seeing this, all of Lo Sciavo's men joined him as he laughed, pointing at the brave men of Amato, but unknown to them, it would be a laugh that was short-lived, a mockery that was flung back in the way of retribution, a vendetta that would be fulfilled. Giovanni surveyed the intruders, pleased to see that they continued their tirade of ridicule. This made them completely vulnerable, with the opportunity so perfect he looked at Donato and then at Giuseppe. A sly smile creased his face as he kneeled in front of his enemy.

What happened next was a blur. Giovanni, as planned, followed the doctor's lead and went down on one knee, holding Lo Sciavo's other hand, also pretending to pledge allegiance. The trap had been set, and with one last look around, Giuseppe also went down on one knee, and as his knee touched the ground, terror struck Lo Sciavo and his men. The sound of gunfire erupted all around the piazza and echoed throughout the hillside and beyond.

At the sound of the first shot, Donato and Giovanni hauled Lo Sciavo down to the ground and held him there with Donato holding a gun to his head and Giovanni holding a knife to his throat.

Then and as if by destiny, the tall, thin man with the pencil mustache began to run. Giuseppe chased him, and as he did, he felt overwhelmed with a sense of victory and excitement. He trembled with the anticipation of catching the bastard and the joy that he would have in killing him. By luck, or some perverted destiny, he tackled him at the very spot where Claudio was murdered.

"How ironic!" Giuseppe whispered in his ear as he held the Luger to his temple. "This, the very spot where you helped that bastard slaughter my son. Now you too shall be slaughtered, but not just yet, not here in this sacred spot. I will not have your filthy blood run the same path as the blood of my son. You, you evil bastard, you will be killed like the pig that you are. You will be hung by your feet in the slaughterhouse, and your squeals will be heard as far away as Palermo."

After Giuseppe said what needed to be said, he raised the butt end of his gun and hammered down hard on his temple, knocking the assassin out. He then dragged him to the fountain where he tied him up next to Lo Sciavo.

Looking around at all his friends, he forced a bitter smile as they moved cautiously toward the square. The battle had been a massacre. Lo Sciavo and his men had been defeated quickly, and as far as Giuseppe could see, they had come through the battle completely unharmed, not even a scratch.

Dr. Donato was guarding Lo Sciavo, who was securely tied to the base of the fountain. The good doctor looked purely evil as he spoke to his prisoner, "Cowards, are we? Weak pathetic men that disgust you? Is that not what you said, Signore Luciano Lo Sciavo? Tell me, great Don, who is afraid now? Did you really think that we would just bow to your every wish? Are you so stupid that you thought we would just let you get away with murdering our sweet child? It is you who is pathetic, you murderous bastard. It is you who disgust me."

Donato paused as he attempted to control his anger, then barely audible but very articulate, he continued, "Look around you, Luciano. See what your evil has caused, see that you have led these poor souls to their demise. Today they died for your sins. Tonight you will join them, but you, my dear Don, will suffer a much more painful death, so painful that it will haunt you for eternity, wherever your evil soul may end up."

Ending his vengeful threat, the good doctor punched the air in victory then fell to his knees as he was overwhelmed by emotion, emotion that had him calling out to Claudio and telling him that his death had been avenged. Giuseppe, leaving the doctor to deal with his own pain, turned his attention to the driver of Lo Sciavo's car, who had surrendered and was begging for mercy. Sorrow and sadness quickly replaced the thrill of the victory. All around the piazza, he saw the enemy dead and dying. Those who were shot but still alive were riddled with bullets and beyond help. Then like the doctor, Giuseppe was also overcome with emotion.

Giovanni's plan had worked like precision, and he was now surveying the aftermath of his work. He was their general and, therefore, took his responsibility very seriously. As he walked around, checking on his men and shaking their hands, the men of Amato saluted him; and as they gathered around him, patting him on his back, they sang songs of victory and echoed shouts of joy.

When Giovanni spoke, he spoke words that only a leader could speak. He told them that the battle they had won there on that momentous day was a battle not only for justice and revenge but also a battle for the future of their children and their children's children.

"This, my dear brothers, was a battle for freedom from those who would believe that they're above the Word of God and the laws of mankind. Yes, we have won this battle, but, my dear friends, the war is far from over. In truth, I fear this war for justice has just begun, and we have been chosen as the front line. Remember, if we stand together as we have done today, we will prevail."

After his moving words, he walked around to check on the enemy's wounded, mercifully giving quarter to those who were suffering with injuries that were beyond the hope of healing. Before ending their suffering, he spoke to each of them, and with death looming, he told them, "Go back to the devil and let him know what happened here today, and tell him that we will be ready for any other bastards he may send our way."

He cried and trembled with emotions so strong that each of his men felt his anger, his strength, and his resolve. Each time he pulled the trigger, their hearts went out to him.

Killing was not easy for Giovanni, but each time he did so, he thanked God for protecting his friends and family and for giving them the strength to overcome the evil that had entered their lives.

CHAPTER 30

VICTORY

T HE BATTLE OF Amato echoed its deadly sounds throughout the cave. The children drew back as the terror was overwhelming and fear was etched on each of their faces. Young and old, they knew that the fight had begun and that the outcome could only mean death. Attempting to calm their uncertainties, Father Michael summoned the group to the back of the cave; he knelt before them, then motioned them to do the same. Together they prayed and they cried quietly, calling out to their loved ones that were charged with the task of protecting them.

They became anxious as the gunfire stopped, then a frightening silence filled the air as each of them wondered if their husband, father, son, or friend was safe. Once again, their eyes looked wearily to the young priest, hoping for some sort of consoling but none came. Sharing their fears, Father Michael went to them and embraced as many as he could. Still, he failed to comfort their distress. Maria, sensing the priest's anguish, entered the middle of the group and called all the children to her.

Quietly whimpering, they migrated to her. The familiar sight of Maria was calming and had them feeling somewhat secure. Then just like she did each Saturday in the piazza, she began to tell them a story, and with this story, she was able to guide them away from the gunfire in the square and transport their minds into the ancient village of Bologna where a simple carpenter was crafting a little doll out of wood.

Father Michael, eyes wide-open and full of apprehension, was amazed at the strength of the young woman. Fumbling in his robes for his Bible, he sent a blessing to them and, again, began to pray. Then just when all seemed to settle, a single blast from a gun was heard, followed by another, and a short time later, yet another shot rang loud, perhaps louder than it really was, but for the group of the villagers holed up in the cave, it might as well have been a blast from a cannon. Their first fear was that Lo Sciavo had won and had begun executing their loved ones. Then as the silence grew unbearable, the young men of the village began to talk of leaving the cave to give aid to their fathers, brothers, and friends.

In his attempt to calm the situation and dispel their fears, Father Michael offered that he would go and check on what had happened, but he would need the boys to stand guard and promise not to leave the cave until he personally returned for them. Then before leaving, Father Michael went to each of the young men to ensure that they understood his orders, and only then did he venture out of the cave.

When the priest entered the square, relief had him falling to his knees. Crossing himself, he thanked God for the victory, then kissed the ground in a symbolic pledge of blessing the earth and the small town. Giovanni, curious to see the priest already in the village, approached him and, with his arm around his shoulder, scolded him for disobeying his orders. His orders were to wait until he was given the all clear. This way, if things went badly, at least he would have been there to provide the guidance for those in the cave. Father Michael simply replied with yet another blessing and then an acknowledgment of his error.

The priest quickly took charge of the happenings in the square and ordered the men to take the bodies to the small church outside the cemetery. There, he said, he would prepare them for burial and give their captured souls the guidance they needed to return to where they belonged. Unlike Lo Sciavo, he told them that these men were young souls who had simply lost their way. He said, "It will not be difficult to guide them back and help them follow their true path." Amused, Father Michael smiled at his audience as a puzzled expression filled the faces of the protectors. Smiling, he looked up to the heavens and then back at his gawking throng of soldiers. "I will explain," he said. "But all in good time, my dear friends."

Four of the men were charged with moving the still-warm cadavers to the church; the rest of the men would clean up the square and remove the explosives from the car. Donato, being the only one knowing how to drive, would take the vehicles and hide them in the slaughterhouse.

The ancient building was erected in the late 1800 and was one of the larger buildings in the town. Although it was still used by the butcher, most of the villagers only used it a couple of times a year. But those were better times, times when they would all get together and make their preserves, their sausages, and salted hams. On occasion, the building would also be used for socials like dances and birthday celebrations, but today would be different; today, the old building would be used as an executioner's chamber.

Giovanni, along with Francesco and Giuseppe, took the responsibility of the five prisoners; the most seriously injured were the two that were tied up to the cactus plants. Dr. Donato treated their cuts and abrasions while the other three were bound, gagged, and taken to the slaughterhouse. There they would remain and wait to be interrogated later that night.

They needed to know if there would be retribution for what they had done, and if so, then they needed to know by whom. As to what would be done with Lo Sciavo, they relied on Father Michael; he would be the one to guide them with who should die and who should be spared.

That evening, after everyone had returned from the cave, they all met in the town hall to celebrate their victory. The baker brought cakes, the butcher brought sausages, the women brought baskets of food, and the mayor gave the order to let the celebration begin.

The men of Amato, now nicknamed the protectors, were basking in all the attention. Surprisingly, even Giovanni was caught up in all the attention, and although the battle had only lasted a few minutes, the war stories went on for hours. There he stood with his daughter at his side as proud as anyone could be. Every few minutes, he would turn, hug, and hold her so close. It was as if it were the last hug he would ever have for her.

From the corner of his eye, he spotted Giuseppe watching them, and seeing the sadness in his eyes, he went to him, followed closely by Maria. Without saying a word, they simply hugged each other, knowing that their minds were consumed with the losses of Rosa and of Claudio. After the embrace, Giuseppe held his niece's hands and told her that her father was a hero and that she should never forget what happened here on this fateful day.

"Maria," he began, and as he did, his system was shocked once again as his identity as Steven Di Carlo surfaced at full speed, and for the first time, he realized that this beautiful young woman, who was his sister's daughter, was also his mother. With this realization, he began to tremble uncontrollably, and as tears began to stream down his face, he asked himself, how was this all possible? When would it all end, and really, did he want it to end? As much as he was terrified, he was also intrigued. Imagine getting to see your own mother as a child. Here she was, barely seventeen, and she was standing right in front of him, holding his hands. Then just like his mother would do in the future when she sensed his distress, she reached up and kissed him on the cheek, telling him that everything would be okay. He thanked her, and then looking into her moist eyes, he tried to smile, and failing miserably, he began to tell her what needed to be told.

"Cara Maria, remembering what happened here this day will help you and your family in the future. My dear girl, you will grow to become a very strong woman and have a wonderful family. I know that you are bravely suffering the loss not only of your cousin Claudio, but especially that of your aunt Rosa. I know that, to you, she was like the mother you never had, and to her, well, you were like the daughter that I was unable to give her."

Remembering Rosa, he smiled and struggled to catch his breath, but still, he continued, "I saw this in the way her spirits lifted every day when you visited and the pride that was her expression whenever she would see you walking in the piazza. She adored you, as you adored her, and Claudio."

Unable to continue looking into her eyes, Giuseppe took Maria into his arms and held her close. With thoughts of his murdered son butchering his soul, he clung tightly to her, trying desperately to swallow the lump that had firmly planted itself in his throat. Somewhat composed, he continued in short spurts and long pauses, "My beautiful girl, you watched over and cared for your little cousin as only an older sister could. Maria, please know that they will watch over you and your family always and that in the future, your memories of today will be of great importance. I want you to have this picture of Claudio. Keep it safe and close to your heart. One day, my dear, it will answer a lot of questions for you."

She thanked him for the picture and then placed her hands on his cheeks and, with her thumbs, wiped away the tears from his face. Staring into his eyes and unable to speak, she embraced him, and then just as she was about to let go of him, she whispered into his ear in perfect English, "I understand, Steven. I understand, my son."

And then, just as quickly as she turned into Steven's mother, she turned back into the seventeen-year-old young lady from Amato as he heard her saying, "*Grazie*, Zio, thank you."

Fully aware of his life as Steven Di Carlo, he watched her as she walked toward her friends. When she was almost there, she turned, and with a sly smile and holding up one finger, she asked him to wait. When she returned, she was with a young man not much older than her. When she introduced him to Steven and he looked into his eyes, he saw his father. He was so amazed that he barely heard her introduction.

"Zio," she said, "may I present to you my friend Roberto Di Carlo. He's from Catanzaro, and when I told him of our trouble, he wanted to help. Papa had him stand guard over us in the cave."

"I'm pleased to meet you," Steven said with a smile and then embraced the young man that would be his father, and while he was looking him over like someone who had just unwrapped a gift, he ordered him to take care of Maria and to always hold her close. The young man, promising to do so, looked concerned at his strange behavior; he then thanked him for giving him that responsibility and promised that he would take it very seriously.

At that moment, Father Michael approached them, and after saying his hellos, he turned to Giuseppe and told him that it was time. The priest, who now appeared to be in charge, ordered Giuseppe to go and get the manuscript; they would wait for him at the slaughterhouse where he would explain to them their existence and their purpose here on earth. He then smiled. "Giuseppe, you must come with an open mind and a righteous heart because only then will you know all that you need to know."

CHAPTER 31

STILL IN 1959

T HE CHILL OF autumn was in the air. The crisp dried leaves that were loud beneath his footsteps seemed to warn all as Giuseppe walked toward the old building, clutching a much older book. As he walked, he was oblivious of the mesmerizing dark blue sky and the brilliance of the peaceful night beneath it. The spectacular beauty of the stars that seemed close enough to touch also went unnoticed as he made his way down the narrow street toward the edge of town.

The manuscript seemed heavier than it was as he held it tightly to his chest. The smell of the old leather, rich within the book, was mingled with the pungent smell of time. The aroma of the ages gone by was so powerful that the memories of writing in it flashed through his mind like bolts of lightning. He knew this book; he knew it from cover to cover, from one painful lifetime to another. This book, filled with the violence of life, was his book; it was his life, and sadly, the manuscript chronicled nine of his lives. All of them, as painful as they were, had a purpose.

In that moment in time, as he walked along the moonlit path, Giuseppe's thoughts were consumed with all the sacrifices he's had to endure, the tears and all the sorrow, the pain, oh, the pain of not only seeing loved ones butchered but also the pain of being a butcher himself.

His mind was on the verge of exploding from all the memories. He Steven, Giuseppe, Thaddeus, or whoever he was—tried to rationalize all of it: his purpose, the so-called path, right from wrong. None of it made sense. *They keep telling me that all this lunacy has a purpose, but where? When? And who has it helped? Are we any better off now than a thousand years ago? Where has it done any good? Are we even winning? Do we even deserve to win?*

In those moments, as he walked toward the slaughterhouse, knowing that he was about to kill again, he felt like taking the old book, torching it and then just running away from all the craziness.

What gives them the right to put all this responsibility on to me? Why is it always my children that get killed? In nine painful lifetimes, I've never seen my children grow up. I have never had a wife long enough to grow old with. Yet I'm forced to live a long life, always alone, and always as a damned messenger of this fucking book.

His legs became heavier with each step, and his powerful back sagged under the weight of the expectations placed on him. Tired and fed up, he was convinced that the dark shadows were apparitions following him down the narrow pathway. The imaginary phantoms lurking in the gloom began talking to him through the breeze. At one point, he thought he heard one say, "Embrace the darkness." Then he was sure he heard it call out his name. "Embrace the darkness, Giuseppe, and it will embrace you."

Freaked out but refusing to run, he instead chose to talk back to them. "Fuck off."

And to his surprise, they did. They were gone as quickly as they came. Feeling overwhelmed, he needed to stop, to rest, and to think.

How can I go in there with all this doubt? I need to be alone. I need time to find myself, and more than anything, I need to be me again, Steven Di Carlo, hanging out with the woman I love, the children that had become my life, living the lifestyle that we had earned and deserved. I'm an advertising suit, not a butcher. I should be at the agency with Robby and Jimmy, planning our next campaign, not here in 19-fucking-59 planning my next execution. I want to be at home in Riverdale, living a normal life. I need all this other shit to just go away.

It was then that Giuseppe turned away from the slaughterhouse and headed for one of the field shacks instead. When he arrived, he sat on the dirt floor, still clutching the manuscript. The smell of mold from the decaying fruit was hardly noticeable, as was the dampness of the earth beneath him. The phantom words began chanting in his mind, *Embrace the darkness, and it will embrace you. Embrace the darkness, and you shall live forever. Embrace, embrace, emb . . .*

Giuseppe and his men at the field shack

He found himself holding the stock of the gun that was tucked in his belt and began to weep with the thoughts of what his mind was telling him to do.

I know. I'm Steven Di Carlo, but I'm still in Giuseppe's body, and I'm in 1959. Why am I still here? God, please, if there is a God and you're listening, then I need to go home. I need to wake up.

Sitting on the dirt floor, holding the gun out but not seeing it, he was no longer thinking like Giuseppe D'Amato. He was totally lost and fully aware of his life as Steven. Not only was he aware of those two lives but also of all the lives that he had lived as an executioner. Nine lives in all, nine murdered wives and eighteen slaughtered children, nine sons and nine daughters.

I'm on a mind-bending fucking roller coaster, he thought as his depression was being overtaken by hope. His hand no longer held on to the gun, the dark phantoms were gone, and a white bearded apparition had arrived.

Never lose hope, my son. Follow your anger and it will lead you to all that you seek.

He smiled, and then just like that, he was gone, and Steven was again thinking of possibilities.

Could this have been a warning that he had sent to himself from 1959 to 2011? After all, if he was really in the past, if this wasn't one of his nightmares, could he, in fact, change the future? More importantly, could he save them? Was it possible? His mind was going crazy with the what-ifs, and the emotional roller coaster just kept on rolling. If he had already tried this once before, why didn't it work?

Am I living in one of those frickin' time warps? How many times have I been back here? Shit, now I'm really driving myself nuts. Or am I? Maybe, just maybe, I'm being given a second chance, a second chance to save my ninth family.

His mind began to think up different scenarios of how he could send the message. He began to feel the excitement of the possibility. And although his life as he knew it would never be the same, at least his family would be alive.

He knew that he had to make some sort of deal with the council, and it would probably be through those that had been assigned to guide him. He also knew that he would still have to fulfill his purpose and follow the path that was designed for him, but instead of being motivated by anger, perhaps now, he could be motivated by fear. The simple knowledge of what would become of them should he fail should be enough to motivate him.

He kept looking around for some sign that someone was listening to him; Rosa or Rachael or Claudio or even the white bearded guy, whoever the fuck he was. He needed someone to tell him that, yes, it was possible. But no one came, no visions, no voices, and no signs. The darkness was suddenly overwhelming; his mind began to fill with thoughts of failure. All the optimism he felt just moments earlier had quickly vanished as the roller coaster was on a deep-down slope. For the first time since seeing his first sign, which was the heart Victoria drew for him in the hospital, he felt totally alone. The dread of nothingness washed over him in waves of horrible memories and, even worse, thoughts. He felt his mind grow heavy as his hand, once again, caressed the handle of the gun.

Alone and looking through the gun, he saw the visions of his dead family; Victoria lying in a pool of blood, Tommy screaming and calling for help that didn't come, and little Cathy hanging dead on the coat hook. Sobbing uncontrollably, his hand shook violently as he brought the barrel of the gun up to his mouth, then leaning back and resting his head on the cold planks that were the walls of the field shack, he closed his eyes. *If I pull the trigger, will I die, or will I finally wake up from this crazy nightmare? I can't really be here. This must be a dream. I have nothing to lose. What more could they take away from me?*

The last thought that entered his mind on this horrible ride was that he should die.

CHAPTER 32

BROTHERS

S TEVEN DI CARLO was restless as Dr. Brunstrom and the duty nurse wheeled him toward the neurology department for yet another MRI. His hands were moving slowly above his face; they seemed to be motioning something. His face twisted beyond recognition just as though he was in severe agony. His lips stretched painfully wide across his face, and his eyes twitched wildly with each movement of his hand when, suddenly, he just stopped. His entire body became relaxed; his shoulders sunk deep into the mattress that had become his home these past weeks, and in his comatose state, he began to cry. Stopping to check on their patient, both Dr. Thomas Brunstrom and his duty nurse were startled as Steven, eyes wide-open, stared straight at them and begged. "I just want to wake up. Please let me wake up," he said somewhat clearly as the pain, once again, began consuming his features. His body tensed as he struggled, and his legs began to flay under his bedsheets when, all at once, he violently slammed his fists down hard on the bed and cried, "I just want to be Steven Di Carlo again." Then as his tortured face crunched itself in what could only be emotional agony, they heard him mumble something else. "I die . . . m . . . dream . . . really die . . . I just wake up?" And then he went silent again. Just like that, his sleep became peaceful and his body was in reprieve.

"His vitals are fine," blurted the duty nurse

"Yes," responded Brunstrom. "Always have been very puzzling. He must be living in some kind of hell in these dreams. I wonder if his mother is there to help him again."

"I hope so," responded the duty nurse.

* * *

Giuseppe's first thoughts after waking up was, why he was still alive? How is this possible? After all, he was certain that he had pulled the trigger, or did he? When his eyes cleared, Father Michael was sitting with him.

Not yet fully awake but completely aware of where he was, he thought back to those moments that seemed to be, just minutes earlier, he was wondering if he would die or if pulling the trigger would simple wake him up from the nightmare. Neither had happened. Clearly, he was still alive and still in 1959. The priest taking the gun from Giuseppe's hand sat beside him, wondering how he would begin, how he would explain that which was unbelievable, that which was the substance of nightmares or horrible fiction.

His worry was all telling on his face; his sadness was evident in his eyes. Silently, he wondered what to do, how to help his dear friend. They needed him to be strong and with a clear mind. So with no alternative, Father Michael decided to tell him the truth, or at least some of it.

"My dear brother, you know that we truly are brothers. You do remember this don't you?" Michael paused to gauge the reaction Giuseppe would have hearing this news. Seeing none, he continued, "Tell me, do you remember Helmut, Thomas, Abraham, Francis, Alexander, Joshua? Tell me, my dear Thaddeus, do you remember yourself those many lifetimes ago?" As Father Michael named off all the characters cast in the many lives of the executioner that had span a millennium, Giuseppe D'Amato quietly listened to the familiar story as flashes of those lives worked their way through his memories just as though they had happened yesterday.

Cupping his hands to his chest, Michael's face was creased with lines, making him look far older than his forty-two years. There was a distant sadness in his eyes, which were moist with recollection. His shoulders were hunched forward, his head was bowed down, staring into his lap, and his chin was almost touching his chest. When he raised his head ever so slightly, it was angled to the right and looking at Giuseppe but also looking through him. He spoke quietly, and when Giuseppe looked at him, the priest appeared defeated; tears glistened in his eyes, and his voice was raspy with emotion.

"My dear, dear friend," he barely spoke the words when he lowered his head and began to cry. Giuseppe reached out to comfort him when the priest continued with his story. "Together we began our quest ten thousand years ago, maybe longer, and together we find ourselves, once again, questioning our chosen path," he said, looking at the ceiling of the old shack and nodding his head in acceptance. "Yes, it has been a difficult existence for us with this enormous task of not only saving humanity but of saving our species as well." Cupping his hands together, he massaged his eyes and then seemed to dry wash his face as the stains from his tears mingled with the tribulations of that day left him looking troubled and lost. Still, he continued with the story that need to be told, "The battle with those that would crush our hopes seems to never end, and like you have done time and again over the centuries, you ask yourself why." He paused briefly to nod his head as though agreeing with an unspoken statement. "As do I, my dear brother, as do I." Then again, wiping the tears from his eyes, he became more composed. "But I ask you to remember the purpose of those we fight against, the atrocities committed by them and of our brother who leads them. Our brother whom we most certainly need to save when the time is right and also of the many young souls that have foolishly believed his promise and joined him in his quest to rule the path."

Giuseppe watched as resolve quietly took over Michael's features. His voice had become more determined, his posture more erect, and his eyes steely. So without interruption, the priest continued, "When our souls were first rescued from the clutches of darkness thousands of years ago, it was the elders, led by our father, who showed us the true path." Then tapping his chest and through gritted teeth, he looked directly into Giuseppe's eyes. "They chose us and others like us to save our existence and to bring all our knowledge and love to this wonderful place. They needed to ensure that the right path was followed so that one day all of us will be able to exist on this earth in our true form, never having to fear disease, violence, or death."

Father Michael paused. His demeanor again softened, and his tone became appreciative. Looking up to the heavens, he continued, "They gave our souls a home in the afterlife where we continue to evolve the ways of the path. They showed us the consequences of failure and the rewards of being triumphant. Then with each human existence, they let us choose our own purpose, our own contribution to our future survival. You know all too well, my dear friend, there is much to do to prepare this wonderful place for our ultimate use. We must continue to cleanse it of its impurities and of its savage and destructive ways. We must recover those lost souls and show them the right path before it's too late for them, and sadly, we must rid the earth of those souls that are beyond saving."

Giuseppe's own lack of resolve was tested, his rekindled memories strengthening his mind as he continued to listen to the story he already knew.

"The recovery of the human souls and embracing them back into the way of the path has proven to be worth the fight and the sacrifices. Remember, death is just the beginning of a new life. As humans, we fear death, especially of those we grow to love. In reality, most souls fear the human existence. For them, being born is like death. Why enter a world full of hate and violence when you can exist as anything you like in our true form? Why willingly choose a life where your purpose is to be born with or contract a painful and deadly disease and then be forced to live a horrible pathetic existence? Why would we choose to be prophets and executioners. Why?"

He paused almost theatrically as excitement of his purpose rid some of the doubt he shared with his executioner. "Why? Because we all have a significant purpose to serve. Some of us, like you and me, are very fortunate and are awakened to the reality of the other side. We, in our quest, need to know and understand our calling in this existence. We need to be aware of our purpose and why while the other poor souls suffer unknowingly. They are left to wonder, why them? Meanwhile, they are unaware of the very important purpose that they have chosen. They don't know the reason for their suffering. For them, there's only the hope of a life after death and of a paradise or heaven as most wish to call it.

"Unfortunately, to cleanse this place, some of us need to contract those awful diseases while others can study them so that we can find cures and, ultimately, rid the earth of them. We have chosen that this amazing place should continue to evolve, but with all the technological wonder and creative genius of our species, we still need a balance. The *Namzu Anunnaki* will provide this balance when the time is right, and only you, my dear brother, can retrieve it."

Then becoming somber once again, he looked down at the dirty floor, breathing deep the smell of the rotting fruit as it mirrored his mood. "You do remember the power of *Namzu Anunnaki,* my dear brother? The book of all of our wisdom, the reason we are able to exist for twenty-three lifetimes." His eyes brightened with the possibilities the ancient science presented for them, but then and all too quickly, his mood became angry once again. "I'm afraid that there are those who wish to steal it from us, those who have chosen to follow the path of evil and create a place that is ruled by fear and manipulation. They dream of an existence that would cater to their own selfish bidding, where a few would control the rest, and the pure souls would cease to return.

"These evil souls bred by us have been searching for the *Namzu Anunnaki* since they first learned of its existence. Some choose to call it the Holy Grail, others choose to call it the fountain of youth. Still, they wish to use the knowledge for their own evil intentions. Their path is to create chaos and prevent the discovery of the cures and the development of solutions to the harmful effects of knowledge. Their path is to encourage wars and terrorism, all in the hope of discouraging us from this place that we hope to call paradise, and when we are gone, this wonderful place would be theirs for the taking, and humanity, as we know, it will cease to exist.

"You see, old friend, we are the ones that can provide the balance that fights this evil path. Our purpose is to block their way, to undo the harm they create, and, ultimately, to rid this place of their evil souls while, at the same time, rescuing the lost ones."

"Listen to me, Michael." It was Steven's persona that had surfaced, pushing back the powerful force that was Giuseppe DAmato. "I understand and remember our purpose," he said with disdain. "But I feel defeated. I feel lost and very lonely. I would willingly and gladly exchange the promise of paradise for one simple human existence, one lifetime shared with a family of my own, enough years to watch my own children grow up and then produce children of their own. My dear brother, I want to grow old and have Victoria grow old with me. I need to see my children, Cathy and Tommy, grow and flourish with life and energy.

"More than ever, I need this. I understand that in the beginning, I needed to be motivated by anger to correct the harm Sebastian is creating, but like this place that we fight so desperately for, I have evolved. The purpose alone is no longer enough to motivate me, and anger is defeating me. Give me my family and I will fulfill my purpose of executing the right plans and preparing this earth for our future. And yes, I will help rid this place of the evil souls, and I will promise paradise."

"My dear Giuseppe, I know not of these people you speak of, but as with all that we have been through and with the wisdom of the elders, it must be of a future life that only you have seen. Listen to me, dear one. We must take care of this threat here in this time before we can think of the challenges you will face in your next life. Your life as Giuseppe D'Amato here and now has a great influence on the challenges that you will face in the future. We have a chance right now to control a very old soul and prevent two others from gaining strength, and there are two very young souls that we must save and return to our path. They must be reminded of our purpose as they both will be with you in your next life. We cannot let this opportunity pass."

"Then, Michael, as my brother and dear friend, tell me why have I come back to this time? Is there some part of the past that needs to be changed? Is it the message that I send to the future? Why am I here, if the reason is other than to save my family?"

"Dear brother, I know nothing of what you speak. You are here in this time fulfilling a purpose that you have chosen. Perhaps, in their wisdom, the elders have shown you a glimpse of what is to come as they did for me. I couldn't imagine being able to travel back in time to change the future. This message that you wish to send is one that you have sent lifetime after lifetime. It helps you to awaken to your next purpose and, more importantly, provides you with the knowledge and belief in our path. This understanding is what separates reality from insanity. It is difficult enough to understand why we need to do what we do. Imagine if we are unable to confirm the reality of our past. Without this knowledge, it would be impossible to continue with our quest. My friend, we have used the manuscript as our bible. It guides us toward the future, and we have lived by its words for over a thousand years. Peppino, ultimately the message you send is designed to prepare you for your next journey and, more importantly, for your next awakening."

Michael turned to face Giuseppe; he looked concerned and seemed to be frightened. His fears were that he was not getting through to him. With his left eye twitching and his right hand rubbing his temple, he fought off the despair that he felt and then continued with more urgency, "Giuseppe, our experiences in this time and place right now are real, and the memories of this time will ensure that your awakening in your next life is full of the knowledge that you will need to succeed. You see, old friend, I will share with you that the visions that I have been shown is of a future where the forces of evil that survive this time are very powerful, and unless we are prepared for them, they will be devastating to our cause. One of those evils is Lo Sciavo. The message that you send is not intended to save your future family. The message you will need is where and how to retrieve the manuscript. The vision that I have been shown is that when the ninth moon is in its sixth day. I am told that one of the most wicked of souls returns to earth, and his return is somehow motivated by Lo Sciavo. We're not certain where this monster will come from, but he will come, and his purpose will be the destruction of our path."

Seeing no immediate reaction from Giuseppe, Michael's mood was on a downward spiral; his eyes had darkened as the pupils within them had grown to three times the size. His face became slack, and jowls had now become visible beneath his pale cheeks. His shoulders sagged in defeat, then, all at once, popped up in frustration. With his mouth pursed in with a grip of anger, Michael hesitantly decided to reveal all.

"Look, Peppino, I shouldn't be telling you this, but I fear that you are lost and worried that the importance of what we have been charged with has escaped you. You should know that it has also been revealed to me that, fifteen months earlier, in the sixth month of 2011, the seed that will thrust Sebastian into his twenty-second existence on earth will have been planted. He will be fathered on that day by the reincarnate of Lo Sciavo. It has been decided by the elders that our brother must be taken from his womb and taught the knowledge of our path, and then we must protect him and raise him with the teachings of our hopes and beliefs. There is no longer any doubt that we will need Sebastian's help to defeat the true evil that will threaten us all."

Steven, now equally sharing the memories of Giuseppe's life, accepted the clarity and knew that what Michael had said to be true. Although he couldn't remember discussing Sebastian's rebirth, he did have a clear memory of the conversation. Sebastian's rebirth was the original motivation for sending the message. Eliminating Lo Sciavo in 1959 would be like wiping out the knowledge of who the father of their brother would be, and in doing so, they would be unable to prepare for his return. The dilemma facing all of them on this day was that if they didn't eliminate him in 1959, then somehow, he would influence the arrival of some kind of very bad evil in 2011. Somewhere along the way, the purpose had changed. Knowledge of this impending malevolence has forced Constantine and the council to redesign the path of Giuseppe's next existence. As Steven, he would have to realize that the picture existed which would lead him to the manuscript and all its revelations, except, of course, for the birth of this wicked soul.

With his thoughts going back to Michael's comments of his future life, he realized why this nightmare had him reliving the past. To reunite the path, they had to enlighten him to the survival of Lo Sciavo's soul in spite of the knowledge of the danger that came with that decision—a decision that would ultimately spawn the arrival of the evilest of all souls, a decision that would allow the awakening of the would-be devil himself.

Though the priest rambled on, Steven could barely hear his words but knew exactly what he was saying. Refusing to believe that his life as Steven Di Carlo was merely a glimpse of his next existence, he continued to formulate a plan in his mind to not only send the critical message but also to send the message that would alert him of the murders of his family. That's when it dawned on him and for Steven; it was like being hit by a ton of bricks.

If the reverse were true and his life as Steven was real and he was, in fact, remembering his life as Giuseppe, then the original message did work. How could he not see it? His life as Steven was being played out in 2011 just a couple of months before this so-called evil is born and ten months before Sebastian's rebirth. *I've been all consumed that the message was to save Victoria and our children, but in fact, it was their deaths that were used as the catalyst that brought me back into this time. They are not dead! The elders had showed me a future where they were killed so that I would be jolted back into the battle of the path.* For Steven, the solution was simple: he just needed a new catalyst, one that would remind him of those deaths, then with that knowledge, he would prevent them!

CHAPTER 33

CONSTANTINE AND SEBASTIAN

WHEN, ONCE AGAIN, Steven tuned Father Michael back in, he was telling him the story of Sebastian who had already lived sixteen lifetimes before Steven's first. He was reunited into the family in the year 936, which was two years before Steven's third existence and eight years before Father Michael's fifteenth. As the older brother, he tried to take hold of their souls and turn them against Constantine, who was and had always been their father.

Constantine Kadopolis was a Greek merchant in the ancient city of Plati. He was an amazing man who was experiencing his twenty-second and final existence on earth, that is, until the path can create an environment safe enough that our oldest of souls, like him, would be able to return. The purpose they shared today was the same as the one they shared back then. With the knowledge contained in the *Namzu Anunnaki*, they hoped to create a utopia where the harmony of souls would ensure a safe and long existence. Unfortunately, a decision he would make during that time would split the path, and Sebastian and their mother would take sides against him.

Their mother, like Steven, was a very young soul, and like all her sons, she was an awakened soul. Althaia Kadopolis was vigilant in her belief of Sebastian's ways and, in the end, became unrecoverable. Eight hundred years later, in 1781 Scotland, Francis McKenzie was forced to give up on this woman that was once his mother and was forced to destroy her soul.

Their father, Constantine, showed them the true way of the path and has guided them from the other side ever since the division. His resilience back then sent Sebastian into hiding for six lifetimes, and when he returned in 1599, he was conceived once again in the womb of the soul that was once Althaia. When Sebastian's presence was felt on his return to earth, it was up to the path to try to eliminate him, but they failed, and once again, he went into hiding and has been in the protection of his realm ever since.

"A soul, as you know, can only be eliminated by its own hand."

Steven could hear the soothing tones in his voice, the conviction of his beliefs, and the concern of his fears as Father Michael continued with his story. "Or by capturing it when it's older than twenty-three existences, and only then can it be destroyed by another. It is said that anything other than a natural death would send an old soul into the abyss. This return for Sebastian will be his twenty-second, and to risk this return, he must be aware of the looming danger, or perhaps it's because it will be my final existence and the last chance for him to eliminate me."

"Michael, how do we know that he will be reborn in the year 2011, and how could we hope to convert him when our father failed this same challenge a thousand years ago? How do we know that Lo Sciavo will be the father, and do we also know who will be the birth mother?"

"So many questions, Peppino, yet you know all the answers. We know of his return because we have both been shown it. Tonight, we will allow his soul to return to Sebastian. Then in the year 1983, we have been shown that his soul will once again enter earth's realm. From all that we know, his awakening will begin on his fourteenth birthday, and as his mind evolves in the understanding of his path, he will be led to the knowledge of his purpose by the memories of this night right here in 1959. Then I am told that in 2009, you yourself, in your next life, will feel his presence. His evil will invade your mind, and on this day in your future, that feeling will be the catalyst that will begin your own awakening.

Steven, absorbed in Father Michael's accounting, was forced to tune the good priest out as the white bearded guy was back. "Do you remember me, my son?" His voice was soft and compassionate. "Father," whispered Steven as he looked deep in to Constantine's dark blue eyes, a sudden tremor convulsed through his body. The hair on his arms spiked up as an uncontrollable chill swept through him. "My son, do you remember in the future when, on that very cold day in the twelfth month, while driving your precious family home, a blinding light sent your chariot out of control? This was the awakening of the evil forces and was your first warning of their existence and all caused by that blinding light. This warning set in motion the events that have brought you to us on this day, allowing your own awakening to manifest." Constantine fell silent, standing in the corner of the shack as he too listened to Michael, who seemed to be oblivious to his presence.

"Peppino, the elders showed me his soul, but that's not all. They also told me of the presence of an intruder in his mind. Our guides have confirmed this, not only with him but also with you. It is described as a pure malevolence, an evil that has grown and developed over the centuries. This evil has been murdering and destroying minds, lurking in the shadows as we unknowingly helped it gain strength."

Steven tried to absorb all that he was hearing, but his mind refused to believe that he was living out a nightmare. "This is too real. Shit, I can smell the air. I can feel the ground. Hell, I can even hear the sounds of the sea beneath this mountain. Dreams just aren't this real." Then contradicting his own thoughts, he asked, "Michael, what if this is a dream and my life as Steven Di Carlo is real? Why can't I just wake up? Why am I completely aware of everything in that time with so much detail? I remember being back here once before, and I remember this conversation, and I know we didn't talk about Sebastian's rebirth. We were only concerned about eliminating Lo Sciavo and his followers. So the way I see it is that this is no dream. I've come back here to the past to change the manuscript."

"Steven, you must believe what your heart tells you to believe. The reason we are here has everything to do with the manuscript and what has been written on its pages. We are also here to somehow ensure that your awakening is with the knowledge of not only the birth but also the consequences of our decisions today."

"So tell me, have I been back here more than once?"

"This my brother. I cannot answer. But it is true that our minds will travel to past lives many times. This is how we are awakened. We come back to absorb the memories. Yes, perhaps they are memories of carving numbers into a door, and yes, perhaps those numbers are of the date that the evil will arrive, or perhaps it is intended to remind you of the *Namzu Anunnaki*."

"My son!" Again, Constantine with his full white beard flowing in the breeze, decided to cut in as Michael continued to speak, which had Steven feeling overwhelmed. "Thaddeus, pray heed to me. The last time we failed to remember the manuscript because we were unable to hold you here. The hopes you had of saving your family thrust you out of this existence back to the other one that is playing havoc within your soul. We had no choice, my son. We had to bring you back to read all that had been written of what we know to be true. This was done a very long time ago, and it was done in your hand. The detail in the manuscript is paramount to your awakening." It was as though a light had been switched on in Steven's mind, and Constantine's words rang clear as he, once again, tried to tune Michael back in.

"Perhaps this crossroads that you face has you questioning the reality that is. It has to be more than just the numbers. Perhaps it is to inform you of the identity of who will mother Sebastian."

"Michael, are you telling me that we know who the birth mother is? If so, then our mission is not as difficult as it sounds. We would simply need to watch her and then seize our brother when he is born."

"Yes, my friend, that is precisely what I am saying, but the woman in question is a resilient feisty soul that will not be so easy to control," Michael said this with a bit of pride in his voice and an almost detectable twinkle in his eyes. "My dear brother, in 1781, we thought that we were rid of our once dear mother, Althaia, but we failed. She did not take her own life. Yes, they would have had us believe this, but in fact, she was killed by one of their own. This rouse was to protect her for Sebastian's return."

Steven, hearing what had been said, was in shock that his first mother still lived. What he felt was not anger or disappointment, but instead it was relief. Althaia's soul still existed, and she lives in 1999. He smiled at the prospects of being reunited with her and was excited that he would have another chance at bringing her back to the path. Then as if he were kicked in the groin, he was brought out of his elation by Michael's next accounting. "My final purpose on this earth will be in that time, and it will be to take the child myself and raise him as my own. I will teach him the ways of our path and convince him of the possibility of coexisting with us in peace and in accord."

"Michael, why would the council risk your final existence to the most powerful soul of the evil path? Why would they do that knowing that on your twenty-third lifetime, he could eliminate you permanently simply by killing you? Why would they think you could succeed, when so many others have failed? Michael, our side cannot afford to lose you. Why not just send him back? If we did this then and it being his twenty-second existence, he would have to remain in the celestial realm until we've achieved our goal."

"Yes, yes. That would be wonderful, but we have no choice, brother. He cannot be eliminated as a child. You know that it is against our beliefs. We will not knowingly send a child into the darkness. To do this would make us as evil as they are." Steven's tone became resigned. His stomach ached as he thought of his older brother. His heart longed for reconciliation, and his head pounded in pain as he thought of it. "Michael, as an adult, he will be too powerful to control, especially after his awakening."

"Yes indeed. This is why we will need to nurture him as a child and learn from our past failures on how to succeed."

"And if we don't succeed and he kills you, then you will be lost forever. Michael, I know it's a horrible thought, but we allow our children to die, to be murdered and sacrificed. Why should it be different with him?"

"The difference, dear one, is that our children choose to die as children. You know this. You know that most of our children die because they wish to remain children for all time. Others simply wish to wait a bit before they serve an older existence. This is their choice, and before accepting an earthly purpose, a soul will dictate themselves when they are to die."

Silence had invaded the small field shack; the distant sound of crashing waves from the sea far below was somewhat soothing. The flapping wings of bats swooshed above the rooftop as voices from the village carried in the wind; meanwhile, they both thought of the atrocities committed by both paths.

"In the future, or in my memories of this future," Steven began as he broke the silence, "this contradicts every human principle. Protection of life is sacred. If we were unknowing souls, we would be appalled at things we say and do."

"Listen to me, Peppino. Within our kind, we are all given the choice of our purpose and taught in our subconscious the ways of the path as well as the rules of survival. As enlightened ones, we kill to save a soul when that soul has been misguided. If the soul is beyond saving, then we find ways to have them kill themselves, thus eliminating them. This is the balance. They do the same on their side as they try to steal souls by having them do their bidding.

"They tried this with the good doctor. If they would have succeeded in having him kill the pope, the guilt that Donato would have felt would have probably sent him into the darkness or would have shamed him into joining Sebastian. Our pope is living his twenty-third existence, and the evil path has not been able to get to him. He is our oldest soul on earth, and we must protect him. His time is near and their last chance to extinguish him was by the hand of Donato, and they failed. Fortunately, we have never failed to protect an old soul, but unfortunately, they have. Five of our friend, despite that they were followers of Sebastian, have sadly perished. This may not sound like much, but there are only fifty-two souls who have experienced more than twenty lives. Our father and our brother are two of those souls. I believe Sebastian can be saved, and you will be there with me in the future to help me save him."

"Michael, I understand all this and will happily try to save our brother, but I need to ask for one thing, and that is to be able to send a message that will awaken me before my family is slaughtered. Victoria is resilient. She would be able to nurture Sebastian as her own. With her at my side, we will bring him back to our path, and then together while we battle the evil threatens to come."

"I understand your wishes and will support them with our father. As you know, he alone cannot approve this. Ultimately, if their death is in your future, the final decision must be made by the souls of the ones you wish to keep on earth. They will have fulfilled their purpose and would have to agree to a new one, but you should know that most souls do not wish an extended life on this earth with all its evil. Now, dear brother, enough of all this talk of the future. We must tend to the task at hand in the present."

Together they left the shack with the understanding that, yes indeed, things could change. The question they both had was how they would change them. As they approached the slaughterhouse, the persona of Giuseppe, who quickly took over from the identity of Steven Di Carlo, and the good priest, pleased at being able to, once again, answer the challenge of bringing his brother back from the edge of darkness, were forced into the reality of what they were about to do. Five lives were in the balance and about to be either saved or extinguished, and unfortunately, there was no way to change this.

CHAPTER 34

THE SLAUGHTER HOUSE

THE SLAUGHTERHOUSE, STANDING alone on the hillside, looked ominous. The massive doors guarding the entrance were made of solid wood that measured at least ten feet wide and must have stood fourteen feet tall. The arches surrounding the doors were carved out of granite, framing the entry like a fifteenth-century castle. The walls, also made completely of stone, had no noticeable windows, just a series of small openings that were designed to allow proper circulation for the curing of meats and preserves and to expel the stench of decay. Two peaks that were separated by a large chimney stack at the center enhanced the roof that was made of black slate. Looking at the slaughterhouse, you would know that you were entering a place of death that touched the boundaries of evil.

The malevolent look of the building gave Giuseppe a sense of confidence and a renewed feeling of control. It was as if the anger had returned and the need to avenge Rosa and Claudio was all he could think about. The intense hate that, just moments earlier, he was trying to fight off was back, and once again, he knew his purpose and understood what needed to be done and why.

When they walked through the massive entrance and entered the dim interior of the old building, Giuseppe was the one the rest looked to for guidance. Even Father Michael fell into step behind him as he too sensed the change in his demeanor.

Giovanni was there to greet them; the look of concern was visible on his face as he quietly motioned them toward the five prisoners. Then embracing Giuseppe, he spoke quietly to him, "*Corraggio fratello*, this is our destiny. The cards we hold must be played for another hand to be dealt. It is time, my brother. *Forza, andiamo.*"

There was no need to have any discussions with Lo Sciavo. Giuseppe simply walked up to him and, then kneeling down close to him, whispered the eternal threat, "You are an evil bastard, and there is no hope to save your pathetic soul. Know this that on this day, I promise that there will be no paradise for you, ever. You, a servant of Sebastian who would kill children, will be sent to the darkness for your sins. The next time you grace us with your evil will be your last. So go back to Sebastian now. Tell him that you failed once again. Tell him that he should prepare you for your extinction, and tell my brother that we are saving you for a much worse fate than a simple bullet to the head."

Then through clenched teeth and venomous eyes, he finished his declaration. "Be grateful that our beliefs, unlike yours, forbid me from inflicting pain when sending a soul back, but I guarantee you that the next time, you won't be so lucky because the next time, we won't be sending you back."

With this said, he raised the gun to his face and pulled the trigger. The shock was evident in the other four prisoners as they cowered at the sight of their leader being mercilessly executed. But it was nothing in comparison to the fear they would soon share.

* * *

The chill in the air was immediate as the gatherers had arrived to claim Lo Sciavo's soul. The icy wind that announced the arrival of the transparent entities seemed to captivate the men of Amato as they looked on in awe. Father Michael was instead gripped with fear as his apprehension for allowing the evil soul to return to Sebastian grew deep within him. Still, the entities moved toward their prize unabated, and then as if they could read his mind, two of the gatherers broke off and briefly hovered near the priest. In the brief pause that seemed to slow time, Father Michael recognized the small entities, and as he looked into their aura, he sensed a deep sadness from within them and then felt an even deeper longing from within himself. Father Michael, with tears forming in his eyes, reached out to the entities, and when he did, the two forms came to touch him. For that brief moment in time, the intense feeling of foreboding had left him, and the slight hope of reconciliation brushed the outer edges of his mind. And then in a blink of an eye, the cruel reality returned with a jolt as the chill intensified into a bitter cold and the entities began to circle Lo Sciavo's body. Then with the appearance of a small tornado, they lifted his soul from its lifeless shell and embraced it for its return to Sebastian's realm. Just as quickly as they had arrived, they were gone. The air in the slaughterhouse returned to normal, but still they stared in awe or, perhaps, in disbelief, searching the room for evidence that they had come.

When reality once again recaptured their minds, they realized that there was still more work to be done. Giuseppe, looking around at the prisoners, moved toward the man with the pencil mustache; the tall man cowered and began to whimper as fear took hold of his emotions. With the gun prominently in his hand, the executioner knelt beside him and asked him his name. The prisoner responded with a terrified babble, blurting out his name as being Angelo Calendino, while, at the same time, sobbing and begging for mercy.

There will be no mercy for an animal like you, Giuseppe thought this to himself when he asked the man if he had experienced the awakening. The thin man answered him instead with a pledge of loyalty and claimed to now understand the evil ways of those he followed. He went on to ask Giuseppe to accept him, and if he did, he would learn their ways and fight for their path. Giuseppe, pretending to listen, motioned for Father Michael to join them. When he did, they began the ritual.

The ritual was a process they had to follow before attempting to eliminate a soul. In his heart, Steven knew this one would fail. He could sense that his existences were many and that this hollow promise was one that he repeated throughout the ages. Nonetheless, it was their duty to be sure, and so Father Michael continued with his questioning, which would eventually reveal all. In the end, they would know all the exploits of not only this poor bastard but also of the others.

Steven left the priest to his task and began preparations of his own. He asked the men to find him the things that he would need.

"Go quickly. Gather what I need and help me send this bastard into extinction." When he gave them his list, some of the men grimaced at the thought of what they were about to do. Giovanni instead smiled and shouted the orders to get them on their way.

The one who called himself Angelo sniveled as his past was being revealed. Steven, ignoring his pleas, went on to the others. Talking to them quickly exposed that they were young souls and that the good father would find a way to save them. He felt an immediate connection with two of their captives. They were the ones that were captured earlier and tied to the cactus. Still licking their wounds, it was evident that they didn't know the ways of the evil path nor were they aware of their purpose.

The last one, Lo Sciavo's driver, was fully aware of his purpose and explained that he did not deserve the forgiveness of the path according to Constantine. He went on to say that this was his second existence serving Sebastian, and he was too much of a coward to face his responsibility and return to his true home.

"How could I ever face them again?" he asked. With tears streaming down his face and his head bowed, his body trembled with grief when he began to tell them of the horrific events that had kept him in the service of the likes of Lo Sciavo for two very long lifetimes.

"The year was 1777." Then there was a long pause before he continued. "I was a schoolteacher in a place called Savannah, Georgia." With unbearable pain, he told his story.

"My purpose was to teach the youngsters right from wrong and develop their subconscious in the way of our beliefs. But then war broke out. Many of the people didn't know which side to take. Did they protect their homes and join the English, or did the fight for freedom and risk losing everything? It was a horrible time. Neighbors were killing neighbors, soldiers were murdering civilians and then burning and pillaging their homes. Women were being raped, children were being slaughtered, all in the name of Mother England. I was terrified! It was as if evil had won, and our path had been destroyed. I thought that all had been lost."

With his hands bound behind his back, he held his head down to his knees to try to control the tremors that surged throughout his entire body as he attempted to continue with his story. The other two prisoners listened with disbelief as their friend was talking of a past life with such detail.

"It was horrible," he blurted out, forcing the lump in his throat to dissolve. "When the English approached our town, fear was everywhere. Their red coats and black hats were a symbol of hatred and destruction. We all hid from them. On that horrible day, I had thirteen children in my classroom, and with no time to get them to the protection of their parents, I hid them in the cellar of the schoolhouse and locked the doors. Then I stood outside the classroom to try to protect them. When the redcoats approached, I tried to act like a loyalist. They asked me which side I was on and what should be done with the patriots, and believing that I had fooled them, I said all patriots should die. They laughed at me and said that I would have to prove my loyalty and ordered me to burn down my schoolhouse.

"When I refused, they swung a rope around a tree and said, 'Then you shall be hung, and we will burn down your little schoolhouse just the same.' I was terrified. They gave me no choice. They would have done horrible things to those children. At least that was my reasoning for trying to save my own life instead of facing the fact that I was a coward. How I wish that I would have died with them. Instead, I torched the schoolhouse, and the screams of those children will echo in my mind throughout eternity. I can still hear them today, almost two hundred years and three lifetimes later.

"Well, after that, the English dragoons took me with them and enlisted me to serve the king and the country, and so from then onward, I've been loyal to Sebastian and have been serving him ever since."

Father Michael had been eavesdropping on the driver's story while he was interrogating the prisoner named Angelo. With his interest now directed toward the driver, he ignored the bullshit that was flowing out of Angelo's mouth and went over to sit with Giuseppe and listened to the driver's painful past. He began by asking the driver his name and then asked him to recount the story for him.

While he did so, Giuseppe called to Giovanni, and the two of them went out for some air. Lighting a cigarette, Giovanni tried to contain his eagerness to find out about the occurrence in the slaughterhouse. Failing, he asked his questions, "Peppino, please tell me if what I saw was real, and if they are evil, why did I feel . . . I don't know how to explain it, but I felt somewhat enlightened. It felt as if I knew them. My friend, I must tell you that I was drawn to them."

"Caro Giovanni, what you felt was true. What you saw was amazing, and yes, you do know them. Evil, I'm not sure that we should refer to them as evil. After all, they are just like us. We are of the same species, you know. Unfortunately, they follow Sebastian, and he leads them in a lie. He tells them that we are the ones who are evil and blames our path for delaying evolution. He blames Constantine for all the plagues that have haunted this world. He blames us for being weak and allowing an old soul to lead us down a path of destruction. And so he tells his followers that we must be eliminated even if it means going against the beliefs of our collective path."

"Why can we not tell them? Why can we not just sit around a table and come up with a solution to this war?"

"Ah, my dear friend, you ask the question we have asked ourselves for a thousand years, but unfortunately, the answer continues to elude us." With that said, the rest of their short walk was in silence as they both pondered the question of peace, and after a couple of cigarettes, they returned to find the priest and the driver embracing like long lost friends.

"My dear brother," Michael was saying, "we have finally found you, and now it is time for you to return home." A few moments later, the good father, still holding the driver, turned to the men and told them that it was time and to behold the power of the path.

The chill was, once again, immediate as the air again became very cold. Feeling the familiar sense of peace flow through his body,

Giuseppe embraced the coldness and waited impatiently for them to arrive. He could see his breath as he explained to Giovanni what he was about to experience. Giovanni turned to him, not knowing whether to smile or to be afraid. Suddenly, a burst of wind rushed through them all, and they could see the white shadows as they entered earth's realm.

Father Michael, the palms of his hands together as if in prayer, accepted the spirits as they arrived. The driver, kneeling beside him, stood up and spread out his arms, and when he did, they floated toward him. One by one, the tiny souls approached the driver, and after each of them had embraced their former teacher, they joined hands, surrounding him. They began to hop and skip like only children knew how to do, and as they did, there was an ambient glow that seemed to swirl around each of them.

They were the thirteen children from his past, and they had come to take him home. Giuseppe felt this incredible sense of exhilaration as he watched the power of the path, then Giovanni, following his lead, began to laugh and once again enjoy the affirmation that there was indeed something else beyond this place and beyond this life.

Suddenly, the room began to glow just as if there was a fire burning at the center. The only darkness surrounded the evil soul of Angelo as he sat there looking terrified. Giuseppe, Giovanni, and Michael stood there in complete awe of everything that was happening when, suddenly, the ceiling began to disappear, and all at once, they were looking up at a bright blue sky.

They were no longer in the slaughterhouse; instead, they were standing on a dirt road under the branches of a beautiful oak tree. In the distance, they could see a bustling small town with white buildings. People in carriages moved slowly down the street while others walked from store to store, shopping for their wares. To their left was a small schoolhouse, which was also painted white. In front of the schoolhouse, playing with their teacher, were the thirteen children. They seemed to be very fond of their teacher as they crowded around him to hear his stories. Then holding hands, they formed a circle around their master and started to sing. As they danced around him, they began to ascend, lifting him toward the heavens, and when they did, the schoolhouse began to burn.

Distant screams followed by gunshots and cannon fire had them looking toward the town. There, they could see some people running while others were being slaughtered. Buildings were being torched and blown apart. Further out, they could see smoke on the horizon as the plantations and their farmhouses fell to the same fate.

After the town was reduced to ashes and rubble and the screams had stopped, a man on horseback stood alone at the bottom of the dirt road. He was wearing a red coat and a black hat and appeared to be staring straight at them. Holding his sword high in the air, he reared his horse back, raising its front legs high, and then with all the splendor of an Errol Flynn movie, he began to attack. He rode hard toward them just as the slaughterhouse began to rematerialize, and as he rode past them, they realized that it wasn't them he charged at. Instead, and to their horror, a small boy holding a gun stood all alone on the road. Watching through the transparent walls of the slaughterhouse, they could see the face of the rider as he brought his sword down on the small child, the same face that now cowered in the corner, begging for his life.

Having fully returned, they watched as Father Michael held on to the limp body of the teacher. With his right hand, he closed the now-sightless eyes and gently lowered his head to the floor. Kneeling in prayer, he thanked the spirit guides for their forgiveness of their teacher and for the answers that they sought. These answers would now help them in their need to deal with this evil soul that still lived in their presence.

CHAPTER 35

ANGELO AND GABRIEL

GABRIEL FELT THE sense of dread immediately. He began squirming in the back seat of his large black Mercedes parked only a block away from the hospital as he could feel invasion of his psyche and felt powerless to do anything about it. His head was spinning out of control as beads of sweat ran down his large slanted forehead and into his eyes. He instinctively began pulling at the short hairs of his mustache as darkness overtook his consciousness.

Gabriel screamed as the sudden smell of decay singed his nostrils and then recoiled when the damp cold air cut through his skin and sounds of desperate moaning pierced his eardrums. The droplets of sweat that ran down his body felt more like droplets of fire that were piercing his flesh. Then as the old building materialized around him and his posh leather seat had turned into a damp cold floor, he tried to run.

"Wake up, wake up!" he screamed to himself. "No, this can't be happening again!" He sobbed. When he opened his eyes, he found himself curled up into a ball on the floor of the slaughterhouse, and although he knew he had entered Steven's dream, he knew all too well the nightmare that was about to begin. He trembled uncontrollably as the knowledge of what was coming terrified him.

Meanwhile, back at the rectory in St. Patrick's Cathedral, the old priest sitting in his warm office tried to contain his smile. He had sensed the evil soul as it hovered the hallways of the hospital, but fortunately, with the help of Maria Di Carlo, they were able to expose him and send him running from Steven's room. And now, with the help of the elders, the old priest had invaded and captured Gabriel's mind. He was now melded with Steven's journey to 1959, reliving the life of Giuseppe D'Amato. The old priest, whose body twitched and trembled regularly since his ninetieth birthday two years ago, felt young again. His hands were steady, and the constant ache of the severe arthritis had left him. He had taken over Gabriel's thoughts and had thrust them into Steven's dream to relive the deserved horror that happened to him fifty years and one lifetime earlier.

* * *

Back in 1959, Francesco and the others had finally returned to the slaughterhouse. It was evident that they had been successful in their quest and had found the things that were needed. The look of disgust on their faces and the way they held the sacks sent a shiver up Giuseppe's spine and chills that ran right through his entire body. The thought of what they were about to do had them all in a paralyzed kind of bewilderment, but as they looked at the monster that helped kill little Claudio, the disdain and repulsion they had for the man returned and quickly warmed them enough to face the task at hand.

First, they stripped him and then soaked his naked body in chicken blood and tied a rope around his ankles. His struggles were desperate as they tied his arms together at the elbows and wound the rope down to his wrists. They then secured the rope around his neck and forced a round cylinder into his mouth; it would keep it open and accessible.

After testing the strength of the knots, Steven threw the rope around a beam that crossed high in the trusses of the ceiling above and then unmercifully pulled him up.

"How does it feel that you're now ready for slaughter? Do you have the same terror you inflicted on my son as you helped murder him? Ah yes, indeed you do feel the fear!" The tall, thin man looked half his size as he hung upside down with chicken blood dripping down his face and through matted black hair. His eyes were saucers of fear, and the internal moaning that resonated through the cylinder in his mouth was excruciating to listen to. "Look at him, my friends," Giuseppe said with a forced smile. He would do what he was about to do but would not admit that it sickened him as he continued his forced charade of pretending to enjoy this horrible atrocity however deserved it was. "Does he not look like the pig that he is? Shall we show him his fate?"

With his head lifted just inches above the floor, Gabriel, reliving his life as Angelo, knew exactly what he was about to see in the sack. Even so, it still horrified him beyond belief, beyond anything that he might expect. He struggled desperately to avoid his cruel destiny, but his screams were mere whimpers followed by hollow echoes that exited the cylinder.

* * *

Back in 2011, Father Michael was finding it difficult to keep Gabriel connected to 1959. His fears and struggles played havoc with the old priest as he began to feel Gabriel's dread. Still, he was determined to show this evil entity the power of the path, so with new resolve, he strengthened his grip on Gabriel's mind.

One block from Steven's hospital room, Gabriel had rolled off his seat and was now wedged on the floor between the front and the back seats. He squirmed now as he did in 1959. With his eyes shut tightly, he tried to force the images away but to no avail as the sack was drawn closer to his head.

* * *

The men of Amato, led by Giuseppe, then placed the sack below him so that it hung open, level to his chin but covering head. When he saw the contents of the sack, the panic that hit him was terrifying and immediate, and when the first of the rats climbed up onto his face, his fear was so overwhelming that he lost consciousness.

Removing the sack, they hit him with another pail of chicken blood that left him gasping as vomit spewed out of the cylinder. Once they were sure he wouldn't choke to death, they continued the ritual and prepared him for self-execution. First, they got his attention by showing him the gun and then explained to him that there was only one bullet. Giuseppe then secured the gun to his hands in such a way that it was pointing directly at his own head. He had one thumb free that could be used to pull the trigger. Other than the thumb, he had very little use of the rest of his hands.

Everyone, including Father Michael, grimaced as they watched Giuseppe and Giovanni pull the sack up once again. This time, though, they brought the sack all the way up and tied the opening around the evil one's ankles. In the sack, there were dozens of hungry rats, and soon they would begin to feast.

The muffled screaming seemed to go on forever, interrupted only when one of the rats would discover the cylinder and venture into his mouth. Then after what seemed to be an eternity but really was only a few minutes, they heard the gun go off and his pathetic body went slack.

As startling as the gunshot was, it was nothing compared to the reaction of the men when they first saw the dark cloud. It appeared almost immediately, bringing with it a whirlwind of shadows that swirled around Angelo's lifeless corpse. They all cowered at the evil that swarmed into the slaughterhouse. They could hear what sounded like a thousand voices chanting in unison and echoing throughout the building, and as the unending parade of dark forms joined in the collection, their mantra had Giuseppe paralyzed once again: "Embrace the darkness, and it will embrace you."

* * *

Gabriel's bloodcurdling screams could be heard a block away from where his car was parked. Passersby jumped away in fright from the gleaming black sedan as they heard them. One man ventured close, trying to peer into the darkly tinted window, only declaring the car to be empty when he unable to see the tall, thin man curled on the floor of the back seat.

When, finally, the vile vision ended, Gabriel remained where he was, holding on to the floor mat that was now curled up in his arms. He wept uncontrollably as tremors rattled his body. He cursed in between gasping for air as he wondered who brought this malevolent memory to him and swore vengeance against those that had done this to him. When, finally, the spasms stopped, he remained on the floor of the big black Mercedes as sleep had mercifully taken him.

The old priest sat in his chair, not knowing what to think. The visions of that day were far worse than he had remembered when, suddenly, he sprang from his chair and hurried toward the chapel, talking to himself as he shuffled down the corridor, "Dear God, the time is near. My, my, we must hurry. We cannot be late. Where are you, dear boy? We cannot be late."

The raspy voice is what Samuel heard first. The excitement within that voice came right after, and the urgency had the old priest screaming for Samuel to hurry. "It is time, lad. The executioner awakens. Come, we must hurry."

* * *

Back in 1959, Giuseppe, breaking loose of the trance, watched the entities as they entered and then covered his mouth and nose as the air became very warm. The stench of death was everywhere. It reeked of burning flesh and stank of sulfur as the whirlwind continued to swarm around Angelo's hanging corpse. When the evil left, they could see his soul being pulled from his body and taken down through the floor into the dark depths of the inferno, a place they knew nothing about, an existence that wasn't one, a destination with no return. At least that is what they hoped, and Father Michael did his best to try and explain.

"My dear friends, as you have witnessed today, good and evil most certainly exist." Saying this, the good priest fell to his knee. His distress was visible; the screams of their victim still rang loudly in his head. He had paled watching Angelo Calendino tortured as he was and sickened at the thoughts of how they had done it. Still, it had to be done if cleansing the earth was their aim. Trying to set aside his feelings of disgust, he continued, "According to all that we know, no soul has ever returned after committing suicide. It has always been the same. The darkness would come, the sounds, the smells, the immediacy, and then it would leave, always the same. We have often wondered and discussed this many times throughout all our existences, wondering what awaited them on the other side, but we could only guess at another realm filled with malice and pain, a dark existence with no escape. Is it hell? I hope so!" The trembling priest bowed his head and prayed that the words he spoke were true. He asked the elders for guidance, and then he asked them for strength as he signaled the men to bring him the body.

After the men cut down the corpse, Father Michael filled his mouth and what was left of his nostrils with wax. He then placed a black hood over his head and tied it tight around his neck. This procedure was repeated with Lo Sciavo's body; superstition has it that by doing this, it will keep the evil thoughts of an evil soul trapped inside the evil head. These two would now be cremated while the driver along with the rest of the gang who were lying in the church would be buried in the cemetery.

Wanting to put an end to this day of bloodshed, Giovanni went to call Dr. Donato while Francesco and the others loaded the three corpses into one of the cars. The two that remained would be dealt with tomorrow as they would be kept alive and taught the way of the path. With their help, the protectors hoped that they would be able to destroy the nest of evil before they had time to retaliate against them.

A long night ahead awaited Giuseppe D'Amato. His identities would continue to fuse and cause havoc with his emotions. Still, it was time to write down all the events of the day as well as those of the prior weeks into the manuscript. Thus, Giuseppe, along with Father Michael, made their way to the empty house with the number nine on the front door. There, they would first open up a bottle of wine and then cut up some strong cheese, all in the hopes of taking away the bad taste of death.

Giuseppe sipped his wine slowly at first, then drained his glass with one gulp as he began to record the events and experiences into the manuscript. When he paused to collect his thoughts, his mind began to wander. His identities of the past, present, and future had, once again, become intertwined. His past encouraged him onward toward the imminent battle they would have to win in 2011. The present cautioned him that not all that will be written will be as it seems and his future as Steven Di Carlo was consumed with the what-ifs. *What if Michael was wrong and this wasn't a dream to remind me of my past? What if they really did die and I blow this chance to send a warning to the future that would save them? What if I could save them? Would it then matter if Michael was right or wrong?* Convinced that he would not risk it, his thoughts went to how he would send the message that would save his family in 2011. And as the present gave way to the future, his identity as Steven Di Carlo took control of his thoughts and played out the possibilities in his mind.

I need to activate my awakening to somehow occur before Victoria and the children are killed. If I could make this happen, I might be able to save them. I need time to think.

Steven reflected on all he had been told and all he had experienced, and in his heart, he felt it to be true and if it was, then September 6, 2012, would be a day of reckoning for him and also the path. The one thing he didn't understand was the constant feeling that 2011 was also a dream, a dream with a different warning—or was it the same? A dream that would be the catalyst for his true awakening, whatever the truth really was. The faint awareness of this other dream ripped at his mind and put all that he knew in a state bewilderment. Still, he knew deep within his soul that he could not fail the path regardless of the cost, regardless of which dream was real and regardless of who died and who lived. So he walked outside and carved 612 next to the 9 that was already on the front door of the small empty house.

CHAPTER 36

CELEBRATING A VICTORY

S TEVEN DI CARLO continued to play out all the scenarios in his mind. Somehow, he knew that he was asleep in his cottage at Lake George, and somehow he also knew that he was in a hospital room, dreaming of being at Lake George. Yet the reality was that he was in the small town of Amato in the south of Italy, perched on a beautiful mountaintop in 1959 and his name was Giuseppe D'Amato. So deciding to believe that the hospital room was the correct dream, he decided then that the message must come from his mother; he could see no other way. Perhaps the message could come from the picture itself. *Yes*, he thought. *I could have her write the warning on the picture and then give it to Steven; to me, at the right time. I just needed to figure out a way of telling this seventeen-year-old girl who will grow up to be my mother a little bit about her future without her thinking that her old uncle Peppino was nuts. It will work. I'm sure of it.* Feeling a bit better, he went back inside and finished journalizing the entries to the manuscript, including his dream within a dream and his message to his future self.

Father Michael, with a look of concern after reading what Steven had written, asked him if he was sure this was the proper thing to do. Steven, with a look of resolve on his face, answered him, which, in turn, had the young priest warn him.

"My dear dear friend, if in your future it is written that the purpose chosen by your family was to be killed at a specific time as a catalyst for another series of event to commence, then, Steven, the souls of the ones you wish to save would ultimately decide if it is to be so."

* * *

The sun shone very brightly on the day after the darkest day in the history of the little village. It seemed to Giuseppe and Father Michael that morning had come before they had a chance to sleep. Maria, as usual, was at the door, bright-eyed, cheerful, and full of questions. She was a pillar of strength for the little village, impressing all in the way she took charge during the crisis. Giuseppe was especially impressed with the preparations she had made for those who were to hide in the cave. She reminded Giuseppe of her father, his brother-in-law; and for the first time through this entire ordeal, as his identities continued creating chaos within his mind, Steven realized that Giovanni was his grandfather. He could see now why she was so remarkable and so courageous.

She brought them some freshly baked bread and some sausage for their morning meal. The bread smelled wonderful. Father Michael tore into it like a man who hadn't eaten in days. The two of them sat on the stoop of the little house and ate the steaming bread with the delicious spicy sausage as Maria kept on questioning them if what she had brought was enough. Looking at Maria, Steven tried to find the words to explain what he needed her to do. He started by asking her to go and fetch the town photographer.

"*Ma perche*, Zio, but why do you need the photographer?" When her uncle ignored her question, she hesitantly left to do as he had asked.

When they returned, he set up the picture to be shot the same as it was in the original. The door was in the background; the tiny window was to the left, and Maria held the picture of Claudio to her heart as a tear slowly ran down her cheek. After the photographer was done, he sat Maria down and, without revealing too much, asked her for her help.

She listened intently as Steven told her what he believed his story to be when he tested her to see if she remembered calling him Steven the night before.

"Zio, why do you joke with me?"

"I wanted to bring a smile to your beautiful face, that's all," he replied, and they both laughed.

After their little laugh, Steven continued to seek her help. When he was finally able to explain it to her, she answered by promising that if she ever lived in America and she had a son named Steven, she would do as he asked. Then she said, "But why would I ever call my son by this silly name?"

Watching her giggle at the thought, Steven realized that his name was the Americanized name for Stefano. His parents had changed it to Steven when his uncle gave their son the same name. After explaining this to Maria, she told him that Stefano Di Carlo was the name of her fiancé's father, her future father-in-law.

It all began to fall into place, and the look in her eyes told him that she would never forget this promise. He hugged her and told her that she was extraordinary and that she would always have the strength and courage of her father, and she would use it well. Steven said goodbye, and ignoring the finality with which he had said it, she reminded him not to be late for dinner. Looking at her with her innocence, Steven couldn't help but hug her one more time.

Soon after Maria had gone, Giovanni and Father Michael accompanied Steven to the cave where, together, they searched for a place to hide the manuscript. They needed a place that would keep it safe for almost fifty years. They found the perfect spot deep in the bowels of the cave; it was exactly what they were looking for, a hole in a rock that was just deep enough to fit the ancient book.

They wrapped the manuscript in the same animal hide casing that had protected it for hundreds of years in Scotland and then placed it in the hole. With the skill of a master mason, Giovanni began to chisel a rock cover that would blend into the wall. When he was done, they secured the rock in the hole and marveled at how invisible the repair was. Even with knowing the exact spot, it was still difficult to see where their hiding place was.

Feeling pleased with himself for securing the manuscript, Giovanni and Father Michael reminded Giuseppe that they still had work to do. They still needed to dispose of the bodies and deal with the two remaining intruders. But Steven, needing some time alone, told them that he would meet them in a short while.

Hesitantly, Giovanni and Michael returned to the village without him. When they were gone, Steven sunk down onto the cold damp ground of the cave with his back to the now-concealed manuscript, then, and perhaps unwillingly, he relived the events of the last few days.

Thinking of all the shit that had happened to them left him feeling that if he was living a dream, then most certainly it was a nightmare. Although this experience to the past seemed as real as real can get, it left him wondering if it all really happened. Consumed by exhaustion, he succumbed to much-needed sleep, then closing his eyes, his mind let go of all the trepidation. His fears, his shame, his worry for the future, it was all gone. Instead, he felt an incredible sense of peace and tranquility; it was as if he were falling in darkness, totally unafraid, completely under control, sort of like flying.

CHAPTER 37

AWAKENED

H IS ARMS WERE spread out like the wings of an eagle; with a simple twist, he could change his direction. Tucking his arms back, he dove straight down, then moving them slightly had him soaring up toward the heavens. The exhilaration was unbelievable. He dove and then climbed; he twisted and turned, and then with a slight movement, he simply floated. "This is very cool!" he said aloud. Then looking down, he saw nothing; it was just an emptiness that couldn't be rationalized, so he began to circle around and around, staring down but seeing nothing.

All at once, he spotted it. It began as a pinhead of light in a sea of grayish black. Steven was immediately attracted to it, so he kept circling, trying to figure out what it was that he had found. He wondered why he was so awed by a simple light, then jumped at the thought that it might be a way out of the dream. So after very little deliberation, he dove straight for it, curious as to what it was. Partway through his dive, Steven thought of caution. The pinhead of light was unknown and might carry danger, so he decided to circle it again. Round and round, he went; it seemed forever but he was getting closer and the pinhead was getting larger. It was amazing, he thought, being able move as fast as you wanted, or if you chose, you could simply hover, always completely in control and filled with a confident sense of peace. The silence was comforting; there were no sounds except for the gentle wind rushing past him and the sounds of his breathing as it echoed softly in the depths of his consciousness.

The light was now the size of a small sphere; it reminded Steven of the long lazy summer nights of his childhood when he would lay on the grass, looking up at the moon. *That's it*, he thought. The sphere reminded him of the moon. The only difference was that, this time, he was looking down on it, and as he circled closer, it grew larger.

* * *

Back in 2011 at Mercy Medical Center, the young priest was impatient as he waited for his mentor who was shuffling as fast as he could down the hospital corridor toward Steven's room. When they finally arrived, the old priest burst through the door, startling Victoria Di Carlo, who was whispering in her husband's ear.

"Father Michael, what is it?" Victoria asked, fearing that something may have happened back home.

"It's nothing, my dear. It's Christmas Eve, and we both had a strong desire to come for a visit," he lied.

"How thoughtful," responded Victoria as the door again opened and Steven's mother, Maria, entered the room. Samuel stood in background, nervous with the anticipation that Steven would finally awaken.

* * *

The light had now grown twice the size of the moon as Steven's flight took him closer to his destination.

"Steven, my darling, please wake up. We miss you and need you to come home. Honey, please wake up." Out of nowhere, he could hear Victoria calling to him.

Her voice was very comforting and soothing and so close that it was as if she were whispering in his ear. He could feel her gentle breath as she spoke words of love and of happiness. Steven tried to answer her but could not vocalize his thoughts. Frustrated, he tried to scream but no sound came out. His anger had disrupted the peacefulness of his flight, and he began to lose control of his descent when, just as suddenly, the calmness returned. He could now hear his mother; she was praying. He could hear her but could not call to her, and just as he was about to give up, she spoke to him, "Steven, my son, look, Father Michael and Father Stewart are here to visit you. You see, God is with you. He knows it's not your time. Please come back to us, son. Your father needs you."

The sphere continued to grow.

Then it was Victoria; she was back. "Oh, how I miss our summers at the lake. Every night I dream of being in your arms, of making love, and of growing old with you. Steven, you know that when I think of you, I think of the fireworks that lit up our lives. I miss you so much, my love. Wake up, my darling. We all need you to come home. It's Christmas Eve. What a present you would be giving us."

The brightness of the sphere had him shielding his eyes.

She was telling him that the children missed him and that his mind was controlling him and that now was time to let his heart take over.

"Believe in your heart, my darling, and it will lead you to us."

The sphere was now so large that it was all Steven could see below him. The air around him began to get warmer, and he could feel the heat emanating from the light. He called to Victoria, but somehow, he knew that she was gone. He could no longer sense her, and the strong presence that, just moments earlier, filled his heart had now emptied his soul. Then as the unwelcomed silence took hold of his mind, Steven once again began to lose control of his flight and tumbled helplessly through the shadows of darkness toward the light.

The sphere was a ball of fire; he watched as explosions of flames were bursting out toward him. Still, he continued to free-fall, and the heat became unbearable. With the outcome seeming inevitable, he succumbed, and he welcomed death. *Why not?* he thought; he was tired, and besides, there was nothing that he could do about it.

Steven closed his eyes and held his breath, waiting for the anticipated impact. It seemed to take an eternity, and just when he thought all was lost, a paralyzing blast of cold air hit him like a monstrous winter wind.

When he opened his eyes, he was at the bank where Victoria worked, and looking through the glass doors, he saw his family. They were being beaten and violated. His mind raced. He didn't understand what was happening. He began slamming his fists into the door but to no avail. He tried again, and the glass dissolved and then solidified around his arms, capturing them in the glass. Horrified and gasping for air, he tried to call for help when, suddenly, the bank was gone, and he was transported to the living room of their house. He was holding Cathy's lifeless body with Rosa at his side. His head was spinning, and the confusion was agonizing. He could hear Tommy calling to him; the helplessness in his voice shattered his state of panic. Steven needed to save him.

Everywhere he looked, he saw death; nine lifetimes of death, his wives past and present, his children, eighteen of them in total, nine boys and nine girls all dead. He was screaming for it to all go away when he saw them. David and Leo were reaching out to him, trying to save him, he thought; then the all-too-brief feeling of tranquility was gone, and Steven's world once again began to roar out of control. It was as if the house was spinning one way and Steven was spinning the other way. It all looked distorted; everything was being stretched from every angle.

Steven ran up the stairs toward Tommy's voice, but the staircase seemed to get longer. For every step he took, another was added, and the harder he ran, the farther away he was from the top. Steven called to Tommy to let him know he was coming; the desperation in his voice was frightening. Then suddenly, everything stopped. The silence seemed to be blasting at him from Tommy's bedroom. His voice was gone, and as painful as it was, he knew that, once again, he had failed to save him.

Then without time to comprehend the scene that was unfolding in front of him, Steven found himself behind the wheel of his Navigator and he was losing control of the big SUV. The roads were icy, and he could hear terror in the screams of Victoria and the kids.

Victoria was yelling at him, something about his seatbelt, and that's when the Lincoln began to slide.

They were heading off the road and into the deep snow when, suddenly, they crashed into a large rock. Steven felt this incredible pain; something had slammed into him, hitting him square in the face. In the distance, he could hear Victoria crying, but the sounds of her screams seemed to be getting farther and farther away. He was sliding face-first along the ice and snow. His mouth and nose seemed to be filling with it; he felt no pain but was having trouble breathing when, mercifully, it all stopped.

He was okay. The pinhead of light was back, the horror was gone, and he was getting another chance, so he started to move his arms, and once again, he was flying, circling toward the light. *Wow this is so cool. I'm getting closer, and this time I'm going to get it right.*

As he continued to descend, he spotted something floating up toward him. When it was close enough, he reached out and grabbed it and was once again holding the manuscript, the articles of proof, the journal of his misery that, once again, had his past identities flashing through his mind, and when he reached the identity of Giuseppe DAmato, it vanished as suddenly as it appeared and then another object was floating toward him. It came straight at him; it was an ornate box that was etched with circles within circles, within circles. When he touched it, a wall materialized in front of him, the same design as was on the box was on the wall. There was a finger, no body, just a finger, and it was pressing the circles on the wall, and as it did, the circles, one at a time, sunk deep within the door until the door hissed open and the box left his grip, floating through the opening in the wall. When the ornate box was out of sight, the door slammed shut, and he was again alone, descending toward the light.

He heard a voice somewhere in the distance. It was calling to him, but refusing to be distracted, Steven continued to fly toward the light. Still, the voice, now closer, beckoned him. He felt annoyed at the intrusion. When, finally, he looked over to see who it was that was disturbing his flight, he saw the vision of an angel. She was dressed in a pure white gown with gold-and-green trim. When he looked deep into her beautiful green eyes, he recognized her. How could he not?

Her fiery red hair blowing in the breeze framed her milky smooth complexion. Her voice, as soothing as it was two hundred years earlier, calmed him, allowing him to regain his composure.

"My darling," she said, "it is not your time yet. Go back to your family." It was Rachael who had come to rescue him, and with her, he saw Rosa and Claudio. Claudio came and embraced him, and then Rosa held his face with both her hands and simply smiled at him. Together they surrounded him and brought him back down to where Victoria was still kneeling in the snow. She looked so helpless and vulnerable that Steven tried desperately to reach out to her but was unable to. She was crying softly as a man was performing CPR on someone.

When Steven looked closer, he was both frightened and shocked. *Hey! That's me. I don't understand. What's going on?*

At that moment, Steven felt so totally disoriented that he had to fight hard to maintain consciousness. He felt very cold as he struggled to breathe. The more he struggled, the harder it was. Once again, he felt himself letting go, so he fought harder to hold on. Anger seemed to take over as he screamed up at the heavens, and then with the name Sebastian echoing in the darkness of his mind and the image of the *Namzu Anunnaki* revealing itself to him, he finally surrendered, and when he did, he shot up fully awake in his hospital bed.

Gasping for air and understanding, Steven was holding on to his throat that felt raw and painful. His body ached with spasms, and his eyes burned from the brightness. When they finally cleared, the first thing he saw was the shock in Victoria's stare, and then just beside her, he saw tears in his mother's eyes. A smiling young priest was at the back of the room, and a very old face that looked a lot like Father Michael was holding his hand.

The Beginning

ABOUT THE AUTHOR

F RANK FRANCO IS a sixty-three-year-old proud father of two wonderful children, the grandfather of five amazing grandchildren aged two to eleven and has been married to his wife, Lina, for the past forty-two years.

Although this is Frank's first novel, I consider him to be a well-seasoned story teller. He began writing The Prophets and the Executioner in 2008, mostly writing on Saturday mornings and while on vacations. Writing a novel was a bucket list item he always dreamed of completing, and after numerous rewrites and the story taking control of the writer, one novel turned into three, and thus, a trilogy was created and the adventures of Steven Di Carlo (the executioner) and Samuel Stewart (his prophet) took him on quite an amazing ride.

The trilogy is lightly based on the author's beliefs and personal experiences of something existing beyond this world—a somewhat mystical connection guiding us through life and then welcoming us home when we die. Although purely fiction, The Prophets and the Executioner explores why we are here, where we came from, and what comes next.

With no formal education as a writer, the intention was to complete the novel, print a few copies, and hand them out to family and friends and cross that one off the bucket list. But coming from a newspaper background and having writers and editors as friends, he was encouraged by us to pursue publishing his story. Now that book 1 is published and book 2 is reading for editing, he has begun working on the final book of this amazing trilogy!

—Fabian Dawson
News Editor Post Media